VANISHED

KATHRYN MACKEL

REALMS
A STRANG COMPANY

Most Strang Communications/Charisma House/Siloam/ FrontLine/Realms products are available at special quantity discounts for bulk purchase for sales promotions, premiums, fund-raising, and educational needs. For details, write Strang Communications/Charisma House/Siloam/FrontLine/Realms, 600 Rinehart Road, Lake Mary, Florida 32746, or telephone (407) 333-0600.

Vanished by Kathryn Mackel
Published by Realms
A Strang Company
600 Rinehart Road
Lake Mary, Florida 32746
www.realmsfiction.com

Scripture quotations are from the Holy Bible, New International Version. Copyright © 1973, 1978, 1984, International Bible Society. Used by permission.

Cover Design: studiogearbox.com
Executive Design Director: Bill Johnson

Published in association with the literary agency of Alive Communications, Inc., 7680 Goddard Street, Suite 200, Colorado Springs, CO 80920; www.alivecommunications.com.

Visit the author's Web sites www.kathrynmackel.com and www.vanishedthebook.com

Library of Congress Cataloging-in-Publication Data:

Mackel, Kathryn, 1950-
  Vanished / by Kathryn Mackel.
    p. cm. -- (Vanished ; bk. 1)
  ISBN 978-1-59979-211-8
  1. Terrorism--Fiction. I. Title.
  PS3613.A2734V36 2007
  813'.6--dc22

                                         2007022536

07 08 09 10 11 — 9 8 7 6 5 4 3 2 1
Printed in the United States of America

To my sisters Mary and Janice,
who have always been where I needed them

acknowledgments

I OWE A BIG THANK YOU AND HUG TO MY HUSBAND, STEVE, who sparked to this idea immediately and encouraged me to keep going with it. Thank you to Bert Ghezzi, who saw the same promise and gave the story a home.

Thank you to my writers group—Bev, Patty, Kathy, Lee, Bob, Judy, Dave D., and Dave H.—for working through the birth pangs with me.

I'm grateful to LB Norton who once again answered the call to bring this book to creation, and to my agent Lee Hough, who always—*always*—is there for me with guidance, encouragement, and wisdom. Thank you to all the people at Strang who shepherded this book through editing, including Debbie, Christianne, and Deb. Thanks to the marketing team of Lucy, Woodley, Margarita, and Tasha, who will make sure readers know about this book.

Victoria James wrote and recorded the lovely song "Oh, Come to Me, Jesus." Thank you, Vicki, for being open to the Lord's leading and understanding the heart of a book you haven't yet read! Go to victoriajamesmusic.com and enjoy this song, as well as many other songs she has written and sung to bless my books.

Now listen, you who say, "Today or tomorrow we will go to this or that city, spend a year there, carry on business and make money." Why, you do not even know what will happen tomorrow. What is your life? You are a mist that appears for a little while and then vanishes.

—James 4:13–14

an august morning

chapter one

THE LETTER ARRIVED AT THE POLICE SUBSTATION special delivery, signature required.

Jason Logan couldn't bear to open it, couldn't bear to see black lines forming letters and letters resolving into words that would destroy his life.

Subject 58RS is negative for paternity.

Five years of pretending would be for nothing once he opened the letter and let the truth out. Back then, he did the research and discovered the combination of genes that would allow a blue-eyed blonde to be born to a sable-haired woman and a part Korean, part who-knows-what guy.

Highly improbable. A million-to-one shot. But statistically possible.

Within hours of Kimmie's birth, Logan had refused to entertain any other possibility. For in truth, wasn't the heart far more than muscle and blood, and parenthood more than the sum—or the discrepancy—of one's DNA?

He and Hilary had named the baby Kim Li after his biological mother, a woman he knew only as a scrawl on his adoption papers. It never mattered that Kimmie didn't have his tawny skin or sturdy build. Logan carried her on his shoulders, kissed away her boo-boos, and chased away the monsters under her bed.

Now the monster under his own bed had reared its evil head.

The door buzzed. Logan shoved the envelope into his pocket, took a deep breath, and turned to greet the visitor.

The guy might as well have been a billboard, he was that obvious. Tailored dark suit, crisp white shirt, modest tie, lean cheeks, almost imperceptible bulge at the waist where his service revolver sat.

"I'm Sergeant Logan. Help you?"

"Stefan Pappas." The visitor presented his credentials.

Logan squinted, not recognizing the bona fides.

"Secret Service. Advance team for President Freeman." Pappas loosened his tie. "Hotter'n blazes out there."

Pappas's salt-and-pepper hair was military short, his eyes dark and intense. Though his voice was a subdued baritone, his straight back and broad shoulders gave an air of authority. Judging from his creased forehead and gnarled fingers, he was in his late forties or early fifties. Which meant he'd have significant seniority backing whatever he was after in Logan's duty area.

"Downtown know you're here?" Logan asked.

"Nope."

Score one for the feds, Logan thought. Downtown was Barcester Police Central, six miles to the southwest. Most of the city subs had closed when the federal money for community policing dried up. A state grant and the public's desire to have a permanent presence in the Flats—the most dangerous neighborhood in Barcester—had kept the University Avenue substation open.

The U-Ave sub was little more than a boxy bungalow with a couple desks, a dispatch system, and a lock-up in the basement. Not the competent luxury a Secret Service guy would be used to. Duty was three cops per shift and no administrative help. Hardly a fast track to a gold shield, but after the Gibbons incident, it had been either run the substation or ride a desk.

Logan chose the former, keeping his pay grade and his self-respect—but losing his wife, who apparently had never been his anyway. Let her have her rich boyfriend and fancy estate. She wasn't getting his little girl.

Pappas cleared his throat.

"So this is an unofficial reach?" Logan asked, trying to focus.

"It's official. Just not orchestrated."

Logan laughed. Downtown loved a good dog and pony show, but it was the beat cops who got stuck with the cleanup. "You're here about the high-speeds."

"Not quite yet. I'm here to check out the bike paths."

The bike paths were Quanta Corporation's gift, a thank-you for allowing them to tunnel under the city for their high-speed train lines. The New York-Boston line and the Providence-Montreal line crossed about a half mile from the U-Ave sub, deep underground. The bike paths had been built on the open land above the trains left by the construction—a win-win for the city and the corporation.

"The high speeds aren't vulnerable to anything above ground," Logan said. "That's what they're claiming."

Pappas opened a pack of mint gum and offered a piece. "Thing is this, Logan. Homeland Security has file cabinets full of threats against the Quanta high-speeds, and we're not talking just eco freaks and Al Qaeda wannabes. These days anyone can put up a Web site and muster an army of fruitcakes. My concern is for the attention junkies who would love to get their mugs on the nightly news. They can't blow up the high-speeds, but they can make things look ugly on your bike paths. And remind the public what is tunneled underneath."

Logan had seen the memos, issued his own memo back to Central PD, and mentally prepared for September chaos when the trains would officially begin their runs. But this was August.

"You're here early. The president isn't scheduled to ride for two months. Columbus Day, right?"

"Which means in four weeks the suits from Homeland and the Service will be out in force. Those visits we'll have to arrange through Barcester Central. Call me a dinosaur, but I'd like to take the pulse of what's above those trains without higher-ups calling the shots for us."

Us. A subtle attempt to persuade Logan to regard him as an ally. Local cops weren't thrilled when the feds came sniffing around, even on matters of national security.

"So are you doing this all the way from New York to Boston? That's the line President Freeman will be riding, correct?"

"I chose Barcester as my area of interest."

"Because of the train crossing."

"Seems reasonable to assume that if anything's gonna go down, it'll be here."

Above ground, the bike paths that followed the train lines met in a rotary known simply as the Circle. Almost the size of a city block, the Circle offered water fountains, park benches, even a little playground.

"Want to cycle it?" Logan asked. "I can lend you a bike and a helmet."

"Nah. I'll walk. I just wanted to stop in, say hello. As a courtesy."

"I'll come with you."

Pappas waved him off. "Not necessary."

"As a courtesy." No fed was going to wander Logan's duty area unescorted.

Pappas glanced about, taking in the empty desks. "Don't you need to man the station?"

"Our mandate is face time on the streets. We're only in here to use the john or to process someone for transport." Or to wait for a heart-shredding letter, special delivery, signature required.

4

Pappas nodded, his expression bland. "In that case—I'd enjoy the company."

"I'm going to trade the blues for a T-shirt and shorts. We've got extras if you'd like."

"I'm fine."

"It's ninety degrees out there. You'll draw a lot of attention with that men-in-black thing you've got going on."

He laughed. "Point taken. OK, I've got stuff in my car."

"Grab it. You can change in here."

Pappas headed out.

Logan went to lock the letter in his desk, then decided to keep it in his pocket, with the irrational notion that—when he finally got the courage to open it—the letters on the page would reveal the real truth.

Subject 58RS is positive for paternity in every way that really matters.

chapter two

KAYA DE LOS SANTOS PEERED THROUGH A CRACK IN THE door. It broke her heart to see Sarah Nolan standing on the porch, baby on her hip.

Just as it broke her heart to have to say, "I'm sorry, Sarah. But we're closed."

Sarah looked around wild-eyed. "Please, Ms. Kaya. I don't know where else to go."

Kaya launched into the spiel that the city attorney had crafted. Every time she recited the words, they caught in her throat. "I can give you a cab voucher so you can go to urgent care at St. Vincent's," she finished.

"But Angie knows you. I know you."

"I'm sorry, Sarah. You received a notification two weeks ago. The clinic is closed until further notice."

Further notice—forever. Kaya had worked her tail off to keep free and convenient medical care in this neighborhood. After the lawsuit, it was unlikely the city would find a replacement for her. Or even try.

Sarah tried to squeeze into the space the security chain allowed between the door and its frame. "We won't make it to the hospital. Please. You've got to let us in."

Kaya focused on the baby, a sweet little girl named Angelina. The baby's color was good, her lips moist. Her breathing was regular, with no obvious rasp other than a weary sobbing. Kaya wiggled a finger, catching Angelina's gaze. Her crying slowed as she focused. Her pupils were normal in size and followed appropriately.

No emergency here.

"It's just a short ride," Kaya said. "The doctors there will take good care of you. I'll call you a cab."

"No! You have to let us in. Please, I am begging you." Sarah rubbed her chest, her breath coming in rapid bursts. Her face drained of color, a panic attack coming on. What was this about? In the two years Sarah had been the clinic's patient, the girl had shown nothing but a dreary apathy.

"OK, but just for a minute. We'll get you out of the heat and get something to drink." Kaya unlatched the chain and took Sarah by the arm to steady her. The city attorney would have a fit if he knew. Would he rather she risk another lawsuit by letting this girl topple off the front steps in a dead faint?

"I've got some OJ in the kitchen," Kaya said.

"Wait. Lock the door."

"I'll only be a minute, hon. We'll get you settled down, then I'll call you a cab."

"No! Don't send us away!" Sarah slammed and locked the front door. "You need to check Angie out for me. She's really hurt."

Sarah thrust Angelina into her arms. The little one nestled against Kaya, her tearstained face dampening the front of her T-shirt. Another complication—had Sarah abused her daughter? That would be uncharacteristic. But if Kaya found any evidence of abuse, she'd have to call youth services.

"I'll take a quick look. But remember, I can't treat her. The clinic's closed."

Kaya led Sarah through the maze of boxes that filled the waiting room. Her son, Ben, was in the laundry room, bundling up sheets and towels to go to the local shelter. She resisted the urge to tell him to turn down his blaring music. This move was hard for him.

Eight years of hard work stuffed into cardboard boxes and taped shut. The clinic's supply of baby food, diapers, shampoos, and soaps would be trucked to the Barcester Food Bank. The prescription samples were designated for St. Vincent's urgent care department. The furniture, equipment, and house were scheduled to be auctioned off to help defray the million-dollar settlement.

Kaya laid the baby on the examining table and pressed the stethoscope to her chest. Angelina Nolan was a beautiful child, with chubby cheeks and silky black curls. Despite the heat, her skin was clammy. Dehydrated, perhaps?

"Sarah, how're you coping with this heat?"

"The welfare gave me an air conditioner. It works. Mostly."

"Is the baby taking enough fluids?"

"She was. Until..." Sarah chewed her fingernail. Sixteen years old with a ten-month-old baby and five months pregnant with her next. Numbers that never added up to anything but heartache.

A quick check showed no obvious bruising. Angelina had quieted.

"Where is she hurt?"

"Maybe her arm."

"Mom?" Ben called from the hall, startling Sarah. "Mr. Wakefield wants me to come in early. He's going nuts down there. Shorthanded."

"Do you mind?" Kaya said. "I'm with a patient."

"Sorry. This'll just be a minute." Her son's voice ran a full octave in one sentence.

"Get in here. Let me speak to Mr. Wakefield."

Ben came into the room, cell phone to his ear. He glanced at Sarah, then at Angelina. "He hung up. I thought the clinic was cl—"

"None of your business. Call him back."

Her son glared at her, all skin and bones and attitude. "It's my last day. Can't you just back off me for one last day?"

Until this summer, Ben had been a mannerly child who read a stack of books a week and devoured Sudoku like chocolate. Now everything was a battle.

"Call him back." Kaya glanced at Sarah. "Sorry."

Ben punched in a number. "Mr. Wakefield? My mother needs to talk to you."

Angelina wrapped her fingers around Kaya's finger. Kaya grinned and waggled her eyebrows at the baby, trying to draw a return smile. On the phone, a raspy-voiced man rattled on about a kid out with an ear infection and another with conjunctivitis.

"Mr. Wakefield, sorry to interrupt, but I'll send my son right over." Kaya closed the phone and pointed it at Ben. "Straight to McDonald's. Nowhere else. You got me?"

He snatched the phone back. "Yeah, I got you."

"Fine. Back home the instant the shift is over."

"Fine." Ben left, stopping just short of slamming the door.

Kaya raised Angelina to a sitting position. Her breathing was good, and again, there was no obvious bruising. She slowly rotated the baby's arm.

Angelina tried to pull away.

A cracked collarbone? Maybe a wrenched elbow or strained shoulder ligament. Common abuse injuries. Injuries that would require an X-ray—and a call to youth services.

"What happened, Sarah?"

The girl shrank into herself. "My boyfriend tried to take her from me."

Kaya held back a sigh. "Is he the baby's father?"

"No."

"Who is he?"

"Just a guy," Sarah said with a shrug.

"What's his name?"

"You don't know him."

"I know half the people in the Flats."

"I can't tell you."

"I'm going to call St. Vincent's," Kaya said. "Set up X-rays and labs for Angelina. I'll have your social worker drive you both over there."

Sarah shook her head so hard her ponytail bounced. "No! Don't do that. He'll kill me if I get the authorities involved. I just need you to fix up Angie. And then we'll take a bus somewhere far away."

"You know I can't let you take her."

"I gotta get out of here."

"Honey, I've been through tough times. I know what it's like."

"Not this. You can't know."

"Tell me, Sarah. Please. Tell me why this guy wants your baby."

Sarah collapsed back into the chair, wrapped her arms over her head as if trying to disappear into herself. "It's horrible. I'm horrible. I never should have—"

"Honey, please tell me what this guy did."

"He sold her."

"He *what*?"

"He said I don't need her anymore. Because I'm pregnant. The people who bought her gave him ten thousand dollars. He says they'll be better parents than me. I wouldn't let him take her. He tried to yank her away from me. That's when he hurt her. He went to—went into the other room, and I ran out the door." Sarah burst into tears. "I love my baby. Please don't let him take her."

Kaya cradled Angelina. "Trust me, he is not getting this child."

"I ran as fast as I could, but I think—" Sarah coughed, choking on her tears. "I think he might know I was coming here."

"Sit, honey. I'll call for help."

"What if he comes in here?"

Kaya forced a smile. "He can't. Haven't you heard? We're *closed*."

chapter three

J ASMINE WAS THE WORLD TO BEN.

He was nothing to her, of course. Just a pencil-necked dope who helped her pass summer-school algebra. The deal had been he'd school her in math and she'd school him in cool.

She had texted him that morning, wanting him to walk the bike path with her. Now, she had typed. A G-BY PICNIC.

IMPOSSIBLE, he typed back. GROUNDED.

And it had been impossible until she'd cooked up the McDonald's story and got someone to impersonate Mr. Wakefield. Jasmine knew how to make things happen.

As she walked toward him, Ben shivered. Even in this heat Jasmine wore her dark curls down instead of in a ponytail or piled on her head. Maybe that was for the better. Something about seeing the sweat running down the back of her neck made his knees wobble.

Her lips were full and her cheeks round with a dimple on the left side. Her skin was nut-brown from the sun. Her orange tube top showed off the gold heart in her belly button, and her short shorts barely covered her backside. She carried a knapsack on one shoulder, its weight pulling her off center.

Ben wore jean shorts and a white tee under his Celtics shirt. Better to be a dork than show off his chicken chest and stringy arms.

"'Sup?" he said, trying to sound smooth. No manual existed for street slang. Either you knew it or you were a loser. Ben had no illusions about which category he fit. Was it possible Jasmine had seen past the glasses and scrawny build? Could she actually *like* him?

She slipped her knapsack onto his left shoulder. "Nice day for a picnic."

"So we really are having a picnic?" He had assumed she was kidding, that she needed his help on legal stuff. Her mother didn't speak a word of English and depended on Jasmine to decipher the Section 8 and MassHealth paperwork. Jasmine— and a whole bunch of other kids—depended on him to navigate them through the tricky waters of government services.

His mother called it his *ministry*, but Ben knew it for what it really was. A way to buy safety and acceptance on the mean streets of the Flats.

Jasmine smiled, crinkling her eyes at the corners. "Of course it's a picnic. You and me. You're the man, so you get to carry the knapsack."

Yes, I finally am *the man*, Ben wanted to bellow. "Where are we going?"

"The Circle."

From the outside, the Circle looked beautiful. The bushes formed a natural canopy, hiding the chain link and razor wire protecting the cement blockhouse with its access stairwell to the tunnels far below. During the day, only squirrels or the Quanta engineers went into those bushes. At night, the junkies and prostitutes took over the area. Not Ben's first choice as a picnic grove.

"We should go over to Hubbard Park."

"Too far."

"It's only a half mile past the Circle. We could sit in the grass next to the water. Stick our toes in." The image of her bare feet in the water made it hard for him to breathe. What a total dork he was.

14

Jasmine pulled away. "Did I say I wanted to go to Hubbard? I told you, I need to go to the Circle."

"*Need* to?"

She snuggled back against him. "Need to because I want to. I go up there all the time."

He stiffened. "With whom?"

"Why do you do that?"

"What?"

Jasmine wrinkled her nose. "Say *whom* instead of who."

"It's proper English," Ben said.

"It marks you. You live in the Flats like the rest of us, but up here..." She danced her fingers across his forehead. "Up here you live in Geeksville."

"Where else would I live?" he asked, annoyed. "I *am* a geek."

"But you're my geek. And I'll prove it to you once we get to the Circle."

"What's in the knapsack, Jazz?"

"Stuff for the picnic, Benjie." She insisted on calling him that, even though his name was Benedict, not Benjamin. But that movie dog is so cute, she'd say, and ruffle his hair.

He wasn't feeling so cute right about now. A queasy dread replaced the heat in Ben's belly. "Stuff? Like what, exactly?"

"Um...OK. Peanut butter and jelly. That's what."

Ben slipped the knapsack off his shoulder and fumbled for the zipper. "I'm hungry. Maybe I'll have some right now."

Jasmine lifted the pack back onto his shoulders and slipped her arm between the straps and his chest, effectively locking the pack in place. "Chill, baby. We'll dig in up at the Circle."

A kid whizzed by on a bike and hooted at them, "Get a room, suckers."

Other than that, the bike path was silent. The trees planted on either side were still too new to cast much shade. Even so, this was a place where a guy could disconnect from the Flats

15

for a mile or so. Pretend that the paved path would take him to a still place where the breezes ran cool. A quiet place where pretty girls didn't lug drugs and pretend they were peanut butter and jelly.

"You're using me as your mule," Ben whispered.

"You watch too much TV." Jasmine tossed her head, her hair catching sunlight. The dimple where her collarbones met looked impossibly soft.

"Answer me. Are there drugs in here?"

Jasmine sighed dramatically. "Look, man. This is no big deal. Some dude is paying me a couple hundred to drop the knapsack off at the Circle, that's all. Happens every day. And don't pretend you don't know that."

"No. No way." Ben tried to jerk away. Her hand through the straps held him fast.

"Please, Benjie, I gotta do this. I owe some people."

"Fine. Do what you have to. Just leave me out of it."

Tears welled in her eyes. "I need you."

Ben scanned the path, worried one of the bike cops would come by. "Why?"

"Because I'm sixteen. There's paper on me."

Possession of pot, she had told him a few weeks back. A talking-to from the judge and probation. Small potatoes for kids from the Flats, but things had a way of adding up. "Why me?"

"Because you're fifteen and clean. Something goes wrong, nothing sticks to you."

His stomach churned. "Is something *going* to go wrong?"

"It's a dumb knapsack. We leave it and book out of there. That simple."

"I don't know, Jazz. Sounds too easy."

"These people I owe? Bad news, Benjie. If I can't pay them back in money, they're gonna take it another way. You wouldn't want that to happen to me, would you?"

"No, of course not." The thought of Jasmine being treated like that almost brought Ben to his knees.

"We'll drop this off and go on to Hubbard. I'll thank you properly when we get there."

"Who hired you to do this?"

"Some guy named Luther." Jasmine tugged at him. "Come on, we gotta walk or someone will think we're up to something."

"How'd you meet up with this Luther?"

"Cannon hooked us up."

"Cannon? You're trusting some dude Cannon knows?"

"I thought you was tight with him."

"Doesn't mean I trust his judgment," Ben said. "He keeps some sketchy company."

"Which is why he does good business." Jasmine shimmied her hips. "All about the connections, baby."

"I don't know…"

"Can't you just man up, Benjie? For me?"

A real man would demand she go to the cops. But if this Luther was a heavyweight, Cannon, Jasmine, and Ben would all end up with lead in their heads. Even if the dude was a small-money, it would come back on Cannon and Jasmine in a bad way. Who was this Luther anyway? Cannon always threw names around, but he'd never mentioned this one.

"I swear you'll be safe. Except…" Jasmine brushed his lips with hers. "…from me."

Ben's blood went from zero to exponential in an instant. He couldn't think past *why not*. This was his last day here. Why not make it something he'd remember for a long time?

chapter four

THESE SECRET SERVICE GUYS MUST TRAIN LIKE MOUNTAIN goats, Logan thought.

He cycled the paths at least once every shift and walked the rest of the time. Without Kimmie to rush home to after work, he was in the gym every evening. Taking his frustration out on the bag, pounding his fists on leather instead of Carlton Reynolds's face.

Hiking up North Spire Boulevard, he poured sweat while Pappas wasn't even breathing hard. It was midmorning, but the sun blazed beyond hot. The dog days of August had emptied the area of traffic, folks taking seriously the weatherman's admonition to go to the beach.

Too hot for trouble—just how Logan liked it. He stopped, uncorked his water bottle. "Thought you were interested in the Circle. What are we doing up here?"

Pappas wiped his forehead with the back of his hand. "Perspective. We have satellite imagery, of course, but nothing beats eyeballing a location. Tell me what I'm looking at."

Though they had walked only half a mile, the steepness of North Spire yielded a good view of the two bike paths and their intersection in the rotary. In the Circle, a mass of lofty rhododendrons and azaleas hid the access stairway to the trains.

All that leafy cover gave Logan the creeps. Let the muckety-mucks from Quanta crawl in under those branches and drag out some meth head who'd OD'd or some drunk

19

who'd passed out in his own vomit. They'd be paving the whole thing over the next day.

Logan pointed to his left. "Down there to the east and southeast are the Flats. Triple deckers, strip malls, some warehouses, a couple old factories. The free clinic."

"Typical old Northeast city."

"You could say that."

Logan gazed at the clinic, thinking about Kaya de los Santos packing up to leave Barcester. She'd be missed in the Flats. Framingham was three towns over—she had promised to come back every Thursday for the divorce support group. But those kinds of promises were seldom kept.

"Over there?" Pappas pointed at the only high-rise in the vista.

"That's the John F. Kennedy public housing. Everyone calls it the Tower. The place has its own security and crawls with narcs. Even your ATF guys go under on occasion, but..."

"Nothing seems to work."

"I didn't say that."

"You didn't need to."

Logan bristled. "For all the lowlifes, there're ten times as many good people in the Flats. They lead honest lives and raise their kids to do the same."

Pappas raised his hands in appeasement. "Hey, man. I'm not here to judge."

Logan clenched his fist, startled by the rush of anger that made him want to punch out the guy. *Not here to judge*—that was a lie. Pappas's presence in Barcester meant the Flats had already been judged as dangerous. Just for being what it was and who its people were.

Just as Logan had been judged.

Two weeks ago a technician had swabbed the inside of his mouth. He had been assigned a number, and his anonymous sample sent to some distant lab, along with the slime from Carlton Reynolds's mouth and a sample from Kimmie and Hilary.

Logan had been unraveled and inspected at the deepest part of his being, all the way down to the level of his DNA. Judged and found lacking.

Today Carlton Reynolds would receive his own letter, special delivery and signature required. Would he be thrilled if his letter read *positive for paternity*, or was Kimmie just the price of admission to Hilary Sousa Logan? A judge had granted Hilary temporary custody, ruling that a stay-at-home mother—even staying in someone else's home—could provide a more stable environment than a hardworking cop.

"You OK?" Pappas said.

"Why wouldn't I be?"

"You're flushed, that's all."

"It's steamin' hot out here."

Pappas nodded at the rocky cliffs that bordered North Spire. "What's up there?"

"The Ledges. Highest spot in this part of the state. The only idiots that venture to the top are rock climbers. Further up the Boulevard is the airport. The runways take off over the cliffs. Kinda dicey if you ask me, but we've never had a crash."

Pappas scanned the area, snapping photos and speaking into a tiny recorder on his wrist. Logan suppressed the urge to pat the small gun and notepad in his back pocket. Talk about a dinosaur.

"Over there? That's quite a contrast." Pappas pointed northwest at the stately homes nestled under leafy oak canopies.

"That's Walden Estates. A gated community. Less than a mile from the Flats, but it might as well be a million."

Kimmie was there now, behind the high walls that set Walden apart from—and above—Barcester. It had taken every ounce of Logan's strength to say good-bye to her this morning.

21

Reynolds's restraining order against him meant Logan's mother had to drive Kimmie back and forth for their weekend visits.

Must be nice to be able to buy a judge with a packet of lies and a bigger packet of promises. *Guy's a cop. Quick temper, quick with the fists. He's made threats.*

Logan was lucky to even have a job after Reynolds's attorney got done with the accusations. He probably would be on desk duty if anyone else on the force wanted the substation job.

Ma said Kimmie had run to Marita with a big hug. Great that she had a connection with her nanny, though why Hilary needed one when she didn't work was just another thorn in his side.

Got to keep his mind on the job, with a fed sniffing around his duty area. Logan took another gulp of water, then turned back to the Circle, sighting directly down the path. "It's hazy, but if you look on the diagonal—there, between East University and South Spire—you'll spot the east side of Barcester Polytech."

Pappas pointed to the west of the Circle to a stretch of trees and water between University and the middle-class neighborhoods that bordered Walden Estates. "Is that Hubbard Park?"

"You've done your homework."

"What can I say? All those great federal resources. And MapQuest."

Logan laughed. "Beyond the park are some nice family neighborhoods. Nothing fancy. Mostly single-family houses. Capes and splits. Straight down Spire you've got small businesses, a few stores. And the fire station."

"If you were going to do some damage, where would you do it?" Pappas asked.

"The obvious is the Circle. But they say the trains are untouchable. They are, aren't they?"

"You already asked me that."

"I'm asking again."

Pappas shrugged. "That's what they say."

"What do *you* say, Agent Pappas?"

Silence.

Logan stepped in front of Pappas so he could see him face-to-face. "Are you being straight with me? Or has there been a threat?"

Pappas smiled. "There's always threats. The question is, which ones are serious?"

"You tell me."

"I'm here on a preemptive mission. So I'll ask again. If not the trains, where?"

Logan turned back toward the Circle. This was a question they had all considered in the aftermath of September 11. Other than the high-speed trains, there was only one target a terrorist might go for.

"The Tech. It's a midlevel engineering school. Word is that there's a boatload of federal money in the grad school, and it's not going for peacetime use. But you already know that."

"*Hmm*," was Pappas's only response.

Logan felt like shoving that *hmm* down the guy's throat, but he knew he'd have to get used to such smugness. In a few weeks Barcester would be crawling with federal agents and intelligence experts who would see trouble on every street corner and under every bush.

Applying threat analysis to the place Logan had sworn to protect and defend.

The place—for better or worse—that he called home.

chapter five

J ONATHAN PERCY LOVED THE SILENCE OF THE TUNNELS.
Even when a Quanta car came through on a test run, it was a mere *whoosh*, gliding between the magnetic guideways like a thought that passes without leaving a memory.

Inside the trains, the quiet was profound. They wouldn't remain like that, of course. Once the high-speeds were filled with passengers, there would be the *toc-toc* of computer keys and the murmur of voices on cell phones. The old-fashioned passengers would rustle newspapers, business contracts, and scientific journals. China and crystal would *ping* on silver trays. Coffee in the morning and cocktails at night—white-gloved treatment for people traveling in the Northeast.

If these two high-speed lines were successful, the United States would be criss-crossed with high-speed city-to-city transport. In the time it took to go to Logan Airport, go through security, wait for boarding, and then take off, the high-speed train could rush a passenger from Boston to New York.

And no hate-spewing terrorist wielding a box cutter would be able to crash a Quanta train into a skyscraper.

Chloe's voice sparked on the walkie-talkie. "Hey, sweetie. Where are you?"

"Just finishing up. Heading down now," Jon said.

Every morning, from Providence to Montreal and from Boston to New York, hundreds of engineering grad students walked the tunnels. They inspected for interrupts on the guideways and checked for cracks in the concrete, gathering the data necessary to prove to Lloyd's of London and to the public that the trains were impeccably safe.

Four prototype trains ran daily. A couple of weeks after Labor Day, the full schedule of high-speeds would come on line. By then, inspection would probably be required only on a monthly basis. For now, this part-time job was easy and the pay excellent. That the train lines crossed in Jon and Chloe's duty area was an amazing coincidence.

The kind of coincidence that could make history.

Chloe had discovered that the Boston-New York train created a hinky magnetic field when it passed in the wake of the Providence-Montreal train. Not strong enough to disrupt the guideways or shake the train, but enough of an irregularity to get Jon thinking.

If they could cause the two inbound and two outbound trains to cross at exactly the same time, they might be able to create an exponentially stronger anomaly. In four separate tunnels, there would be absolutely no danger to the trains. In fact, when the full schedule came online in the fall, the trains would cross a couple times a day. Jon and Chloe would no longer have access to the tunnels once the prototype phase ended. It was now or never to see if they could harness this magnetic burst as a poor-man's particle accelerator.

Every great mind in physics was on the hunt for the one theoretical particle—the *unifier*—that was supposed to point to that which bound all forces together. After billions of dollars spent on particle accelerators in the United States and Switzerland, this theoretical boson still hadn't been detected. Some had begun to whisper that perhaps there wasn't a unifying force after all.

Jon didn't believe that. Something held the universe together. Otherwise, mathematics and physics would just be scrawls on a blackboard and not the definition of mass and energy and everything that made the world an amazing place.

They worked for months, Jon creating a makeshift particle detector while Chloe installed the conduit. No one knew—neither the university nor Quanta could be allowed to, though it was perfectly harmless. It was a matter of protecting their intellectual property—by the time Quanta scientists or their own professors had gone down with them, Chloe and Jon would be listed as a footnote in this experiment, rather than the brilliant minds who conceived and executed it.

The guideways had been in place for almost two years, so no one noticed a superconductive pipe barely wider than an inch. Even when the master engineers and Quanta big shots came by, their attention went to the roof and walls of the tunnel, wary of the tons of earth pressing down on them. They were oblivious to what lay right under their feet.

This experiment was a touch insane, but weren't all great discoveries? If two grad students from Barcester Tech could use the Quanta high-speeds as their acceletron, what a slap in the face that would be to MIT and Caltech.

What a glorious boost to their own careers.

Today, due to their elegant hack job to the software that controlled the trains' speeds, the four prototypes would cross. For one miniscule moment, the polarities on magnets on all four guideways would align. Not long enough to cause anything more than perhaps a tiny shudder on the trains.

But long enough to spark a tremendous magnetic burst.

After the crossing, the hacked computer program would readjust the speeds so the four prototypes arrived precisely on time. The few people on board wouldn't even notice—they'd be busy playing video games, watching DVDs, or getting some paperwork done. That's how safe and well programmed the trains were. The code would then delete itself and restore the original programming.

No one would ever know until they were ready to publish their findings. And then Chloe Walter and Jonathan Percy would be scientific superstars, pursued by prestigious labs and foundations that had never even heard of Barcester Polytechnical Institute.

Not long now until 10:00 a.m. Moment Zero, they called it. If they wanted to get mushy about it, they could term it the first moment of the rest of their lives.

Jon jogged down the stairs, trying not to stop and fiddle with the particle detector that he and Chloe had installed before this morning's inspection. The ones at Cern and Illinois were half the size of a house. His was little bigger than a suitcase. Should this experiment produce results, they'd apply for huge grants and build a larger model. They'd likely get a big bonus from Quanta, which would be thrilled to show another use for the high-speeds besides ferrying privileged passengers.

Just one particle. That's all it would take to show this could work.

Jon came out of the stairway and spotted his wife leaning against the wall. Chloe's fingers twitched in some daydream where she deciphered the universe one equation at a time.

"Hey, beauty," he said.

Chloe greeted him with a slow smile. "Hey, beast."

Of Egyptian ancestry, she was graced with elegant features and silky black hair that hung down to her waist. Why a stunning woman like her had married a pear-bodied physicist with snowy blond hair and a receding chin was the one question Jon would never be able to solve.

Why should he even try? There existed no particle trap for joy.

Except perhaps this. Jon pressed his hand to his wife's abdomen, where deep inside their child grew.

Yes, certainly this.

chapter six

ENTERING THE CIRCLE, BEN TOOK CARE TO KEEP ON the proper side of the yellow line. This was not the time to draw attention to themselves by straying into the cycling lane.

"What if someone comes in there while you're leaving it?" Ben whispered.

Jasmine rolled her eyes. "No one's gonna come under those bushes. It's so hot, no one's even out."

They'd only seen a couple cyclists since getting onto the bike path. Even on the street, traffic was unusually light. August meant a lot of people on vacation. The playground program at Tapley School was closed for the day. The city had bused all the little kids to the beach, even the toddlers in the day-care programs.

After a quick look around to make sure no one was watching, Ben and Jasmine pushed through the outer bushes. Anyone who spotted them would assume they were two horny kids looking for privacy.

The lofty branches of the rhododendrons provided welcome shade. Beer cans, snack papers, and condom wrappers littered the ground. In the middle was a chain-link pen topped with razor wire—the access stairway down to the trains.

Ben slid the pack off his shoulders. "OK, we're done. Let's get out of here."

"Wait. What time is it?"

"It's 9:47."

"We've still got three minutes before I'm supposed to leave it and get out of here." Jasmine pulled Ben to a patch of ground that had been cleared of trash. "Come on."

"Come on *what?*"

"Let's sit."

Ben's heart drummed like a jackhammer. This was seriously whacked, but so what? When she leaned against him, time seemed to stop.

Jasmine slipped her arm around his waist and nestled against him. "I'm going to do you a favor, Benjie. Ever get wet?"

"What?"

"You are such a geek. Take a hit." Jasmine sniffed.

"Is that what's in this thing? Coke?" As if he didn't know.

What Ben did know was that something was off here. A backpack filled with bags of cocaine was too valuable to trust to a dimwit like Jasmine. She leaned against him, her lips a whisper away from his own. Making it so hard to think. What kind of fool was he?

"Check it out." She unzipped the knapsack and shoved it in his lap. Inside was a freezer bag filled with white powder.

"What's that stuff doing in the Flats? That's rich dudes' playground."

Jasmine shrugged. "Just going for a ride up the chain, I guess. Come on, let's pretend we're in some Boston penthouse and playin'. One hit, Benjie. No one's gonna know."

Somewhere in the dim mist of Ben's mind, common sense said *walk away.*

"No." Spineless—he should yank her by the elbow and get her out of here. Fast—before what really was going down came down on them.

She laughed. "You've never gone high, huh? A little E or weed, even?"

He cleared his throat, trying to muster nonchalance. "Never wanted to."

"Everyone *wants to*. But not everyone dares." Jasmine traced her finger along the sweet spot under his ear.

Every nerve ending in his body fired.

"OK," he said. "Real quick, though."

Jasmine coated her finger with the powder and slid it into Ben's mouth. "Feel the buzz?"

He shrugged.

"Here, try it again." Jasmine rubbed her finger under his upper lip.

Ben licked his lips, wanting the kick. Feeling cheated. "It tastes sweet."

"Don't be dumb, Benjie. It's supposed to be tangy, and give you a little..." Jasmine ran her finger under her own lip. She frowned.

"What's wrong?" Ben said.

She shoved the baggie back into the knapsack. "We gotta book it outta here. Luther's running some sort of scam."

"What scam?"

"It's sugar, you fool."

"Wait. Maybe they put a bag of sugar on top because they knew you would dig into it."

Ben unzipped the pack all the way so he could get a better look. Underneath the bags of powder was something any kid who had seen an action flick would recognize.

Plastique explosives, with a detonator attached and a digital clock set to 10:00 a.m.

chapter seven

OGAN AND PAPPAS STOOD ON NORTH SPIRE, STARING down at the Circle. Pappas droned on about the precautions for the president's train ride. Quanta planned a party atmosphere, with President Freeman taking in an afternoon game at Yankee Stadium and then a night game at Fenway.

The high-speeds were that fast.

Is that what we've been reduced to? Logan wondered. Burrowing underground so the enemy can't get us? Maybe he should have taken the same route. Gone underground by moving his family out of Barcester right after Kimmie was born. But Hilary had been so loving that he never breathed one doubt about why their daughter didn't look a bit like him. If she had been unfaithful, it was over and done with. He had silently forgiven her, and they became a family, happy together for almost five years.

And then, out of the blue, Hilary announced she wanted a divorce.

Homeland security—what a joke. Logan couldn't even protect the sanctity of his own home, and Pappas was blabbing on about arrangements for Columbus Day?

His cell buzzed, a welcome diversion. Logan glanced at the screen. *Private caller.* Better answer it. It could be Hilary or maybe Marita. He pushed *talk*. "Sergeant Logan."

"Hello? Sergeant Logan?" A kid with a hitch in his voice.

"This is. Can I help you?"

Silence.

"Son, is there something—"

"You gave us a card. Said if there was ever any problem, we could call this number." The kid spoke so fast that Logan could barely catch what he was saying.

"A what?"

"A business card. Two nights ago."

The curfew sweep. Sixteen boys and seven girls trucked to the substation. Most of them thought it was a party, an arrest that would be their first badge of honor. Logan had given them his cell number so they could talk without having to go through the PD switchboard.

"What can I do for you, son?"

"There's a bomb."

"What?"

The kid's voice hushed. "I can't say it again. Someone might be watching us."

"You said *bomb.*"

Pappas jerked to attention. Motioning him close, Logan upped the volume on his phone.

"Yeah," the kid said.

"Where?"

"The Circle."

Pappas frowned. Logan held up his index finger. *Wait.* Hot summer days and bored kids bred pranks. "Are you there now?"

"Nearby. It's set to blow."

Logan peered down the boulevard. They were too far away and the bushes too dense for him to spot anyone. "Talk to me, son. Where exactly are you?"

"I'm calling from..." The kid stopped.

"It's OK. You can tell me."

"I'm outside the Circle on one of the paths."

"Which path?"

"One of 'em, that's all. I told people to get away, said I saw a big snake in the bushes. There were only a couple of kids out anyway. Too hot to cycle."

"Ask him how he knows," Pappas whispered.

"How do you know it's a bomb?" Logan said.

"I was in the bushes. Just hanging out. I...um...found a knapsack in there. There was plastique."

Logan handed his two-way to Pappas. *Call Central,* he mouthed. *Tell them to stand by.*

Pappas got on, speaking low, eyes on Logan.

"You know what plastique looks like?"

"Kinda."

"You want the bomb squad?" Pappas whispered.

Logan held up his index finger again. "If this is a prank, son, you'd better fess up now."

"No prank. I swear. There was a timer attached. It looks like it was set for ten o'clock."

Logan's watch read 9:56.

"Son, go to the substation and wait for me there, OK? Pappas, tell 'em to send the works. I gotta get down there."

Logan broke into a run.

Half a mile and downhill all the way, but suddenly the Circle seemed a hundred miles away.

chapter eight

BULLETS RIPPED THROUGH THE BACK DOOR.

Kaya unlocked the bolts of the front door with one arm while holding the baby in the other. Nearly catatonic with fear, Sarah clung to her shirt like a toddler.

The back door shattered. The man was on them before Kaya could get the last bolt unlocked.

"Give me that baby."

His eyes were narrowed, an animal ready to strike. His hair was ragged, his face gaunt. His arms were marked with tiny scabs, and his pupils were dilated. Clearly a meth head.

"OK, OK. But don't shoot. Please," Kaya said.

"Get out where I can see you." He motioned them into the middle of the waiting room.

"Please," Kaya said. "We only want what's best for your daughter."

"She's not his," Sarah whispered. "Don't say that."

"Shut up, slut. She's mine if I say she is." The man glared at Kaya. "Give her over."

What did her one hour of hostage training teach her? *Make the encounter personal. Find a common ground, a point of meeting.* "I'm Kaya de los Santos, the clinic director. And your name is—"

"Now!"

"Stone," Sarah said. "Please."

He slammed Sarah on the cheek with the butt of the gun. She went down to one knee without making a sound.

"Mr. Stone," Kaya said.

"Just Stone," he said.

"Can I get Sarah some ice? From the fridge behind the desk?"

Stone smacked his palm on the desk. "Hurry up. I see a gun, I'm gonna blow your head off."

"No guns. See?" Clutching Angelina to her chest, Kaya pulled the tiny tray of cubes from the freezer and sat down.

"What're you doing?" Stone was tall and thin. His neck was heavily tattooed and his eyebrows pierced with heavy studs. Reeking of smoke, even now he patted his T-shirt, looking for a cigarette.

Kaya almost laughed when he pulled out a pack of low-tars. "Looking for something to wrap the ice in."

She pulled her chair in all the way. Underneath the desk was the panic button that Jason Logan had installed. She pressed her knee against it and felt it vibrate to indicate the signal had gone out.

"OK, I've got the ice wrapped. Can I give it to her?"

"No. The slut will come get it." Stone turned to Sarah. "Get up."

Sarah held the ice in her hand, apparently unable to stir enough energy to put it to the bruise. Kaya guided the girl's hand to her face.

"Give me the baby." Stone's cheek twitched despite the deep draughts of nicotine. Likely coming off his high.

How long before the cops would get here? Even though the clinic was closed, Jason Logan had insisted on keeping the alarm active.

Kaya liked the sergeant's calm manner, had found herself stealing glances at him in Bible study. His black hair, long enough on top to shine under the lights. His warrior's eyes, fierce until he grinned and showed his dimples. His football build was imposing, but she'd seen him gently cradle an abused child.

Jason's wife had left him a few months back and taken his little girl with her. Stupid woman. If Kaya had a man like Jason Logan, she'd glue herself to him.

Where did that come from? *Survival compensation*—the mind reached for the trivial to alleviate the obvious. Kaya took a deep breath, forced herself to focus. "Stone, this little girl really needs to be looked at before she goes home."

"You're the doc. Look at her."

"I'm not a doctor. I'm a nurse practitioner."

"What you are is stalling. And I'm not liking that, lady."

"I'm not, I swear. Something's wrong with the baby's shoulder."

Come on, Jason. Where are you? He and his people must all be out on patrol. Even so, the alarm should signal a call to his cell. If the substation didn't acknowledge the alert, the signal would be transferred to Barcester Central. Downtown meant an extra eight minutes in response time.

Stone tossed the cigarette to the floor, ground it with his heel into the carpet. "I don't have all day, lady. I'm taking my kid."

The phone rang. In the empty waiting room, it sounded like a fire alarm. After ten rings it stopped, going to voice mail. Probably Central trying to ascertain if the signal for help was genuine. They didn't expect anyone to be here, would likely assign it a low-priority—the work of kids who broke in and were messing around.

"Let me splint her shoulder, OK? Otherwise Angelina will be unmanageable."

"She don't look unmanageable."

"That's because I'm holding her carefully. So her shoulder won't slip."

"OK, OK. After you show me your driver's license."

"What? Why?"

Stone shot into the ceiling, raining down plaster. "I said, give me the license."

39

"Sarah, could you get my license out of my wallet? Is it all right if she does, Stone? I don't want to move Angelina. It might jar that shoulder."

"Whatever. Just give it to me."

The baby grasped at Kaya's shirt, and for the thousandth time her heart ached. Perhaps it was good she had been forced to close the clinic. How many more Sarahs and Angelinas could she bear to heal with medicine, only to see them lost to the likes of Stone?

Sarah's hand shook as she passed the license to Stone. He studied it, then tossed it to the floor. "Good."

"Good what?" Kaya asked.

"Now I know where you live. If you mess with me, I'll return the favor ten times over. So let's go fix that little girl's shoulder, and then her mama and I are taking her home."

"And then what?"

Stone jammed the gun into Kaya's face. "*Then what* ain't your business."

chapter nine

J ASMINE TUGGED AT BEN. "Let's go," she said. "We gotta get out of here."

"We can't. We have to keep everyone away from the Circle until the cops come. Kids. Oh, no, little kids on their bikes. Jazz, they gotta be told to keep away."

There was no buyer, and there were no drugs. Only a stupid girl who for two hundred bucks had carried the pack to a spot where an explosion would devastate the whole neighborhood. If you can't be safe on a bike path with your little kid and her little training-wheels bike, where can you be safe?

They stood about three hundred feet east of the Circle on the edge of the University Avenue path. Ben had tried to get Jasmine to go to the opposite side to warn people, but she refused to leave him.

His watch read 9:59.

A cyclist raced toward them, a stern-faced man in fiery spandex and one of those sleek helmets with the point at the back. Head down, legs pumping, the guy paid no attention to Ben as he waved for him to stop.

"No, don't go in there! Stop!"

The guy had to have heard him. No—he had wires coming out of his helmet, listening to an iPod. Ben flung a rock and screamed, "There's a bomb, fool!"

The man kept riding, head down.

Go fast, Ben hoped, and then he prayed, *God, make him fast.* If the Big Guy wasn't around for times like these, what was His job description anyway?

Ben's watch turned over to ten o'clock. Traffic on the Avenue had picked up, people out on errands. Two men ran across the bridge from Spire Boulevard. Sergeant Logan and some other guy—which meant Ben and Jasmine could finally get out of here.

"Come on. Let's go." Ben scrambled down the bank and headed onto University Ave. "Jasmine?"

"Luther. Omigosh, there's Luther!" Jasmine jerked around and ran back toward the Circle.

The wrong way.

Ben wanted to follow her, to catch her and yank her back, but before he could find the courage to turn his body around, the world exploded—

•••

Kaya splinted Angelina's shoulder, still praying about what to do about Stone when the world made the decision for her.

There was a distant *boom*, followed by bigger bangs from further away. Stone stretched and shrank, as if he had become a rubber band.

Sarah broke out of her stupor long enough to say *oh*, a tiny exclamation echoing on and on until Kaya thought she'd go mad with the girl's everlasting despair.

She swam against the tide, striving against a mighty swell of the moon as it stretched and snapped every tide that had ever rolled in and out.

Shrinking and stretching, snapping and shaking.

The world shook into a billion pieces, but Kaya refused to be shaken because she had splinted a precious baby to herself, and even if the world insisted on falling apart around her, she would not. Grace held her steady in the vortex, giving her time to remember a love that was before all things, and so she found the will to pray—

—*please, God, watch over Ben, wherever he may be.*

•••

Ben watched as the first blast blew Jasmine backward, her eyes wide with confusion until—

—another blast came, and still another until the earth rose up in protest and Ben saw Jasmine come apart in such pains-taking slowness that he was intimate with every bone and muscle and cell in her body—

—and he cried for mercy for her because God must be squeezing this world until it bled, for all he could see was red—

—but that was his blood, not hers, and he watched in fasci-nation as his own DNA wound and unwound, over and over until—

—the sins of the father came to Ben, who vowed in this unending moment that he would never visit his sins on his sons, or his sons on his sins—

—but how could he escape his own blood—

—yet he did because even as the world bent into itself, he knew one thing with certainty—

—that somewhere in this breaking apart, his mother had named him to the heart of God—

•••

For some reason, though the train had gone by Jon and Chloe, it kept on coming—and did so with a huge *bang.*

The world folded in two, and Chloe bent with it, her mouth open as if to protest the warping of the air and the stretching of the tunnel and the persistent train that just kept coming, even though it had gone by.

43

Jon saw the particle. One particle that became a hundred, a million, an infinite array of particles as the big bang from above split the world into its endless possibilities. Too many to count, to calculate, to do anything but wonder.

Suddenly Jon was one person, a hundred, a million, an infinite array of flesh and mind and spirit. Disarrayed as was never meant to be, yet refusing to realign because the stars had lost their alignment. *Give me a minute*, Jon told the universe.

Being of a generous nature, the universe gave him far more.

•••

A flash of fire and the *boom-boom-boom* of one blast after another. Logan spent a lifetime in the air, a lifetime in which—

—a fist of fire swept down from the sun and up from the heart of the earth, roaring a song that couldn't be heard anyway because who was left to listen?

Pappas perhaps, but where was the man in black now?

Where was Logan now? Where was *now*, now?

Why didn't the air stop screaming?

Why didn't the sky stop shredding?

Why did the fire rise up only to cool and rise up again until each finger flame wiggled its own self into existence?

As the blast ripped Logan out of the air and slammed him against the pavement, he uttered the only words he could think of.

Jesus, my Jesus, what is happening?

the first hour

W HEN THE WORLD CEASED ITS STRETCHING, LOGAN sat up and tried to figure out what to do next.

"The trains," he said, taking a strange pride in figuring out the obvious. "They've blown up the trains."

A knot swelled on the back of his head. A thousand bits of dust had pinpricked his skin. He looked down, not surprised to see he had been blown right out of his sneakers.

Pappas's feet were bright white in crisp sport socks, though debris and smoke were everywhere. His face was frozen with shock, but his mouth streamed steady curses aimed at the explosion, the panic, and Osama bleepin' bin Laden.

The *bleeping* was real, alarms from the cars crashed along University Avenue. People cried out, their hands on their heads, looking skyward as if trying to find someone to blame and someone to save them.

Surely Kimmie was in the gated estates where no bomb could get her. *Please, God* was all the prayer Logan could summon, because he had work to do. He stood, pain like a second blast erupting in his lower back. Must be a broken vertebra or ruptured disk. If that was the worst of it, he'd be grateful.

The Circle blazed, the greenery dissolved in flame. If he and Pappas had been on the bike path instead of the boulevard, they'd be feeding the conflagration right now.

Why was the fire silent?

Logan's hearing had become selective, that was it. Which must be why he wasn't hearing sirens though it had been at least two minutes, and maybe more, since Pappas had called for the bomb squad. Yet he could hear the car alarms and people crying, cursing, screaming.

One motorist—insurance info in hand—motioned to a woman to roll down her car window. The familiar amidst the terrible.

Logan held out Pappas's sneakers. "Come on, man. We've got to get moving."

"My shoulder is dislocated. You need to fix it for me. Grab here and here." Pappas pointed to a spot above his elbow and another behind his shoulder. "Now pull that way, and when I yell, push it into the socket."

"The ambulances are coming—"

"Do it!"

Logan did.

Pappas cried out once, then hung his head. "OK, OK. It's manageable now, but I need to splint it."

Logan ripped up his own shirt and fashioned a sling. Pappas pulled it over his head and gingerly slid his arm in.

Logan tied Pappas's sneakers for him, thinking of this morning when he had buckled Kimmie's sandals. All he wanted was to dash up to Walden Estates and make sure she was all right.

And he would do that as soon as help arrived.

A woman ran at him, cradling a young boy. "Someone help, please! My son's not breathing!"

Logan laid the boy on the grass, mindful of burning embers all about. The boy's lips were blue and his eyes rolled back, only white showing. No pulse and no respiration.

"What happened, ma'am?"

"Josh was out with his friends, skateboarding. There was the blast, and he took a bad spill. I ran out, and he sat up and said, 'My head hurts.' Then he just...went over." The woman sobbed, took a breath, and found her voice again. "Please, help him."

"Does he have any condition I should know about?"

"A seizure disorder, but it's controlled. He takes medicine."

It had been a good minute since the bomb. Almost four now since Pappas had called Central. Logan needed to begin CPR, but he could paralyze this kid if he had a neck injury. Then again, if he didn't revive him soon, that would be a moot point.

Logan tipped the boy's head back, squeezed the boy's nose, and gave him a breath. The boy smelled like Doritos. The rise of his chest meant his airway was clear.

Logan began the chest compressions, remembering not to press too hard.

One two three four five. Breathe.

"Come on, Josh."

One two three four five. Breathe. One two three four five.

"I tried to call 911," the mother said. She was a thin woman with spiked brown hair. "The phones are dead."

One two three four five. Breathe. One two three four five.

Time passed—one minute, maybe another. Where were the paramedics?

The blue in Josh's lips faded. A guy in UPS brown tried to put a shipping blanket under his head.

"No. I need his airway open," Logan said. "But you could cover his legs for me."

He looked around, saw Pappas bending over a woman in a yellow sundress. The cheerful color of her dress against cracked pavement was an affront to America, where a woman had the right to stroll on a sidewalk, sun splashing on her shoulders—not broken by a bomb no one saw coming.

One two three four five. Breathe. One two three four five. Breathe.

The mother pressed her face to the sidewalk. "Please, God," she whispered.

49

Logan pressed his ear to the boy's chest. A sickly thub rewarded him. No spontaneous respiration yet.

A dark-haired man stared out of the crowd that had gathered, his eyes eager. Drawn by accidents and violence, his kind were the worst.

Josh gasped.

"Thank God," the mother cried.

"Amen," Logan said. "Keep him warm and comfortable. I'll send the EMTs down here as soon as they arrive."

He got up and went to help Pappas.

chapter eleven

STONE SPRAWLED ON THE FLOOR, UNCONSCIOUS UNDER boxes of baby formula.

Kaya cradled Angelina and tried to get her bearings. Had a plane crashed nearby? Or perhaps it had been an earthquake. That wouldn't account for that strange instant—that instant that seemed to last forever—in which the world stretched out of shape.

Sarah leaned against the wall, dazed. "What happened?"

"I'm not sure." Kaya punched in 911, but her cell was dead. That didn't make sense. She had charged it this morning, had made only a couple of calls.

Stone groaned, his fingers twitching as if looking for the gun. It wasn't anywhere in sight—maybe he had fallen on it.

"We've got to get out of here." Kaya steered Sarah out the front door. In her haste, the girl almost pitched headfirst off the front porch—the bottom step had cracked in the blast.

The scene out on the street was surreal. It was the same old neighborhood Kaya saw every day—huge oaks and pines lining the street, old Victorian houses that had been broken up into multiple apartments, driveways crammed with cars from so many tenants, bikes and riding toys, basketball hoops and baseball pitch-backs, Fenway Variety Store on one corner, the Starlight Diner on another.

But the crash or explosion or whatever it was had changed everything.

The lack of engine sounds was unnerving. In this neighborhood, the background noise of cars, trucks, and factories was a constant reality. People were out but not going about their business. Instead they grouped on the sidewalk, a teen in gang colors talking to a man in a sport coat, an anxious mother with a toddler being consoled by a woman with a walker.

The sky was so overcast that Kaya couldn't see the sun, but the air was strangely clean, as if whatever had caused the booms had purged it.

She unlocked her car, motioned for Sarah to get in. She slid Angelina onto the girl's lap—no time to hunt down a car seat.

The front door of the clinic banged open. Stone stood there, gun in hand, eyes searching them out. Kaya desperately turned the ignition but only got *click-click-click*. She glanced around, realized no cars were moving.

"We've got to run for it. Hurry up." She grabbed Angelina from Sarah and dashed down the driveway.

"Get back here," Stone bellowed.

Kaya stumbled and fell to her knees, clutching the baby to keep from dropping her. Something *pop-pop-popped* over her head, a dreaded noise she knew too well from growing up here.

"Get down," she cried, but Sarah froze, and before Kaya could yank her down, more shots rang out.

Sarah crumpled, a crimson splotch blossoming on her throat. Only enough breath left to gasp, "Don't let...him..." before the light in her eyes died.

Kaya crept into the street, found cover behind a car. Angelina dug little fingers into her neck but could only muster a whimper.

"Give me that baby," Stone shouted, "or you're next."

Lord, save us, she prayed because she couldn't give this baby to a madman.

Stone stormed off the porch and lunged forward, bashing into the sidewalk as he tripped on the same cracked step.

Kaya ran down University Avenue for her life, and for Angelina's.

chapter twelve

J ON HELPED CHLOE TO HER FEET, RUNNING HIS HANDS over her face and shoulders, cupping her belly.

"What happened?" Chloe's voice cracked, as if she hadn't spoken in a hundred years.

"I don't know. Are you OK?"

"Sweetie, I'm fine. We were just trying to push one particle," Chloe said. "Just harnessing a natural anomaly. How could we—"

"We didn't. The *booms* came from high above us. It was an external event."

A series of muffled blasts had come from above just as the Boston-New York flew by, a silent missile speeding through the explosions.

"That just *happened* to occur at the same time we were running our experiment?"

"We need more information before drawing any conclusions." Jon tuned his walkie-talkie to the command frequency. Static burst from the speaker.

"Maybe it's broken," Chloe said.

"No, it looks OK. Something's happened up there."

"Could we have triggered a gas explosion?"

"You know the topography. There aren't any gas lines anywhere near the tunnels."

"An earthquake or a plane crash? Maybe even some weird sonic anomaly?"

"Or the obvious—someone trying to blow up the trains." Jon looked east and west, the tunnels empty as far as he could see. The walls were intact and the lights burned bright. He had been trained to spot any flaw in the guideways or tunnel. None was apparent.

"We're OK," Chloe said. "These tunnels are built to withstand anything."

Jon pulled her close. "You really all right? You took a good fall."

"No bleeding or cramping. We're both fine, sweetie."

"OK. Good. Listen—this place will be crawling with Quanta security in a little while. Before anything else, we'd better retrieve the particle collector."

"Jon. What if the trains...?"

"They're fine. Besides, they weren't carrying passengers. A few engineers, maybe a cheap politician who wants a photo op. Stupid terrorists were two months early with their bomb."

"If it was terrorists that caused this," Chloe said, "it happened at Moment Zero—our moment zero."

"We did nothing more than run a small cable and tweak the trains so they'd cross in Barcester. They've done that before and will do that many times a day when they're in operation. It was our bad luck that the bomb went off at the same instant."

"Scientific reasoning doesn't allow for coincidences, nasty or otherwise."

"Common sense does," Jon said. "For now, that's the hypothesis under which we should operate. We'll go to the stairway, get the detector, and make a quiet exit."

Chloe slipped her arm through his, and together they walked toward the access stairway.

"Maybe it was... some sort of sonic blast?" Jon said. "Why are we thinking the worst just because of a few loud bangs?"

"Dread."

"Don't get all poetic on me."

"I can't help it. Dread is the only appropriate concept for the sinking feeling in my belly."

Jon stopped. "You said you were all right."

"I am. Individually. But as for corporately, for Barcester or even the United States or..." She stopped, panting.

"You're hyperventilating. Honey, it's going to be OK."

"Not an anxiety attack, idiot. Look—the fans aren't going."

Sure enough, the blades that were visible through the grate were not moving. "The vents must be closed. That's one of the antiterrorism controls, right?"

"I thought the fans were supposed to go double-speed. In case of, like, sarin gas or something."

"I don't know, Chloe. Some close, others vent. I just don't know."

She tightened her grip on his arm. "You're panting, too."

"There's too much volume to diminish the air supply yet. We'll be OK. You, me, the baby."

"Promise?"

"Absolute promise." He slipped into their little mantra. "As in zero or space or vacuum or—"

"Oh, Jon. *Vacuum.* The train must have created some sort of vacuum that ordinarily is back-filled by the vents and fans. The air is depressurizing to fill that vacuum. Getting thinner and thinner—"

"No, we don't know that. Besides, vacuum requires a limited space. The tunnels stretch too far to be..."

She nodded, hardly in need of a lecture on Quanta architecture or basic physics. They walked the few hundred feet to the access stairway in silence.

The door was open.

"It shouldn't be," Chloe said.

"Emergency measures," Jon said, making it up as he went along. "The locks must release automatically."

"It's bright. Too bright for the lights." Chloe stepped back, her eyes wide. "The stairwell is on fire."

"It can't be," Jon said, no scientist now as he tried to pretend that what he saw was not what *was*. A steady flame filled the stairwell, casting tremendous light but little heat. "There's no smoke."

"Too hot for smoke. Pure combustion."

"It's not hot at all. Do you feel any heat? And precisely what is burning? The stairs are cast in concrete and the railing is steel."

"We go by facts, Jon. We see fire. Therefore, there is fuel for it to burn."

Jon looked at his feet, expecting to see the walkway shift under him as reason slipped sideways. His stomach roiled, and he had to swallow hard to keep from vomiting. He bent over, taking deep breaths.

"Are you OK?" Chloe patted his back. Always cool in crisis, though the worst crisis they had faced up to now was telling her traditional parents that they had eloped.

Nothing like this—whatever *this* was. "The numbers don't add up," Jon muttered.

"What?"

"Nothing, just thinking." He couldn't figure out this atypical fire simply because he didn't have all the facts. There was no mystery—*no impossibility*. Just a calculation still waiting for its variables to be plugged in before he could solve it.

"Come on. We have to get away from this until we know what it is."

"Yeah. OK."

"We should follow the train west. To the next access stairway. That's what—four kilometers?"

"Yeah." Jon turned with her, heading in the direction of the New York line. "Just for something to do. While we wait for someone to come."

"Will someone come?"

"I promise they will," Jon said, not daring to make it absolute.

chapter thirteen

BEN RACED AWAY AS FAST AS HIS BATTERED BODY WOULD allow. He could outrun the cops but not the scent of Jasmine's perfume on his shirt, the feel of her touch on his skin.

The image of her being blown apart.

Not just her. Other people, bodies lying around, scorched and broken. The worst ones were those who were still alive and moaning. Deep, guttural sounds, like wounded animals. At least Jasmine had been spared that, though Ben would live with the smell of burnt flesh for the rest of his life.

Which might not be much longer.

How terrifying had this Luther been to send her running into the bomb? Or had she simply not believed Ben when he said the mound of clay was plastique and the tiny wires and Blackberry-type device a detonator?

He'd be blamed for the whole thing.

Even if no one remembered Ben carrying the knapsack, witnesses would recall him warning people away from the Circle. How long would it be before his description was on FOX News, along with a sketch of a geek with thick glasses and a Celtics shirt?

Slow down, don't run. People would notice running. Ben shoved his glasses into his pocket and hunched his shoulders like most kids in the Flats. As he cut down a side street, no one even gave him a second look. Almost everyone moved in the opposite direction, more interested in seeing danger than fleeing it.

Was that something in the shadows? Maybe just the wind ruffling the leaves of a small birch tree. Or—maybe not. Maybe Luther had spotted him and wanted to turn him into the same red mist Jasmine had become. Would a bullet to the head be more merciful than getting blown up by a bomb?

Ben ran down another block and into the alley next to Pizza King. He climbed onto the Dumpster and hopped onto the roof of the shop. When he, Cannon, and Tripp were little kids—in those innocent days before they had to worry about their status on the "street"—they used to shoot acorns down on people coming out of the store, then flatten to the shingles and try not to laugh.

The street in front of Pizza King was empty. The quiet gave him goose bumps. Where were the fire trucks and the bomb squad people? It was almost ten minutes since the blast. Had bombs exploded somewhere else in Barcester? That would explain why there hadn't been a response yet. In a citywide disaster, the Flats was the last place the cops would come.

What if the attack was even more widespread? Maybe Boston or even all of the Northeast. But ground zero had to be the Circle—the whole world knew the two train lines crossed there. Stupid Quanta had bragged they were terrorist-proof. Hadn't they ever seen *Titanic*?

Mom was probably freaked. Hopefully she'd see on television that the damage was confined to the Circle and assume he was safe at McDonald's. People were probably hanging out there now, like they did after 9/11. Looking for water or a soda, just wanting to be near others, even people they didn't know.

Where were the news copters? They were always first on any scene. Ben rolled over on the roof and looked up at the sky.

The smoke hung like a gray curtain, fluttering like tinsel on a Christmas tree. He jammed his fists into his eyes to clear his vision. An illusion, that was it—created by a new kind of bomb.

Which meant Ben had really messed up this time. He felt marked, as if a giant arrow hung over his head, flashing a neon sign that read: Here's the sucker who carried the bomb.

Think, loser. It's the only thing you're good at. Think.

Jasmine said Cannon had hooked her up with Luther. If Ben could get a description—or, better yet, find out where the guy hung out—he might be able to clue the cops where to nab this Luther. And convince them that he hadn't meant for this to happen.

If Cannon even knew. He wasn't the sharpest skate on the ice. A fringe player in the Flats, his talent was in connecting people up. He ran schemes, bullied his brother, dissed his mother. But he had always been good to Ben, covering him with his word so the street wouldn't eat him alive.

Ben opened his cell and speed-dialed Cannon. Stupid phone—not even a no service screen. That didn't make sense. He was fully charged and in close range of the nearest tower, the steeple of Grace Community Church. He could see it from this vantage point, even make out the dish behind the clock tower.

What if someone had taken out the satellites?

Was he blaming Osama bin Laden for something that would require a world power to pull off? Too many nuclear weapons from the old Soviet Union were still unaccounted for. North Korea and Iran were both involved in high-level weapons development. And where did those weapons of mass destruction really go?

Not enough information. And no way for a fifteen-year-old fool from the Flats to stop it if some rogue power wanted to blow up the best country in the world.

Think locally, loser. One terrorist at a time.

Visualize success, the therapist in fifth grade had told him. After the old man—he would never be "Dad"—had punched him out, Mom had wanted someone safe for him to talk to.

But then she yanked him because she didn't agree with that kind of behavioral therapy.

What was the difference between a therapist teaching him positive visualization and a Sunday school teacher telling him the invisible and unprovable Holy Spirit would present his prayers to God? People believed what they wanted to believe. Didn't make it true.

Mom admitted that she desperately believed the old man would stop beating on her. Old man—weird term for a guy who hadn't reached forty yet. But Ben would never call Gus Murdoch his father, even though the jerk was responsible for half of his DNA.

Not that Gus would admit it. When he wasn't outright cursing, he called Ben a half-breed. "You wouldn't catch me dead watching Discovery Channel. Or reading all those books," he'd say and pop another brew.

"Gus was my mistake," Mom always said. "Not yours, Benedict. You're nothing like him, nothing at all. You're my blessing."

Would she say that if she found out he was the one who carried the bomb? He'd already done the stupid thing today. Now he'd do the right thing. Track down some information from Cannon, pass it to Sergeant Logan or whoever they sent looking for him.

Instead of being the kid who carried the bomb, Ben Murdoch would be the kid who caught the dirtbag who blew up the trains.

chapter fourteen

IRST-RESPONDER PRIORITIES.

Communicate with Central. Not going to happen. Logan's two-way was dead, as was his cell phone. Where were Jamie Walsh and Paul Wells, his other cops on duty? He hoped their training would kick in.

Establish a perimeter. No need, at least right here on East University. No one was eager to approach the flames. Strange clusters of smoke roiled up from around the Circle, trailing so high overhead that he couldn't see the sun.

Logan's knees wobbled. No, he couldn't deal with any pain or fear, not right now. Work to be done. First on the scene, respond appropriately.

Deal with casualties. It was too late for the poor souls who had been in the Circle when the bomb blew, but there were plenty who needed attention. Those closest to the blast, like Pappas and himself, had shock injuries that would need to be evaluated. Other people were hurt by flying glass and debris. The numerous vehicle crashes would have spawned injuries.

Where were the ambulances? Logan had to start triage and needed more help than the one-armed Pappas could provide.

"Can I have your attention, folks? Listen up for a minute. I'm Sergeant Logan, Barcester PD." He hoped some would recognize him even though he was bare-chested and dressed in shorts. "We need people with medical training."

No one came forward.

"Nurses, technicians, EMTs. Even if it's just first-aid training. Come on, folks. We need you."

Two women and one man moved out of the crowd. They identified themselves as a physical therapist, a nurse's aide, and a lab tech respectively.

"Now I need at least two volunteers for each of these medical folks."

A thin woman in a miniskirt shook an accusatory finger at him. "The EMTs will come and take care of this. The rest of us should just go home."

A man with a bushy white mustache glared at her. "How? Your car working?"

Then a dam burst, shock erupting into fear, anger, and worry. *I need to get home...I left my elderly mother...Someone's trapped a couple hundred feet back...I hurt my neck...My car is wrecked...Why aren't the cell phones working?*

Logan took a deep breath, waved his arms. "If you're willing to help, step up. Otherwise, stay on the sidewalks and out of the way."

"Why won't the cars start?" someone shouted.

"I don't know," Logan said. "But we need them moved. If anyone is a good runner, you can head down the street, tell people to roll cars out of the way. We need a clear path for when emergency vehicles arrive."

A thin woman in a flowered skirt raised her hand. Logan recognized her as Dorothy Britain from Muir's Hair Salon. "I can do that," she said.

"Thanks. If there's something I need to know about, send someone back this way."

"You got it." Dorothy jogged down University, shoulders squared with purpose. In the face of chaos, any measure of control was comforting.

"What about the bodies?" someone yelled out.

Pappas had covered the face of the woman in the yellow sundress with newspaper. There were four other fatalities that Logan could see, but who knows how many others had been caught too close? A dark-haired girl had run toward the Circle just as the bomb blew.

Triage—help those who can be helped and grieve later.

"Sergeant." An older woman touched his arm. "What about the bodies?"

"Leave them for now."

"Can't we at least cover them up?"

"That would taint the investigation."

"We don't need no investigation," a man in paint-covered overalls roared. "We know who did this."

"If someone can round up some sheets or towels, just lay them over the faces. But please, don't touch anything or move anyone."

Logan bent over, trying to clear his head. *First-responder duties.* Circle the blast site, see who else needs help.

Wait for word from Central—Boston—Washington—telling him what to do.

"Sarge!" One of his patrolmen pulled up on his bike. Paul Wells was a muscled stud and rough around the edges, which made him perfect for the Flats. "They're saying someone blew up the trains?"

"I don't know. Maybe. Listen, I need you to get to Babin's Pharmacy, load up on supplies, and get them to my medical responders. Tell Chet I sent you. He's on the disaster plan—he'll know what to do."

Logan scanned the crowd, waved over two kids on bikes. "You kids go with Officer Wells. Do as he tells you."

"Rockin'," one of the kids said. "We get to help!"

"Have Chet ring everything up. The city will reimburse him. We need sterile water, bandages, soap, ice packs. Get those boys knapsacks or something to haul stuff—"

Wells swung back onto his bike. "I got it, man."

"Yeah, OK. Go."

A chunky teen handed Logan a Coke. "Look like you need this."

"Hey. Thanks. I guess I do."

"I got you this, too." He held up a gray T-shirt with a New England Patriots logo on it.

"Wow. I owe you, man." Logan slugged down the soda, the sugar restoring a bit of what adrenaline had drained. He pulled on the shirt. A size too small, but at least he didn't look like Tarzan now.

First-responder priorities. Go around the fire, see if there are injuries on Spire or West University.

He found the nurse's aide trying to gently remove a rollerblade from a young boy's broken ankle.

"I need to check the rest of the immediate area," Logan told her. "Are you OK for now?"

"For now, but..." She stood, blocking the boy's view. "Where are the ambulances? It's been almost ten minutes."

"They're coming. We called for them befo—" He caught himself.

"Before?" She squinted. "Before what?"

"They've been called, and they'll be here." Logan turned away. If word got out that he'd had advance notice of the bomb—even by only a couple of minutes—people would be on him.

Pappas caught up to him, his face still gray and his shirt soaked with perspiration. "I've done what I can here. I'm going back to the substation and try to get communication established."

Logan's cop radar kicked in. The man had flashed credentials, dressed like a fed, sounded like a cop. But without Central's blessing, how could Logan really know? *Pappas shows up, and an hour later a bomb blows. Maybe a coincidence. Maybe Homeland Security knew of some threat.*

Or maybe Pappas was the bomber, wanting to see his own handiwork.

"After we assess the rest of the blast area."

"Sergeant, you've got your priorities. I've got mine."

"Let's get this perimeter managed, and then I'll take you down there."

Pappas's eyes narrowed. "I expect your cooperation. As will your superiors."

Logan folded his arms across his chest, feeling ridiculous as the sleeves of the undersized T-shirt tugged on his biceps. "Unless you got President Freeman in your pocket, you've got no jurisdiction here. Since I do, I'm going to make sure there's no one on the other side of that fire who needs help. You can come with me or I can cuff you to a lamppost so you'll stay out of trouble. Which is it, Pappas?"

"Your lack of cooperation doesn't bode well."

"Nothing bodes well today. Or haven't you noticed?" Logan climbed the embankment to the bike path and headed for the Circle.

Pappas caught up to him. "Sure you want to get this close? What if it's a dirty bomb?"

"Then we're dead already. Soaked through with radiation, right? But maybe you know something I don't."

"What're you saying?"

"What are you *not* saying?"

"I don't have time for this, Logan. Just say what's on your mind."

"I want to know how you knew when and where a bomb was going to explode. And why you didn't warn us."

"Straight up—we got a tip."

"Homeland gets lots of tips. That's what you said."

"Some gangbanger dropped a dime. Said this mutt was asking around, looking for a courier. Implied it was a simple drug drop, but this guy—calling himself Luther—was way off profile for the Flats. Gave the snitch the creeps. No one in DC or Boston paid much attention. Too many threats, too little time. Even so, this one was shunted our way because of the possible link with the trains. The rest is just as I told it, Logan. I got a gut feeling. When someone on the street decides something stinks, you've got to sniff it for yourself. So I arranged this stop-by."

"Did you know the timing?"

"No clue. We knew this Luther wanted a courier, but that was it. The rest is just brutal coincidence."

In the rotary, Logan headed counterclockwise, heading toward South Spire Boulevard. A scorched, earthy odor lingered in the air from the smoldering roots of the rhododendrons and azaleas. The fire blazed on one side, showing no sign of lessening. The smoke was bizarre—shimmering as if it were threaded with silver, making Logan more nervous than ever about some sort of radiation. More mist than smoke, it had no smell but felt cold against his skin. And it billowed out from the fire and curved over their heads, forming what seemed like a mushroom cap that bent all the way to the ground and closed them in.

A deadly tunnel, Logan thought. We'll never survive this.

His skin crawled with the sense of utter abandonment. Pastor Rich, the guy who led the Thursday night Bible study, said God was with you wherever you went. Hard to believe that here or most places. The pastor might see the kingdom of God in the here-and-now, but it was Logan's job to clean up after hell on earth had its way.

Like now. He had a job to do, so he kept walking in this tunnel of mist and fire.

After a few more steps, Logan heard familiar sounds, similar to what he'd left behind on University—shock, anger, fear. Desperate people, looking for someone to tell them what to do next.

For better or for worse, that someone was him.

chapter fifteen

THE OTHER SHOE, ALEXIS LATHAM THOUGHT.

Hadn't they been waiting since September 11 for the other shoe to drop? These terrorists were termites. You could spray the corners and cloak your foundations, drill holes and drop poison. But when you least expected it, they'd bring down your house around your ears.

It was good that this happened during the day while she was at the store. As general manager and owner of Donnelly's Supermarket, Alexis had the fierce will and common sense to make sure all her customers—and the store—would be taken care of.

And she had her gun.

Licensed to carry, trained to shoot, Alexis could protect what was hers. As she shoved her Lady Smith & Wesson 9-mil and an extra clip into her pocket, she flipped on the office television. Snow was all she got. No signal, no emergency broadcast. Just white static.

The emergency lights were on. Power was out on the street, but after 9/11 she had installed three top-flight emergency generators. As long as her diesel held out, the freezers and refrigerators would, too.

Alexis took the stairs from her office carefully, in case they had come loose in the blast. From up here she had a good view of the windows—or what was left of them. Somewhere in the cyclone of sound that followed the first explosion, she had heard the glass shatter. The breaking apart seemed to take forever, as if she counted every shard as it hit the floor.

Shoppers huddled near a display of Life cereal, some banging on cell phones, others clutching children. An elderly couple clung to each other, and a middle-aged man comforted a squalling preschooler. Other than the windows, the store seemed intact. A display of beach toys had toppled, but the season was almost over anyway.

Only three checkouts had been manned to handle the midmorning lull. Alexis wasn't the praying type, but she cast a vague thought heavenward, hoping that she wouldn't find her girls dead at their registers.

"Bev, where are you?" she called.

"We're here." Her senior cashier waved from under her register. She huddled with Kate and Jenny, the teens who worked summers.

"It's OK. Come on out."

"What happened?" The tremble that seized Kate seemed unable to exhaust itself.

"Shush, dear." Alexis rubbed her back. The girl was skin and bones, expecting to graduate high school and become America's next top whatever. "Breathe deep. Come on, that's a girl."

Bev grasped Alexis's shoulder hard enough to bruise. "I need to talk to you."

"Jenny, hold on to her. That's good." Alexis moved away, Bev still holding tight to her.

"Ralph," she whispered.

Alexis glanced at the door, saw Ralph Pepper lying in a mound of glass and blood. So much blood. She took a long breath, willed her voice to be steady. "I'll take care of it. I mean, him."

"I've got to get home. My kids." Bev's children were ten and twelve, old enough to fend for themselves while she worked.

"Sure. Go out the back. Keep away from..." *Ralph*, they both knew, but Alexis said, "...the glass."

Seventy-five years old and a retired bus driver, Ralph had supplemented his retirement by jockeying carts. His eyes were closed and his mouth serene, as if a gentle hand had said *hush, dear* rather than shoving a shard of glass through the back of his neck.

Alexis reached for a plastic bag to cover his face. But he won't be able to breathe, she thought, then rebuked herself because now was not the time to be irrational. Ralph wouldn't ever breathe again, and despite that shocking fact, someone had to remain calm.

Alexis had long ago elected herself to that job.

She untied his apron and covered his face and neck with it. Ralph had just been diagnosed with advanced bowel cancer, though she was the only person at the store who knew. What mercy had ensured that he'd been the only person near the windows when the bomb went off?

Shoppers moved cautiously toward the front of the store, caught between the horror of Ralph's body and curiosity about what was going on outside.

An overweight woman in a Red Sox cap shook her phone at Alexis. "My cell phone's not working."

"Mine either." This from a worried mother with a baby pressed to her shoulder. "Why won't they work?"

"I don't know," Alexis said.

Shoppers looked at her, recognizing the authority of her straight back and white manager's coat. "Look, keep calm, everyone. I'll see if I can find out what's happening out there. You all wait here."

Alexis grabbed Ralph's broom and punched out the glass shards that still remained in the door frame. Then she stepped outside.

It looked like a war zone.

Windows were blown out in all the stores on the block. Vehicles were crashed up and down University Avenue, mostly fender benders. One SUV had flipped over, and a UPS truck had plowed into a telephone pole. Maybe that's why power was out. Some people attended to the injured, helping them out of cars, trying to keep them calm. Others wandered about, unsure what to do or knocking their cell phones against their palms. Some walked purposefully, purses, knapsacks, or briefcases over their shoulders. Like Bev, their instinct was just to get home.

Not Alexis, though. No reason to go home. Her daughters lived in California, one working as a screenwriter and the other as a makeup artist. They were safe, she knew, because her gut would have told her if they weren't. Even her cat was self-sufficient, and antisocial to boot.

A haze cloaked the sky, a gelatinous mass of gray and blue. It vibrated, making Alexis want to tremble, too. But no, there was work to be done. A store—a neighborhood—needed her.

In her parents' time, the Flats had been a respectable working-class neighborhood. Social programs and cultural disarray of the sixties had paved the way for drugs and other afflictions. Now decay ate away at a good neighborhood the way Ralph's tumors ate away at him. Alexis could have put her hard-earned money into a store in Vermont or Idaho, but there was work to be done in the Flats. People needed to eat.

People needed someone who was one of them to believe in them.

Dawn Martinez waved from Exotic Nails across the street. Next door to her, Harry Kontos stood in front of his dry-cleaning shop. He had given up smoking ten years ago but joked often that he'd take it up again right before he died. He puffed on a cigar like he was enjoying the end of the world.

"What happened?" Alexis called out.

Harry took a deep lungful of smoke, blew it over his head. "Bomb at the Circle."

At the police substation a few doors down and across the street, a slender, dark-haired woman banged at the door. Alexis's heart ached at sight of a baby in the woman's arms. So young to be exposed to terror. Despite the woman's knocking, no one buzzed her in. What few cops the city gave this neighborhood would all be down at the blast site helping out.

The woman spotted Alexis and waved frantically. It was the nurse who ran the clinic. Correction: *used* to run it, until the fools on the city council and the scum ambulance-chaser put an end to all the good work she had done.

The woman ran across the street, holding the baby to her chest.

"Something wrong?" Alexis said. "Other than the bomb, that is."

"A bomb? That's what it was?"

"That's what they're saying." The clinic was six blocks east of Donnelly's. Too far to hear the explosion, perhaps. "I'm sorry, I've known you for years, but we've never met. I'm Alexis Latham."

"Kaya de los Santos."

"I know. Is this your baby?"

"No, she belongs to one of my patients." Kaya's shirt was drenched with sweat. Despite her dark hair and eyes, her skin was pasty. "OK if we go inside?"

Alexis took a long look around. Thankfully, Donnelly's parking lot was nearly empty—the Monday morning lull after the weekend shopping. Her fellow merchants stood protectively in front of their stores. There seemed to be no immediate threat she needed to watch out for. "Sure. But I need to warn you, we've got a fatality inside. My bag boy. Not a boy—he's over seventy. Poor guy."

"I'm so sorry—but trust me, that won't stop me." Kaya ducked through the door and scurried to the back of the store.

Alexis glanced up at the security mirrors to make sure no one was light-fingering in the cosmetic aisle. She caught up to Kaya at the display of twelve-pack sodas stacked almost to the ceiling. Good thing those hadn't come down during the blast. Talk about a lawsuit waiting to happen.

"What can I do for you?" Alexis said.

Kaya stroked the baby's hair. The little girl hadn't squirmed or cried. Poor thing seemed as shocked as everyone else. "I need you to take this baby. Please."

"What? You're asking me to babysit her?"

"No. I am begging you to *protect* her."

"Why?"

Kaya blinked back tears. She was a pretty woman—beautiful, really, no matter the gray at her temples and the lines around her mouth. The closing of the clinic and the ridiculous publicity must have been a huge strain.

"There's been a shooting," Kaya said. "Her mother—"

Alexis slipped her hand into the pocket of her jacket, felt her steel security blanket. "Honey, you're safe here. Tell me what happened."

Kaya poured out a tale so ugly that even Alexis was shocked.

"I'm not even sure if this man Stone is still alive," Kaya said. "But if I can hide the baby while I find Sergeant Logan, at least I'll know she's safe."

This was insane, Alexis thought. She had a dead body to contend with, a store to button up against shoplifters and—if this bomb thing wasn't resolved in the next couple of hours— maybe looters to worry about.

When was the last time she had even held an infant? It'd been twenty-five years since Virginia was a baby. She had blue eyes, the same color as Alexis's. Jessie had big brown eyes like Brad's. Big brown eyes, like this baby's.

She stroked the child's cheek with the back of her fingers. So soft. All she had been through, but she didn't cry—just looked at Alexis as if she knew she could trust her.

"What's her name?"

"Angelina."

"Straight from the tabloids."

"Listen, Alexis. I understand why you'd say no. But this man Stone is looking for her with me. He won't know to come here."

"Just let him try." Alexis took the baby, held her close. "Just let him try to take her from me."

chapter sixteen

LOGAN AND PAPPAS SKITTERED DOWN FROM THE BIKE path and onto South Spire Boulevard. Jamie Walsh ran up to meet them. She was small for a cop, but strong, with a friendly manner that was a good fit for community policing.

"Sarge, thank heavens. I've been waiting for backup. What happened?"

He introduced Pappas and gave her the standard answer. "Some sort of bomb. That's all we know. Do you have casualties?"

"'Fraid so. I've got two." She pointed to the bodies on the side of the path. "I grabbed tarps from Lorden's Hardware to cover them with. Didn't know what else to do."

"You did good."

"Hal Monroe's been helping me. Hey, Hal! Come here."

Hal Monroe trotted over, a retired cop who spent his time shooting the breeze either at the U-Ave sub or the Starlight Diner.

"Logan. What the—"

Jamie gripped his arm. "Tell Sarge about going down to the firehouse."

"We worked with the injured, counting the seconds until help arrived. A minute went by, and another, but we still didn't hear sirens. Jamie and me figured one of us better go looking. I hopped on the gal's bike. Haven't been on two wheels in forty years, but we couldn't get any of the cars started. Pedaled down South Spire. Cars stalled everywhere, all the way down. One of those weird bombs, I figured. Worried that madman from North Korea—no offense, Sergeant."

"None taken."

"Anyway, I worried he might hit us someday. Here we are."

Logan held back a smile. Hal was a veteran of the Korean War, still thought Communist first and Al Qaeda a distant second.

"Anyway, I kept pedaling and pedaling," Hal said. "And then I notice the smoke or whatever it is—it's coming down on me."

"I don't follow," Logan said, though perhaps he did. At the Circle, the smoke had curled around the bike path, forming that strange tunnel.

"The further I got down the Boulevard, the lower it got. And I'm still hearing no sirens, nothing to indicate the fire station or Barcester Central or the bloomin' Federal Bureau of Interference was doing anything to help us. And then the smoke reached the ground in a solid wall. I skidded to a stop on the bike, practically breaking my neck. Logan, I don't mind telling you I was afraid. I took a couple steps into it, wound up confused and dizzy. I'm old, but I ain't that old. So I came back. I'm sorry I couldn't find any help though."

Logan clapped him on the shoulder. "Hey, man, thanks for all you're doing. Can you stick around? We might still need you."

"You bet, Sarge."

"Jamie, what's your triage status?"

"Most injuries are from flying glass and debris. But Sarge, I've got a little girl with a neck injury. The woman with her—I'm assuming her mother—was one of the fatalities." Jamie's voice cracked. "I think the little girl is paralyzed."

Logan exploded. "We've been flapping on about Hal on a bike ride and you've got a child down?"

"Sergeant, I attended to her quickly and have people with her now. My priority was to find help for everyone." Jamie's jaw clenched. "*Everyone.*"

"Where is she?"

"I was afraid to move her, so we've got her where she fell. On the far side of the path." Jamie pointed to the grassy slope a couple hundred feet from the rotary, opposite from where he and Pappas had come out from the Circle.

Logan ran, pain not an issue because if *his* daughter—whom he should have never allowed to go back to that slime Reynolds, no matter what any judge said—if this was *his* Kimmie, then terror truly had found its mark.

A man and a woman huddled over the little form. Logan shoved the man out of the way and bent down to the girl, hating himself for the surge of relief in his chest.

She was an African-American child, with huge brown eyes that locked on him. "You're the police guy, right?" she whispered.

"Yeah, sweetheart. I'm Sergeant Logan. Tell me your name again."

"Natasha."

She and her mother were always on the bike path. The mom had lost forty pounds, and little Natasha had lost her training wheels.

"You took a spill, I see."

Natasha blinked slowly, as if she wanted to nod. The woman on her other side looked across at Logan, the message in her eyes clear. *This is a nightmare.*

Logan stroked Natasha's cheek. "Do you hurt anywhere, honey?"

She nibbled her lower lip. "My shoulder. But I can't rub it."

"Better that you don't, then. One of us will rub it for you." He nodded at the woman and mouthed the word *gently.*

Then tears came, hot drops down the child's cheeks, followed by a confused look because she couldn't wipe them away. "I'm scared."

"I know, sweetie. It's a scary time, but we've got people to help you. I want you to hold still, OK?"

Natasha broke into sobs. "I can't move, so don't tell me not to."

"Oh, honey, I'm such a dope. I'm sorry." Logan wiped away her tears. "We're going to take you to the hospital and get you all better."

"Where's my mommy?" she hiccupped.

"She fell off her bike, too. We've got people helping her." Logan hated the lie, but the truth would be merciless. "Just hold on for a few minutes while I go looking for the ambulance. Can you do that for me?"

"OK."

He pressed his lips to her forehead. "You forgive me for being a dope?"

She nodded, showed the beginning of a smile. "OK."

Logan tried to stand, couldn't get his back to cooperate. The man he had shoved offered a hand, helped him up. Someone else forgiving him for being a dope.

"Don't let her turn her head. OK?"

"You got it."

He started back toward Jamie.

"Thank you, Sergeant," Natasha called after him.

Logan's heart hammered. If he learned that Stefan Pappas was involved in the bombing that had hurt this little girl, he'd break him in two.

He took Jamie aside. "I need to see the woman's body."

"She's gone, Sarge."

"I might be able to identify her for sure."

Jamie led him back toward the Circle, keeping to the bottom of the embankment. "We figure Natasha was well ahead of her mother on the path. You know how kids like to race ahead."

Two corpses sprawled to the far side of the embankment. One was a charred body of indeterminate gender, melded with his or her bike. The other was a woman whose safety helmet had been shattered and her back burned.

Logan bent down. Indeed, this was Natasha's mother, but her name wouldn't come. Come on, come on—what was her name? She deserved to be known.

Trina. Trina Perkins.

"We'll take care of your baby for you, Trina," he whispered. "I promise."

chapter seventeen

I F THE BOMB HADN'T BLOWN THE GIRL TO MIST, LUTHER would have had to put a bullet in her head.

Shame, really. Little Jasmine was fiery and fresh, the way he liked them. Not much in the scheme of things, but genuine, through and through. The same girl when she died as when she had been born.

He was a different matter, of course. Wearing so many faces, speaking in so many tongues that some days he forgot his own real name. Forgot where he had come from, whom he had loved.

Not why he was here though. Never that.

He had been a mole so long that the light of day bleached his true identity. It took a long mental squint to grasp who he had been before burrowing underground and coming back up as someone entirely different each time.

His own cause couldn't nurture him, of course. Not like they did the young ones who were brought in as dewy-eyed kids. Taught in groups that drummed the cause through their skin, they couldn't breathe without gasping for victory. Sent out to mission fields, some carried money, some carried the message, some carried the bombs.

He was of the elite few who called the shots. Buried so deep that he could manipulate with a mere whisper. Indeed, he was the epitome of that marvelous piece of Christian irony—*the first shall be last and the last first.*

It would take a day or so for some cop to backtrack the girl's pathetic life and come up with a name. They'd be hard-pressed to come up with a face. The oversized shades and cap took care of that. Shoulder padding, skin coloring, and a gold tooth monogrammed with the blocky *L* ensured that anyone's recollection would be the tooth and little else.

Yet Jasmine had recognized him. How'd she do that when he was stripped of his street persona, looking as close to his own self as he ever did? Perhaps it was an intuitive leap, that psychic grace he had seen in other victims in the last moment before their deaths.

That boy would have to be accounted for, of course. No telling if the skinny kid actually registered a face when the little tramp called out his name, but he didn't get where he was by leaving such things to chance.

He would hold on to this character for a while, at least in his mind. The explosion was so fresh that his own name seemed dangerous, even as a passing thought. And wasn't this a moment of triumph for Luther, the extent of which had yet to be revealed?

Stalled cars were only the first sign. When power finally was restored, these suckers would discover that anything with a computer chip had been fried. The geeks at Barcester Tech would be the first to howl, but wait until Mary Sunshine tried to use the microwave to heat her tea, the couch potatoes tried to fire up their plasma screens, or some nurse stuck a digital thermometer in a kid's ear.

And what of the Quantas? Time would tell, though the corporation wouldn't. Mustn't interfere with their stock offering, of course.

He would find a way to get those classified reports and see what the actual damage was. If nothing else, the high-speeds had been stopped dead. Theoretically, they couldn't crash—nothing to bump into down in those tunnels. But an electromagnetic pulse the size of a small sunspot would have shaken those babies enough to put a scare into potential riders.

Enough to derail—*gotta love the pun*—the massive Quanta corporation.

The United States mourned the three thousand lost in 9/11, but what he and his people admired were the trillions of dollars blown to bits, the businesses crippled or smashed into dust. Paper flying over Manhattan, lifetimes of information spit out like confetti. Yet this country still hadn't grasped the notion that the greatest act of terrorism would be one that systematically shredded their economy.

That truth was buried deep under Barcester. The collateral damage was nice, but the terror dawning on the faces of these fools as they realized their world had been rocked was his real reward. Stripped of cars and cell phones, they wandered in a daze, waiting for someone to restore order.

Which was exactly what he was waiting for.

Order restored meant order that could be blown apart. And once again, the suckers would never see it coming.

chapter eighteen

"**P**APPAS." Logan motioned him close so he could speak low. "Is there some Homeland Security protocol that could account for the delayed response?"

"Maybe they're running some aerosol test, making sure this mist isn't bioreactive."

"Not good enough. These people need help, and they need it now."

Pappas shrugged his good shoulder. "You pulled rank, Logan. So you get to decide what we're going to do."

"If emergency services won't come here, then I'll go drag them out of their safe little station house."

"What makes you think you'll have more luck than your friend Monroe?"

"Nothing," Logan said. "But I have to try. Do what you can to help Jamie and Hal until I get back."

"No flippin' way. You got your job, I got mine. Give me those keys."

"Sorry, Agent Pappas. But we need as many trained personnel on the street as we can get." Maybe Logan was being hardheaded, but the thought of Pappas alone in the sub didn't sit well. Not that there was much there. The radio, some files, a first-aid kit, keys to the cruisers. And the gun safe.

"I got a long memory, Logan. And I sure as blazes won't be afraid to use it when your superiors arrive."

Pappas stomped back to work, doling the ice packs Hal had pilfered from the Kiddie Academy. Retired or not, Hal had slipped right back into his tough cop persona.

Logan hopped onto Jamie's bike and rode it onto the path. He preferred its relative solitude to the Boulevard where people milled about, cursing their stalled cars or shaking their cell phones. Yet for every whiner, there were two people wanting to know what they could do to help.

He glanced over his shoulder, hoping to make out Walden Estates up on the hill. But the mist hung heavy over the blast site, obscuring everything north of the Circle. He couldn't see to the east or west either, as if the mist blossomed out around the bike path. In one sense, it put him eerily in mind of the doughnut-shaped cloud generated by nuclear bombs, except for the opening where the bike path intersected the rotary.

He cycled south, ignoring his back spasms and flaming sciatic nerve.

Looking down the boulevard, he could see mist obscuring the top stories of the Werner Insurance building. The fire station was a block past Werner. The air vibrated, reminding Logan of his junior high science class when Mr. Lester explained about the movement of electrons. The whole universe was in motion, if one were to believe the physicists and the Discovery Channel. That the earth under their feet felt solid was an illusion.

Logan rode on, trying to pray for Kimmie and little Natasha and the lady in the sundress and the girl who had run into the bomb instead of away from it. One block, four blocks, six blocks, praying for Jamie and Hal to do good duty and for Pappas to be friend and not mortal enemy.

Was God even listening?

When he was within three blocks of the Spire firehouse, he rode down the grassy border until he was back on the Boulevard. Even here, nearly a mile south of the Circle, cars and trucks had stalled, though the fronts of buildings were intact. No windows were broken, nor was anything charred.

Another phenomenon was in play here, Logan thought, something that must have driven people to move north toward the Circle. As Hal had described, the mist curved down to the ground, a barrier to emergency responders who were either too frightened to pass into the mist—or had been ordered not to.

Was the mist a by-product of the bomb or its real intent? Was everyone in the Flats already the walking dead?

Logan's anger hardened, a rock-solid resolve to steal an ambulance or rescue truck and drive it back himself. People needed help, and they needed it now.

The mist hung before him, a veil draped from the sky, close enough so he could stretch out his arm and see his hand disappear into it. It was translucent, like one of his mother's sheer curtains, but it refracted light in some odd way. If he stared hard enough at it, he could see an endless stretch of trees and sky. The green and blue vibrated as before, but now that he was up close, Logan saw the movement in lines, like a clear tinsel hung from above.

Just a mirage, some trick of light. Nothing to fear here—he knew exactly what lay on the other side, and it sure as spit wasn't a forest. Hadn't he walked or biked these streets his whole life?

What was that old line from World War II that Grampie Logan used to quote? Nothing to fear but fear itself.

Logan straightened his shoulders and walked into the mist.

chapter nineteen

"**O**H, NO," CHLOE SAID. "There's the train."

The Quanta car sat about a quarter mile down the guideway, wrapped in a dark haze. She broke into a run. Jon caught up, stopped her. "Slow down. The air is thin."

She yanked away. "Don't treat me like a child."

"I'm treating you like the *mother* of a child. Our child. Slow down."

"We've got to do something."

"I'll run up there, check things out. You meet me there in a couple of minutes. Swear you'll walk at a nice, easy pace. OK?"

"I hate playing the little woman."

"Play the big mommy then," Jon said.

"Yeah, yeah. OK. But you wait until I get there to perform your manly heroics. You'll want an audience."

"You bet." Jon kissed her forehead, then took off at a jog.

Wider than a conventional rail car, the Quanta train was streamlined for speed but spacious for comfort. When the magnets were powered up, the cars hovered between the guideways, propelled forward by the alternating states of electromagnetic attraction and repulsion.

Though the lights still shone overhead, there was no glow to the guideway. The circuits to the trains had been broken, which meant computer control had somehow been disrupted. Without the magnetic force to elevate it, the train had sunk between the guideways. Jon could only see half of a single car buried in mud. Indeed, the entire tunnel was blocked by mud.

What if their little hack job had caused this catastrophe? What if they had killed someone?

Out of breath, he had to stop and squat down. No time for what-ifs now, even though unraveling such what-ifs had driven Jon's whole life.

"You all right?" Chloe's voice echoed from down the tunnel.

"Totally out of shape." As if he had ever been in shape. "Take it slow, babe."

Obviously the tunnel had been breached, but where did the water come from to turn earth into mud? Barcester was chosen for the train crossing because of its granite-based topography. Geological surveys had shown no water tables or faults.

Someone called out from inside the train.

Jon jumped down onto the platform and pushed through the door. The car seemed empty. "Is someone in here?"

"Here! I'm up front."

Jon moved quickly, barely taking in the fine leather seats and mahogany panels. The car was dim, emergency beacons supplying the only light.

Mud had seeped into the front half of the car.

A man was wedged under a seat. His gray sport coat, black silk shirt, and sleek hair marked him as a corporate wonk.

"Are you hurt?" Jon asked.

"I can't tell. My legs are trapped under the seat. They're numb. Who're you?"

"I'm one of the inspectors. Jon Percy."

"Thomas Hansen, VP marketing. Tom."

"What happened?"

"The car slammed to a stop. I got thrown forward and then jerked back onto the floor. My legs caught under the seat, and this blasted mud avalanched in around me before I could even try to get unstuck. Why the blazes are you just looking at me? Do something!"

"Of course. Let me see if I can move that seat." Jon pressed his shoulder against the side. As he pushed, Chloe came up behind him, with a quiet touch to his back.

"You're moving it the wrong way," Hansen said. "It's crushing me."

"I'm not moving it at all. I can't."

"The mud," Chloe said. "It's rising."

"Call for help. Hurry up, before this muck swallows me."

"We can't," Chloe said. "We lost communications, and the closest access stairway is blocked."

"Who're you?" Hansen said.

"Chloe Walter. Jon's wife."

"How many were on the train with you?" Jon asked.

"Four others."

"Four others? Were they...?" Jon was absolutely sick at the thought of them buried under the mud—and the possibility that he and Chloe had caused this.

"Everybody else was in the front car. Could you two get this seat off me, please?"

"Yes, of course," Jon said. "But Chloe can't push. She's pregnant."

"Brute force shouldn't be our first consideration anyway," Chloe said. "We need a lever."

Jon took a long look around. They could try to rip apart the luggage compartments, but even if they could break off the chrome flashing, it would snap under the weight of the mud. Nothing else was sturdy enough or long enough to break off. Given the data, there was only one possible solution.

"I'll be the lever," Jon said.

"What?" Chloe gaped at him.

"I'll jam my shoulder under that rack of seats. Once I lift it—just an inch—Chloe, you pull him out. But be careful. Use your legs, not your stomach. Tom, push hard with your arms. Do most of the work."

Hansen squirmed, trying to get his arms up on the seat behind him.

Chloe dragged Jon down the aisle. "I don't want you in that mud. Try jamming the top of the seat with your shoulder, pushing with your legs."

"I already tried that. That mud is acting like a seal. We need to break it."

"I don't like the look of that stuff. There's something not right about it. It's kind of..."

"Glowing?"

"That's a little twilight zonish for me, but yes...it's got some sort of luminescence. An unknown phenomenon—we need to step back, consider what it might mean."

"I don't think we've got the time."

"But what if more mud comes through while we're trying to get him out? He would still be stuck, and you would, too."

"Hey, you two! I'm not deaf," Hansen yelled.

"We're going to get you out of this." Jon knelt next to the seat and wiggled his hand into the mud. His fingers numbed. The weight of the mud, cutting off his circulation already?

"What's wrong?" Hansen asked.

"Nothing. I just can't find the bottom of the seat."

"It's right here, man. It's got to be."

Hansen was correct, of course. Even so, an irrational notion seized Jon—that the mud had somehow displaced the bottom of the seat, along with Hansen's legs and any hope of ever seeing daylight again. Like that episode of *Twilight Zone* where a child rolls out of bed and falls into another dimension.

No, he couldn't think like that. Jonathan Percy was a scientist, trained in rational investigation. He accepted only what he could measure, see, quantify, define. He could speculate on the possible forever, but dwelling on the impossible was a waste of time.

And he had little time to waste. The mud had seeped to Thomas Hansen's ribs.

Just do it, Jon thought, amused that a commercial slogan would provide the impetus his own conscience couldn't seem to muster.

He jammed his arm into the mud up to his shoulder. He felt the seat—maybe—but couldn't seem to get hold of it. He pulled his arm out, looked up at Chloe. "I have to get down under it. It's the only way it will move."

"No," she said. "I won't let you."

Hansen's eyes said it all. *Please.*

Jon took a deep breath and pushed headfirst into the mud. It flowed around him as smoothly as if it were a resting place prepared just for him.

Was this what a hibernating frog felt like? Embracing mother earth like a womb and having the faith that, when the air warmed once again and the sun rose higher in the sky, it would find its way out?

For Jon, faith didn't add up to anything beyond a slippery slope.

He tried to back out and regroup, but the mud held him. Odd formulas whirled through his mind, strange music that made sense only on the highest plane of existence, that apex where math and physics existed in purity.

How many times had he and Chloe sung the same song, exulting that they were able to calculate the essence of energy and matter, proud that they could look into the heart of creation and measure each beat?

Yet the mud drew Jon elsewhere, directing its song to where all his intelligence and education couldn't guide him. Hadn't his entire career—his entire life—been directed at grasping that *elsewhere*, that unifying force that brought together weak and strong attractions?

He and Chloe believed in a particle that no one could see, the first particle to speak its existence after the universe banged its way into being. Was it such a leap to believe that a mighty finger had flung that particle into what *was not* and sang as the universe formed out of what *couldn't be*?

Chloe pounded on his back, signaling him to come out. Buried in the mud's embrace, panic was a rational response. Though the air in Jon's lungs grew heavy with carbon dioxide, something stirred deeper in him.

A notion that hope in what could not be could also be rational.

If Jon dared to hope, would there be light? As physics and biology and chemistry proved, light was life. For surely, his minutes—seconds now—were numbered. Without hope, he would die in wet earth with no air or light or life, with nothing except some crazy song the mud knew to sing but he did not.

His shoulder bumped against something.

With his last ounce of strength, Jon pushed upward. The song of the mud resolved into a mighty sucking sound and a sensation of pushing against the tide, something his own child would know in five months as he fought his way into the light.

The mud snapped, light broke through, Chloe cried out, and Hansen came free.

Jon didn't have time to catch more than a quick breath before the mud dragged him back in. It was as if someone was needed to pay a price. But what was Jon's infraction? Was it in expecting concrete and steel made by the hands of men could outlast dirt and water made by...*whose* hands?

Jon's body demanded oxygen, the stolen breath too quickly converted to carbon dioxide, the signal that his body needed more, screaming in every cell that he needed to open his mouth and breathe.

If he did, the mud would fill his throat.

Yet frogs could take oxygen in this way—a creature of such a low order that it wasn't even warm-blooded. Was it a blessing not to be able to sing the song of matter and energy, not to know the words of $E=mc^2$, not to follow the steps of pi to their illogical eternity?

Though Jon had little faith it would ever be answered, he dared to throw one last question into the mud.

Are You out there somewhere, God?

chapter twenty

THE KID WASN'T COMING BACK.

Half an hour ago Ben had slipped a kid ten bucks to go into the Tower and bring Cannon back to him. Kid was probably laughing his fool head off now, fist-tappin' his friends about the stupid geek hiding in the bushes.

He'd have to go in, but not through the front entrance. Too much of a crowd in the courtyard. He pulled his cap down over his face, hoping he looked like just another ratty kid walking across the playing fields behind the housing project.

Usually the air stunk back in here, a sharp chemical odor from the plastics factory. The fans on the roof always whirred steadily, dueling with the Tower's air conditioning units. Today the air smelled strangely clean, maybe because the fans were silent.

Power was out, which meant no elevators, and the stairways would be lit only by emergency lights—and that only if no one had broken them in the past week.

At seventeen stories, the John F. Kennedy housing complex was the only high-rise in all the Flats. Cannon lived on the fourteenth floor. That would be a long way to go in the dark.

Ben dashed for the back of the building, expecting at any moment to hear shots ring out. If he caught one in the head, would he actually feel it, or would he be gone before his brain registered the bullet? Jasmine had probably gotten up this morning thinking she'd live forever.

And now look. Life stinks, and then you die.

99

He slipped into the recessed bay that was supposed to let sunlight into the basement. Every kid in this project and most their friends knew that the window grill had enough give to let someone slender slip in.

Ben wormed through and dropped in.

Emergency lights glowed an eerie red in the basement corners. Cobwebs cast spiderlike shadows across the floor. Ben carefully sidestepped piles of junk. Take a header down here today and the rats would be down to his bone marrow before anyone found him.

By the time he hiked up to Cannon's floor, Ben's lungs were bursting. Madeline Sheffield answered the door. Eight years old and chubby-cheeked, she was always making goo-goo eyes at him.

"Where's your brother?" he said.

"Tripp's out."

"You know who I mean."

"Out there on the balcony, showing off."

Dressed only in a pair of gym shorts, Cannon was doing curls with a barbell that Ben couldn't hoist with a forklift. A serious lifter, the kid could be a college wideout or point guard if he didn't keep getting thrown out of school.

"Yo," Ben said.

"'Sup?"

"We gotta talk." Ben closed the slider. Madeline pressed her face against it.

"You wanna keep that face, Mad Dog, you better get to your room and don't come out until I say!" Cannon put the barbell down and slammed a hand against the glass, and Madeline disappeared.

Ben leaned on the railing, clearing his throat and trying not to cry. No way to say it but to say it. "Jasmine's dead."

"Wow." Cannon swiped his hand over his face. "Man, that's really cruel. How did it happen?"

"The bomb got her."

"Oh. Man."

"You hooked her up. A carry job?" Ben said.

Cannon straightened, pulling on his cool like someone else might pull on a T-shirt. "Who's wantin' to know?"

"She said you did."

"Dude had business. She had need. So what if I did?"

"She carried the bomb. Thought it was a drug drop for your pal Luther."

Cannon stepped into him. "Don't you get in my grill on this. I just made the hellos. Jazz made the deal herself."

Ben opened his palms in a hands-off gesture. "I just need to know what he looks like. In case he comes after me. Know what I'm sayin'?"

"What's your hook in this?"

"I was stupid enough to go with her on the job."

"But you didn't get clocked out with her."

"Obviously not, moron."

Cannon's eyes narrowed. "Don't you disrespect me, boy."

"Tell me what the guy looks like."

"Better just to mind your own biz, you know what I'm sayin'?"

"Come on, man. I'm trying to keep alive here. Give me something to work with."

"Dark skin, but not a brother. Not Latino, either. He had a gold tooth with a diamond-crusted L. Bling on his fingers, but Euro-bling, you know what I'm sayin'?"

Ben nodded. Jewelry not only marked a guy's status but also who his people were. He wore none himself, which was a good thing. Kept him in neutral and out of trouble—until today. "How big was he?"

"My height."

Over six feet, then. "Weight?"

"Now that you're asking...I can't land on that. Man wore a silk shirt. The kind you don't tuck. Didn't see his biceps, but he had forearms tighter'n mine." Cannon flexed for emphasis. "So I would've made him for a lifter except..."

"Except what?"

"Dude had a gut. Which doesn't make sense, now I'm recallin'."

"Maybe he was a boozer. They get those big stomachs."

Cannon nodded. They both had alcoholic fathers. Gus Murdoch was in the joint and Cannon's old man was over in Worcester, running numbers and drinking his take, last anyone heard.

"What about eye color?"

"I only seen him once without the shades. His eyes were real dark. Black. And he squinted."

"Like he couldn't see?"

"More like'n his eyes bugged him. Know what I'm sayin'?"

"Hair?"

"He covered his head."

"Do'rag?"

"No. Like a whatchamacall...watch cap. Dude was one walking fashion disaster, but he had this thing about him. Like you wouldn't dare look sideways at him."

"What's your best guess on where he was from? Like, did he talk with any accent?"

"No. Sounded like the rest of us, though, now I'm thinkin' on it—he maybe posed hard on that one. He coulda been a Greek, Turk, any of those Euro-types. Or one of those Arabs? I never made him for that, Ben, or I woulda taken action. My word's on that."

"Sure, man. Age?"

"What's with the questions? You aimin' to become a cop?"

"Aimin' to keep in one piece, man."

Cannon frowned. "The cap and shades, man. It was distractin', if you know what I mean. Not that I cared—his money was green, same's anyone else's."

"How did you meet him?"

"Gotta take five on that one."

The pass meant this Luther was likely a customer. Cannon was a small-time dealer. Pot mostly. His bigger business was in employment, mostly younger boys as runners. He made sure no one had any interest in the kids other than to run errands. Especially when he found jobs for the girls, even fools like Jasmine.

Then again, who had been the bigger moron? At least Jasmine got paid for her idiocy. Ben had gone along because his hormones had blown what little common sense he had right out of his ears.

Not that any of that mattered now.

Ben leaned over the railing. The tears would pass, but not the regret. Never the regret. And maybe not the fear either. It all depended on finding this Luther before Luther found him.

A fifteen-year-old dork versus a bomb-blowing terrorist—those were some seriously fearsome odds.

chapter twenty-one

THIS WAS A VERY BAD IDEA, LOGAN REALIZED.

The mist had engulfed him so he couldn't tell where he was going or where he had come from. He must have wandered off the bike path, because he couldn't feel the pavement anymore. Instead, there was grass under his feet, lush and springy with motion. A biting chill gripped him, taking his breath away.

Too proud to call for help, he tried to walk in a straight line. Sooner or later he'd walk into a building, bump into a telephone pole, or stumble back onto the path. He just had to keep going.

Then he heard voices.

A man cursed. A woman cried out, a high voice in a language Logan couldn't understand.

The mist cleared. Dizzy and confused, Logan couldn't understand why he saw a sordid room instead of sidewalk and street. There was a mat on the floor, a bottle of booze on a low table, too much cigarette smoke to see clearly. The smoke swirled into the mist so that he could only glimpse—

—a woman, a face that would be beautiful if not contorted with fear as a man flung her against a wall, stunning her—

—a man with a shadowed face, bearing down on her—

Logan moved to stop him, but with each step the mist swirled and he was still no closer. He drew his gun, aimed, but couldn't shoot the man without getting the woman too.

Soundless in her despair, she turned dark eyes to him and whispered *Jae Sun.*

"No!" he cried. "No, no, no!"

Someone yanked his arm. Pappas, pulling him out of the mist. Dizzy and confused, Logan couldn't make out what was real and what was a dream.

A federal agent. *A cruel man.*

A bomb. *A rape.*

People hurt. *A woman helpless.*

No one coming to help. *Jae Sun had tried…*

Like thinking through mush. Logan couldn't sort it out.

"You OK?" Pappas said. "You were yelling at someone."

"Yeah. What're you doing here?"

"Hal got Jamie spooked about this fog or whatever it is. Finally, I said I'd come check up on you. You OK?"

Logan bent at the waist, hands on his knees. "Give me a minute."

It had to have been a hallucination. Maybe the mist was some sort of a biological weapon, spawning madness that mocked reality.

"Did you get down to the fire station?" Pappas said.

"No. I guess…I got lost." Had to get it together. He couldn't show vulnerability in front of this guy. Logan picked up the bike and headed with Pappas back toward the Circle. "Is this mist some sort of new weapon?"

"A psychotropic bomb? Maybe," Pappas said. "But that doesn't explain the effect on engines."

Jae Sun. Hilary called him that, but his biological mother was the one who had named him. The delusion was a product of his own longing, yet it felt real.

"Did you hear me?" Pappas said. "What I said about pulse bombs?"

"Yeah. I'm just trying to process. I thought those were an urban myth."

Pappas's smile was tight-lipped. "They exist."

"Pulse—what did you call it?"

106

"Electromagnetic Pulse Bomb. It's the only thing that—"

"There they are!" someone yelled out. People rushed to them, voices edged with anxiety as they demanded answers.

Logan held up his hands, took a deep breath to compose himself. "Help will come soon. Until then, we need to help each other out. We're Americans—we see someone in need, we do what needs to be done."

Like a wave ebbing from the shore, the panic subsided, but it would be back unless he gave these folks something to hold onto.

"There will be an informational meeting at…" Logan's watch read 10:56. Less than an hour since the blast. It seemed like an eternity.

Pappas nudged him. "They want to know when the meeting is."

"Two o'clock. At Grace Community Church on East University."

"What can we do to help?" Hal Monroe asked, playing straight man.

"Go door to door, check up on the elderly. Look for kids who might be home without an adult. Pair up. Better yet, go in threes so you have someone to act as gofer."

People nodded, relieved for something to do.

"I need someone to organize this effort," Logan said.

A woman in a navy business suit and silk blouse raised her hand. "I'll do it."

"Thanks. See if you can find me more people with medical training. A retired doctor, a nurse, EMT. Anyone. Have them report to Patrolman Walsh. She's the woman with the curly hair over there. If she asks for help, you all do what she says."

Logan gave Jamie some last-minute instructions, then checked up on Natasha. It broke his heart to see her so still, and so trusting that someone would make her OK.

Then he grabbed Hal Monroe to come with him and Pappas. Pressed back into service as a cop, Hal suddenly seemed twenty years younger. But when they headed into the Circle, the old man cursed a blue streak at the mist, the terrorists, and the weenie staties and feds who were keeping his friends at the fire station from coming in to help them.

Logan breathed with relief when they came out on West University. This end of the street was mostly residential. Fewer vehicles had been involved in crashes. Injuries were mostly cuts and bruises. They left Hal to forage supplies from nearby homes so he could patch up the injured.

He and Pappas went back up to the Circle. Logan held his breath, worried about even brushing the mist. He had to focus. If he could figure out what the mist was, maybe he'd understand what he saw when he was in there.

"Strange how the mist groups here," Logan said.

"The bomb," Pappas said.

"But it's weird how the only openings in the mist are on the bike paths themselves. What could do that?"

"Maybe the magnetic fields from the high-speeds are attracting or repelling the haze."

"The trains are a hundred feet underground."

Pappas shrugged his good shoulder. "That's as far as I can take it. Let the scientists do the postmortem."

They left the Circle at North Spire where they found only one injury—a woman who had fallen from her bike and broken her wrist. When she heard the ambulances had been delayed, she said she'd hike home to Walden. Logan used her fanny pack to splint her arm and locked up her bike for her.

It took everything in him not to walk the woman up to the Estates himself, and then keep walking to the palatial estate that Hilary now called home—where, Logan prayed, Kimmie waited in safety.

the second hour

chapter twenty-two

ALEXIS COULDN'T WORRY ABOUT WHAT HAD happened—*some bomb*—or who had done it—*some terrorist*—or what the worst of it might be—*the end of the United States as we know it.*

Now that the baby was sleeping, she had work to do.

How many times had she planned for this? Sitting up in the manager's office, her orders placed, her schedules made, her checkouts fully manned. A free five minutes, once or twice a day, to feed that pit in her stomach. The dread that some other shoe would drop.

Today her planning had paid off, though she still couldn't figure out one thing: why Barcester?

People passed through this city on their way to Providence or Boston or Hartford, but seldom few regarded it as a destination. It proclaimed itself a college town, but who was Barcester kidding? Barcester State was the safety school for UMASS and Barcester Tech the safety for Worcester Polytech.

People outside Massachusetts couldn't even say Barcester properly, injecting syllables and consonants that might exist but should never be voiced. Spoken by the locals, it became *Bahstah*, a second-class imitation of Boston.

Alexis had been born, schooled, married, widowed, healed, and successful in this city. And now some terrorist was trying to take it away from her.

She scanned University Avenue, where people still roamed about, stunned. Word had come from Sergeant Logan, somewhere up near the Circle where they said the blast had taken place. *Move the cars; clear the road.*

Two toughs wearing hooded sweatshirts had pretended to help, but she'd spotted them stealing stereos and cell phones. They took off down a side street, but they wouldn't be the last, not if power and phone didn't come on soon.

Alexis had planned for that, too. Her generators were locked up in a cinderblock shed behind chain-link fencing, and her oil tanks were underground. If need be, lights would burn all night at Donnelly's, keeping the darkness—and the evil roaming in it—at bay.

Most of the staff had gone home, some gearing up to walk two miles or more. That was understandable, and it was good. Fewer people to keep an eye on. Alexis had loaded them up with juice drinks and kept an eye on the younger ones, making sure they didn't pocket an item or two from the snack aisle.

Before sneaking out the back door, Kaya de los Santos had helped Alexis wrap Ralph's body in a tarp and move it into the meat cooler. It just didn't seem right to leave him out like that. Mopping his blood from the floor was one of the most heart-breaking things Alexis had ever done.

Kate and Jenny had asked to be allowed to stay. Too far to walk, they said, and their homes were in opposite directions from each other. And then there was Tripp Sheffield. The kid had been in the store, buying macaroni and cheese for lunch, when the bomb blew.

He had begged to be allowed to stay, offered to work. His older brother was trouble, but Tripp was a good kid, still on the fence between the straight way and the street way. Alexis and he had had a meeting of the minds a few months back—she wouldn't harass him if he would tuck in his shirt when he came into the store. To him a loose shirt was cool; to her it was a shield for shoplifting.

Job one was to pull down the grates. Alexis had had them installed in anticipation of expanding the store to include a pharmacy. With the windows out, the grates would be the only thing securing the store. That, and Alexis's gun.

Though the store had power, the grates didn't respond to their computerized controls. She'd have to pull them down manually—a tough job, but she had just the guy for it.

Tripp was a fireplug of a kid, would have been an offensive lineman on the football team if he had any meanness to him.

He gazed out at University Avenue. "Why're they doing that?"

"Doing what? Moving the cars, you mean?" She held the stepladder steady while Tripp climbed up and grabbed the handle on the first grate.

"Yeah."

"Someone said they're all stalled." Alexis hadn't thought it through until this moment. She had done her reading—knew all about EMP bombs. Best not to speculate aloud, however.

"Yeah, but why're they moving 'em?"

"To clear a path for emergency vehicles."

Tripp rode the grate to the ground, silly grin on his face. "So why ain't they coming?"

The innocence and stupidity of youth, Alexis thought. "They probably already did. The firehouse is down on South Spire. They wouldn't pass this way to get to the Circle."

"Then why did Sergeant Logan want us to move the cars?" Tripp said.

Maybe for the same reason she had asked Jenny and Kate to squeeze the air out of the beach balls and fold them into storage boxes, Alexis thought. Something to do.

A scream came from the back of the store. Alexis went running and found Jenny in the bake shop, cupcakes at her feet. "Whatever is wrong?"

113

"I...came back here to get something to eat. Kate and me, we're hungry. We're gonna pay for them, honest."

Right. "And you screamed because...?"

She pointed at the safety shower in the corner. "I heard something in the drain. This clicking sound."

"Water dripping."

"It can't be. We don't have any water."

Wonderful, Alexis thought. First power and phones, now water. "Jenny, I'm really busy up front. I'm sure it's nothing."

"I think you ought to look. In case, like, there's another bomb or something."

A bomb in the pipes would almost be fitting for Barcester. No important buildings to blow up, so first they blow up dirt and bushes, and then they blow up the sewers.

Jenny twisted her hands. "Please, could you just look?"

Alexis squatted down and shined her penlight into the drain. And sat back hard when she actually saw something—

"What!" Jenny cried. "What's there?"

—something reptilian.

She had to get a grip. This was a weak moment, that's all. Nothing was down there. To prove it, she put her face almost flush with the grate and looked into the drain. The narrow beam of light showed metal pipe, dull with age. Was that something gray and silky far below? Just a bit of vapor backwashing into the pipes.

"There's nothing there, Jenny."

"I heard something, Ms. Latham. I know I did."

"It's an old building. Things creak."

Jenny shivered, rubbed her arms. "Are you sure?"

"Absolutely. You don't have to worry, hon. You're here, and you're safe." She smiled and handed Jenny another box of cupcakes. "Go ahead, you and Kate enjoy. Just save a couple for Tripp."

After a last glance at the shower drain, Jenny went back to the front of the store.

Alexis picked up the spilled cupcakes and tossed them in the trash. Three dollars and fifty cents wasted, but what could you do?

Hysterical girls would be—well, hysterical girls.

chapter twenty-three

C HLOE PUMMELED JON WITH HER FISTS. "Don't you ever"—*whack*—"do that"—*slap*—"again!"—*shove.*

"Hey, trust me. I have no intention of ever doing that again." Jon pawed mud out of his eyes, trying not to lose his contact lenses.

Chloe burst into tears and squeezed him like she'd never let go.

"I'm all right. Shush." Jon kissed the top of her head, his hand to her throat so he could monitor her pulse. From the moment that pregnancy stick glowed positive, he had had an irrational fear of losing the baby. It was as if he thought that by factoring profound happiness into his life, something dire would be required to balance the equation.

Chloe pulled away, now covered with mud. "I know what you're doing. Stop it."

"Making sure you're OK is a crime?"

"Playing hovering husband is downright felonious. Besides, you're the one who went swimming in primeval ooze, not me."

"And I, for one, cannot thank you enough." Thomas Hansen squeezed mud out of his shirt. "Hey, you guys hear that?"

Chloe squinted. "What?"

"That."

Something dragged on the roof of the car.

"Mudslide!" Jon yelled.

As he pushed Chloe toward the exit, the ceiling creaked and bowed. The weight of the mud deformed the door. He leaned his shoulder into it but couldn't budge it.

"Get out of the way!" Hansen kicked the door off its hinges.

They jumped out and ran a few hundred feet down the walkway before daring to glance back. The top of the Quanta car bent but hadn't collapsed.

Chloe stared. "First fire, then mud."

Hansen doubled over, then sat hard on the walkway.

"Are you hurt?" Jon asked.

"I jammed my ankle busting through the door. Not as tough as I thought I was. What's this about a fire?"

As Chloe explained, Hansen shook his head, incredulous. "A fire that burns without fuel. Maybe you two were delirious or something. From the explosion."

"So you think that's what it was?" Jon said. "An explosion?"

"What else could it be?"

Chloe met his eye. Jon didn't even blink. This guy was sharp—he'd pick up anything between them. They helped him up and started walking. Fifteen minutes later, they were back at the access stairway.

Hansen stared at the fire, mouth ajar. "Impossible," he finally said.

"It's reality," Chloe said. "Therefore it cannot be impossible."

"It hasn't diminished one bit," Jon said. "Maybe it's an underground pocket of gas feeding the flame."

"We should try to find a way past it to the stairs," Chloe said.

"The stairs are long gone," Jon said.

"No, they aren't. If you look hard enough, you can see them on the other side."

Jon didn't want to look. Something immeasurable was in play here, something they shouldn't mess with. He reached out, mystified to feel no heat. This fire was an affront to the natural laws of the universe.

He had to figure this out—observe, measure, deduce, decide. If they could discern the true nature of this thing that appeared to be fire, perhaps they could also find a way to pass by it and get to the stairs.

"Chloe, honey. Stand with Tom. OK?" Jon said.

"You're not approaching the fire," she said.

"We'll do it together," Jon said. "Make ourselves a chain so I can get close, check it out."

"No. I don't like it."

"He'll be all right," Hansen said. "We won't let him fall in."

Jon needed something to extend into the flame. Their two-ways had been lost in the mudslide. The particle collector was on the far side of the fire. He bent down, untied his sneaker, handed it to Chloe. He stripped off his sock, handed that to Hansen, then put his sneaker back on. He balled his sock and tied it into a fat knot. It wasn't much of a measurement device but he wasn't ready to sacrifice his sneaker to the fire.

This would be a simple experiment—either the sock would burn or it wouldn't.

"Tom, you hold onto me, and Chloe, you hold onto him. But no straining."

They linked up, hands clutched to forearms. Jon inched forward, averting his gaze because the flames were mesmerizing. If he stared into them, he suspected that he'd uncover a great truth. But maybe some things were best left hidden, though he had never believed that until this very moment. And did he truly believe that now—or was truth forcing itself on him, so he had no choice but to believe?

"Jon, you're veering sideways," Chloe said. "Focus."

Yes. He needed to focus. It was the stairs that mattered. The fire was irrelevant except as an obstacle.

Three feet away now. Creeping forward. The fire was mute. Like starlight is mute, Jon thought. Unless one is walking into a fiery sun, and then it's elementary, Watson. No, *elemental.* Get it straight, Sherlock. The interaction of hydrogen and helium cast photons out as light into the void in a vast miracle of power and might.

What if he broke away and let the fire take him? Would the hydrogen and oxygen, carbon and nitrogen that formed Jonathan David Percy become a solitary photon before he burned out?

Could he make his own light?

"Jon, you're pulling too hard," Chloe said. "Come on, slow down."

Her words drew him back into focus.

Observe—this fire burned without fuel and spoke without a voice.

Measure—this fire burned without warmth and without an apparent beginning or end.

Deduce—this fire was impossible, and therefore could not exist. That it did exist meant either their definition of fire was wrong or it was limited by their means of observation and measurement.

Decide—touch, feel, know.

That was what Jon wanted most, wasn't it? To know. Or was it *being known* that he needed? Science teased him, strutting out the laws of the universe with glory and majesty, trailing him and Chloe in its wake. *Know this,* science said, but when Jon knew, she'd uncloak the next mystery to be pawed over by him and his fellow scientists. A pack of wolves ripping apart the fabric of time and space and matter, clinging to their own scrap of flesh and howling that they were the ones to pierce the heart of the matter, raw tatters of the mystery clinging to their fangs while the lifeblood flowed freely away—

—Jon smelled blood now, longed to drink deeply of its nature, not as a beast hungers for blood but as a child cries for milk, because he would die if he didn't know and so he followed the blood to the fire—

—when something slammed against him. Jon kicked and punched, trying to get to the fire. Almost there, reaching out his hand, stretching, his body aching to be taller, bigger, smarter, better so he could actually touch it—

—then Chloe slapped his face.

Jon coughed, found his voice. "Sorry, I don't know what...I just didn't know..."

"I told you not to do it," Chloe said. "You have to stop playing hero."

"I'm sorry. I should have listened. I am so sorry."

"OK, I get it. You're both sorry," Hansen said. "What's done is done. At least we know that those stairs aren't a viable option."

"Then what is?" Chloe snapped. "Jon, are you listening?"

He stared at the sock on his hand. The knot had been sheared off, a perfect line with no threads hanging, no scorch marks, no wrinkles.

Chloe unrolled the sock from his hand, gasped. "Oh, Jon, oh, baby."

The tips of his fingers had been cleaved off. Impossibly, no blood flowed, though Jon could see the capillaries, bones, and tiny muscles. He felt no pain and no shock because, like the sock, the margins of the cut were perfect.

As if scored by a laser, he thought. *Laser*—light amplification by stimulated emission of radiation.

"We've got to get away from here," Jon said. "We've got to go right now."

chapter twenty-four

L OGAN WAS AMAZED WITH WHAT HAD BEEN DONE OVER ON East University. Cars pushed out of the way. Younger adults helping the elderly and corralling kids.

Law and order served with a whopping dose of patience.

How long would this last? There had been no looting after 9/11. But Hurricane Katrina had been a national nightmare from which New Orleans still hadn't fully recovered.

"The ambulances will be along soon," Logan said in response to the constant questions. When pressed, he told people about the informational meeting at two o'clock. Totally bogus, but it gave them something to hold on to while they waited for the official responders to arrive.

The injured were a concern. Some had been bandaged and splinted, but those with significant wounds suffered considerably.

"Chet won't give me real painkillers," Paul Wells said. "Not without a licensed medical person to write prescriptions. So we loaded 'em up on Advil and promised help was coming. It is coming, isn't it, Sarge?"

"Sure," Logan said. "Any minute now. Listen, I'll talk to Chet in a little while. Meanwhile, can you get some supplies over to South Spire? Jamie's got her hands full over there."

Wells eyed the Circle. "That looks pretty gnarly."

"We went around the fire. Even Hal Monroe did. But if you're unsure..."

"Hey! I was just sayin', that's all."

123

They left Wells loading up a couple of knapsacks and Hal watching over the injured, and headed down a couple of blocks to the police substation.

As soon as they got inside, Logan went straight for the bottle of Tylenol. The pain running down his lower back and into his leg felt like a knife.

Pappas sat at the dispatch system, punched buttons, and cursed up a storm. After a minute of getting nothing but white noise, he tried to manually dial in the emergency bands.

Finally, he grabbed the Tylenol Logan had left on the counter and slugged down a couple. "The radio is fried, too. Like the cars and everything else."

"You saying an EMP blast took out everything?" Logan said.

"Everything's digitally based these days. Anything from microwaves to kids' toys to those musical greeting cards." Pappas frowned. "Then again, the pulse would fade over distance. This place is almost ground zero, but over on South Spire we were almost a mile from the Circle. I'm surprised the cars that far away from the blast were affected."

"Which means the trains might have been as well. Assuming one was passing when the bomb went off."

"Quanta sold shares based on the high-speeds being terrorist proof. Nothing like waving a red flag—saying you can't blow 'em up. What better way to derail a MagLev train than with an EMP blast?"

"Why now?" Logan said. "Why not wait until the president was riding?"

"We would have found the bombs by then. There were plans in place to bring in large-scale metal detectors and check out the whole line. This was probably the last window of opportunity."

"Bombs, plural? We only saw one."

"An initial detonation. Or maybe just something above ground to make a splash, something to show on the nightly news. I'd bet the EMP devices were planted in the Circle—in the ground, as smaller devices linked in a series. Quanta ran security checks on everyone involved in the construction and design, but I'm betting no one vetted the landscapers."

Logan's neck prickled. Maybe the power was out, but his cop radar was working overtime. "You've got all the answers."

"Just doing my job."

"Your alleged job."

"What's that supposed to mean?"

"Kinda strange how you knew nothing before the explosion, but you're a font of information now that it's too late."

"You always this paranoid, Logan?"

"Only on days when a bomb blows up in my face."

Pappas came around the desk, got in his face. "I'm getting sick of your insinuations."

"It's my home turf. So deal with it."

"If help doesn't come, you'll need me," Pappas said.

"Help will come."

"Dream on, buddy."

Logan had a good four inches on Pappas, but the guy didn't back down. "Another tip?"

"I've been on the job longer than you, son."

"Don't you call me *son*."

"I got twenty years on you, most of 'em hard-earned. Point is, Sergeant, my gut tells me this is bad. You've been a cop long enough. You sense it, don't you? That razor-scrape in your stomach—don't you?"

Pappas's voice was soothing now, inviting trust.

Maybe I am being a jerk, Logan thought. "I don't know what I know—or who I can trust. You're just gonna have to live with that."

The spell was broken by a hard knock at the door.

Logan unlocked it and let in Johnny Beck. The neighborhood baker, Johnny handed out free cookies every Friday to the neighborhood kids. He knew each one by name—his own brand of community policing. "I've been looking for you, Sergeant," Johnny said.

"You OK?"

"Yeah, yeah. I just wanted to tell you what I heard."

"What's that?"

Johnny glanced nervously at Pappas. "OK to talk in front of him?"

Pappas met Logan's glance, steel-eyed.

He nodded. "Mr. Pappas is a federal agent."

"So they are starting to arrive? People are nervous, saying no one's come. Glad to see that ain't true."

No reason to tell him otherwise. "You had something to tell me, Johnny?"

"Some kids came into the store looking for a place to chill. So I gave 'em cupcakes. Day like today, everyone's family, right? They were talking about this kid they saw, screaming at people to get out of the Circle right before the bomb went off. The kid bolted when he saw you coming."

"Did you get a description?"

Johnny took a scrap of paper from his apron pocket. "Glasses, longish brown hair, skinny. Wore a Celtics shirt. Kids remembered that because, as they put it, only geekoids wear Celtics shirts in the summer."

"Did they see where he went?"

"They followed him to the Tower. According to them, he's still there. Out on the balcony with that big kid that goes by the name of Cannon." Johnny checked his paper again. "The fourteenth floor. Sixth balcony from the left side on the front side of the building."

"Wow, talk about good surveillance. Thanks, Johnny."

"They wanted to know if there was a reward."

Logan opened his mouth, unsure how to respond.

Johnny waved him off. "No, no, Sergeant. I already told them doing the right thing was their reward."

"Good. Thank you."

"I gotta get back to the store. I locked it tight, but times like these..." The baker paused on his way out the door. "Sergeant?"

"Yeah?"

"We gonna be OK?"

Logan forced a smile. "Of course. We're OK now."

Johnny nodded and left.

Pappas started out the door after him. "I gotta get that kid."

"You can't go into the housing project by yourself," Logan said. "I'm going with you."

"Good. I'll be right back." Pappas went out to his car, returned a minute later with two M16 semiautomatics nestled in his good arm. He held one out to Logan. "Know how to use this?"

"Yeah, but...we're only going after a kid. Not to war."

"We are at war, Logan. Or haven't you figured that out yet?"

chapter twenty-five

KAYA COULDN'T FIND BEN ANYWHERE.

He had not only *not* gone into work early, he hadn't shown up at all, according to Mr. Wakefield. Hearing that, she had run home, terrified that Stone had gone there. The house was blessedly empty—but that left her son still missing.

The video arcade was dark and locked. A block over, she ran into Ben's friend Derek. He hadn't seen Ben but thought maybe he'd be at the Tower with the Sheffield kid. By the time Kaya got there, her legs were wobbly from all the running—and from knowing that she was making it very easy for Stone to catch up with her.

Many of the people milling about on the sidewalks or front lawn of the Tower were patients of hers and knew Ben. No one had seen him anywhere.

The whisper of panic in her stomach had become a shriek—what if the bomb had gotten him or Stone had kidnapped him or he had simply run away because he didn't want to move to Framingham?

When she couldn't think of anywhere else to look, Kaya went back to the University Avenue substation and pounded on the door. When Jason Logan opened it, she leaped into his arms.

"Thank goodness," they said at the same time.

Behind the desk, a man with salt-and-pepper hair and a military bearing fumbled with the dispatch system. Definitely not from the Flats, he reeked of authority.

"Jason, my son is missing," she said.

"Refresh my memory," Logan said. "How old is he?"

"Fifteen."

"First things first—there are no teenaged boys among the injured."

"Thank You, Lord," she said.

Logan rubbed his face, strain showing in red circles under his eyes. He was a tall man, sturdily built. Someone said he had been a football star in high school. She pressed her hand to his forehead. "How about you, Jason? Are you injured?"

"We've got people a lot more seriously hurt." Grimacing, he leaned against his desk. Beads of sweat popped out across his forehead.

"St. Vincent's and UMASS Medical are on DM, aren't they?" Disaster mode status would bring all area medical personnel in to the hospitals or out to the actual disaster site.

"We've had no response from Barcester Central. No fire trucks, no ambulances, no DM instructions."

"Then who's treating the injured?"

"Agent Pappas and I did triage the best we could. I rounded up some volunteers, but we have no one with real expertise."

Upon mention of his name, the man behind the desk looked her way. "Stefan Pappas," he said. "Secret Service."

"Sorry. This is Kaya de los Santos. She runs the free medical clinic."

"Used to." Kaya stepped back. "Secret Service? Is the president here?"

Logan took her through the account of Pappas's involvement and how they had seen the bomb explode. Kaya took it in, her heart thudding.

"Where are the injured?"

"Mostly scattered up near the blast site. We didn't want to move them because we've been expecting the ambulances to come."

She closed her eyes, willing it to be tomorrow when she would wake up in her new condo and go to her new job, reviewing medical exams for a big insurance company. Never again would she have to look a confused teenager in the eye and tell her she was pregnant or explain to some ex-user who had turned his life around that his HIV was now full-blown AIDS.

Instinct took over, or maybe something more essential that no lawsuit or bureaucratic nightmare could ever drive out of her. "We need to get those people under shelter," she said. "Someplace centrally located. Can we transport down to Rose of Sharon?"

"We haven't found any car that will start. Besides, I went down Spire, trying to drag responders, but…"

"But what?"

"I couldn't seem to get through the mist."

She squinted at him. "That's ridiculous."

"No. It's not." He ran his hand over his forehead, bristling his black hair. "Sorry, Kaya. Didn't mean to snap at you."

"I know you're not given to flights of fancy." Kaya clicked her fingernails together, as if trying to fire up a plan. "OK, we'll get the injured to Grace Church, then. That's where the neighborhood's civil defense supplies are, right?"

"What little we've got of 'em, yeah. I'm sorry, I should have thought of that myself."

"You can't think of everything, Jason. I'll make a record of who we've got and what we've done for them so I can give a good report when we hand them over to the DM teams."

Logan's relief was obvious. "Thank you. By the way, I've been telling people there's an informational meeting at the church at two o'clock."

"I thought you didn't have any communication with—"

"We don't." He kneaded his temples. "I just had to tell people something. So if they come by, just send them up to the sanctuary. I'm sure Pastor Rich won't mind."

"Sure. But before I get up there…" Kaya launched into the tale of what had happened at the clinic.

"I'm sorry that you had to go through that." Logan leaned against his desk, his right leg twitching.

"You're really hurt." Kaya glanced over at Pappas. "And I'm hoping that's a dislocation and not a fracture."

"Good eye, ma'am," Pappas said. "Logan popped it back in for me."

Kaya tried not to imagine the tissue damage. "And you, Jason?"

"Back injury. I took some Tylenol, but look, you are so much more important than I am right now. I'll get you protection in case that maniac Stone comes looking for you. Is the baby OK?"

"She's locked up inside Donnelly's. She should be all right for a couple of hours."

"OK, we'll take care of the situation at the clinic. And get someone to look for your son. It's all going to work out."

She followed him into the basement. It was musty and dank, with two cells on one wall and a refrigerator and a banged-up table against the other. A row of lockers abutted a grimy washroom.

The gun safe was on the far side of the furnace. Logan dialed in some numbers and opened it. "Here," he said, passing her a bulletproof vest.

Kaya wrapped her arms about herself. She had witnessed a murder, endured a bomb, seen her son go missing—but somehow the vest unsettled her, as if it made everything so horrifically official.

"This is serious, isn't it?" she whispered.

His gaze cut right through her. "Dead serious."

Kaya hugged him. "I'll pray for you, Jason. For all of us."

chapter twenty-six

A<small>S LOGAN CLIMBED THE BASEMENT STAIRS, HE HAD TO</small> steady himself against the rail.

"You need to sit down," Kaya said.

"Not now." He and Pappas needed to get to the Tower, apprehend the kid who might give them a lead on the bombing. "Kaya, you can write prescriptions, right?"

"Yeah, I'm certified."

"Chet Babin is balking at handing out pain meds and the like. I don't blame him. He needs some assurance that our volunteers aren't just out there partying."

"I'll get you something. I can tell from the way you're moving, you're in terrific pain."

"I'm not talking about me."

"You'll function better with something more potent than Tylenol."

"Yeah, maybe later. But for now, if you could get Chet to dispense what the injured need."

Pappas had donned a bulletproof vest with a big ATF on the back. Logan had forgotten the Secret Service reported to the Bureau of Alcohol, Tobbaco, and Firearms.

Kaya helped Pappas get into the sling they found in the first-aid kit, while Logan slipped on his bike-uniform shirt and a navy polo with BPD on the back. Unlike Pappas, he wore his vest underneath. No reason to advertise where not to shoot, if the kid in the Celtics shirt had a gun.

He gave Kaya the key to Grace Community Church. She fingered it nervously.

"We'll get down to the clinic as soon as we can," Logan said. "And we'll track down your son."

She forced a smile. "Thanks."

Shouldering various bags of equipment and supplies, the three went outside. Logan blasted the air horn. Within seconds, people crowded around. "Is there anyone here who's been a cop? Or maybe in the military police?"

A young woman and a man in his sixties worked their way to him. Logan took them aside one by one and grilled them in hushed tones. He sent the man back with a thank-you and brought the woman to Kaya. "This is Leah McKellan. She's done two tours in Iraq as an officer."

"I understand you need someone to watch your back," Leah said. "I have two marksmen medals, ma'am."

Kaya's face reflected his own thoughts—the pretty blonde might be a lieutenant in the army, but she looked about twelve. As he had with everything else since the bomb blew, Logan had to make do with what they had, not worry about what they needed.

He picked through his bag, brought out a Glock 17. "Can you manage a 9-mil?"

Leah turned it over in her hands, checked the slide and the magazine. "Yes, sir."

He turned to Kaya. "Pappas and I will secure the clinic, do a couple other things down that way. Do you have a picture of Ben?"

"I..." Kaya patted her pockets. "No. But you picked him up a couple nights back. The curfew sweep."

"I would have remembered a de los Santos. And I'd have remembered talking to you."

"My neighbor had to pick him up because I was having my exit interview with the council. And Ben's stuck with his father's name until he's eighteen. His full name is Benedict Murdoch. He's about five six, weighs next to nothing. Brown hair, shaggy because he hasn't had a cut since school let out. Glasses."

Logan shook his head. "Sorry, half the kids his age look like that. What's he wearing today?"

"A sports tank top. One of those basketball things. Green."

Chills ran down his neck. "Celtics?"

"Yeah, that's it. It had a name on the back. Pierce maybe? Is that a player on the Celtics?"

"Paul Pierce." *Only geekoids wear Celtics shirts in the summer.*

Pappas cleared his throat.

"Is something wrong?" Kaya said.

"No, no. We'll find him."

Kaya squeezed. "You're a good man, Jason Logan."

"Just doing my duty, ma'am." Logan forced a smile. Trying not to think about the duty that would require him to go after Kaya's son—and perhaps arrest him.

•••

Logan and Pappas headed for the Tower, where Ben Murdoch had been spotted.

Most of the people on the front stoops or sidewalks knew Logan by sight. He'd give anything for a little anonymity right about now. People crowded them, peppering him with questions.

"Who did this? Was it bin Laden?"

"Why doesn't my cell phone work?"

"When's power coming up?"

One question was a steady refrain: "My *husband-daughter-son-friend-mom* works in *Boston-Providence-Leominister-Sturbridge.* Why can't I get in touch with them?"

Another was a steady concern: "Where are the *ambulances-fire trucks-soldiers?*"

Logan held up his hands. "There's an informational meeting at two o'clock at Grace Community Church. We'll address all these issues then."

"Will the mayor be there?"

"If he can get away," Logan said.

The so-called meeting was just about two hours away now—a delaying tactic that might come back to bite them. Both he and Pappas had assumed that the lack of official response was due to a hesitation to enter the mist. The technicians were probably on the other side, trouncing about in biohazard suits, taking air and soil samples, trying to decide if it was safe.

But what if there was another explanation?

One woman clutched his shirt, another pushed against him.

Pappas gave a long blast of the air horn. "Back off! Good, that's good. Folks, we know you have questions. But you are hampering recovery efforts. Find something useful to do or just get out of the way."

"Thanks," Logan said.

"Just wanted you all to myself."

"Yeah, I'm such pleasant company."

"So when you going to tell Ms. de los Santos that her kid is mixed up in this?"

"When we know for sure."

"What's their story?"

"Kaya was born and raised in the Flats. Same as me."

Pappas looked at him sideways. "*Hmm.*"

Logan's laughter was welcome release. "OK, so I was born in Seoul. I'm an adopted kid with an Irish father and Polish mother. Got a brother from Colombia and twin sisters from Vietnam. We're quite the mix."

"Which makes you downright American."

Patronizing him? Or did Pappas really get what the Flats was all about? What did he see as they walked past the triple-deckers? Laundry hanging from the back porches. Pitted front lawns and old cars. Houses in need of paint, and roofs with tattered shingles.

Did Pappas see inner city and think *trouble*? Or did he understand that people here worked hard, loved their kids, and tried to make a better life for the next generation?

"What about Kaya de los Santos?" Pappas said.

"What about her?"

Pappas held up his good hand in appeasement. "I'm just trying to dig out anything in the Murdoch boy's background that might link him to a known group."

"Kaya was a couple years ahead of me in high school, though we didn't know each other back then. No deep family secrets that I'm aware of."

"The kid's old man?"

"In prison. Anything beyond that..."

"Is what?"

"Private."

"You her lawyer or something?"

"Something."

"Come on, Logan."

"Look, I'm in this support group with her. For divorced adults. She went through it years ago but was asked to stay on, help counsel people in my situation." A Bible study, actually, but Pappas didn't need to know that. Logan had no desire to discuss this whole faith thing. He hadn't yet figured it out for himself.

"Yeah. OK. So?"

"Things shared there are confidential."

Pappas glared at an elderly woman who approached them. As she reversed course, he turned his withering look to Logan. "This is not the time to play goody-goody."

"If I knew something that was relevant, I'd tell you."

"Maybe the father hooked up with a radical group on the inside?"

"I don't know. But I can tell you this much: the kid hasn't kept in touch."

"Because that's what Mama thinks? Ms. de los Santos may think her son isn't interested in Daddy, but kids—adolescent sons especially—see incarcerated fathers in a different light. When manhood breathes down their scrawny necks, they want that relationship. And this is a tough neighborhood. Being in jail has street cred."

"No. Trust me on this. The kid would not have reconnected."

Seven years ago, Gus Murdoch had broken half of Kaya's ribs, then turned on his son. No way Pappas needed to know this, unless it became absolutely necessary.

When the lawsuit against the clinic and Kaya was made public, Logan tried to find some way to reach out. Three years earlier, he had had his own incident to endure but with different ramifications. When he beat the stuffing out of Marco Gibbons, a child molester he had caught in the act, the local paper called him a hero. His superiors did, too, until the *Boston Globe* called him a vigilante; then the chief of police shuffled him out of Central to the U-Ave substation.

At least people in the Flats still thought he was a hero. In Kaya's case, the public—stirred up by a vicious, bloodsucking lawyer—had called for her dismissal.

"What's your gut say about the kid, Logan?"

"I don't know Ben. Which means he's a quiet kid. Stays off the street."

"Smart kids—especially if they're marginalized—are often drawn into causes."

"I can't see it, based on who the mother is. She'd know. Trust me, Kaya would know."

"The baker—what was his name?"

"Johnny Beck."

Pappas grimaced. "His account of what the kids had told him was very detailed. Based on that and the phone call you got, this kid was involved somehow."

"And he'll explain."

Pappas shook his head. "If Ben Murdoch was going to 'explain,' he would have already. Don't you think?"

the third hour

chapter twenty-seven

NERO FIDDLES WHILE ROME BURNS, BEN THOUGHT. The bomber was still on the loose, but all Cannon could think to do was play hoops with a Nerf ball and plastic basket.

Ben plopped down on the sofa and watched Cannon pretending to be Kobe Bryant. The FaztBox sat on top of the television, a silent reminder that power was out. Not as trendy as the Xbox 360 or Nintendo Wii, all of their friends still preferred that game system to the others. The go-back button meant FaztBox games were forgiving. Players could learn from their mistakes, go back a couple levels and play better the second or third time.

If life had a go-back button, Ben would push that sucker hard.

He'd go back to that moment when Jasmine texted him about a "good-bye picnic." Hard to believe that was only three hours ago. Jasmine was dead, the Flats was a mess, and his life was in the toilet. If Luther didn't get him, the cops would.

Maybe he'd go back further, to when this Luther began hanging around Cannon. He'd put himself in the scene and say, "Hey, man. Something's not right here. Better roll off on this dude."

Why not go all the way back? Stop his mother from getting involved with that scum of the earth, Gus Murdoch. Pair his mom off with decent man, get himself a real father. Then maybe he wouldn't have come to this very moment when he couldn't change one stupid instant of what had gone before.

"Cannon, we've got to do something. We can't just sit here."

"Hey, man. I got no notion where this Luther hangs."

Madeline peeked into the room. "Ben?"

"Huh? What?"

"Didn't I tell you to stay in your room, Mad Dog?" Cannon said.

She squeezed next to Ben, looking at her brother from behind him. "I thought Ben should know that that man came here this morning while you were asleep."

Ben jerked his head around. "What man?"

"The guy you were talking about. Mr. Luther."

Cannon jumped to his feet, loomed over his little sister with his hand raised. "Luther came here? Why didn't you wake me up?"

"Chill, man," Ben said.

"I tried to. You swore and rolled over. That man said it was OK, that he didn't need to speak to you. He offered me a job."

"You're too young to be messing in this stuff. A million times I told you, but will you listen?"

"Cannon, stop. Let her talk. We need to know what happened. What did the man want, Mad Dog?"

"He said his little girl left her knapsack at his house, but his ex-wife would kill him if he brought it over there. So he asked me to bring it back for him." She folded her arms over her chest. "And my name is Madeline."

"Why didn't you tell me when I got up?" Cannon said.

"He said not to. Said you might want a commission. Said I should keep all the money myself."

"Did you look inside the knapsack?" Ben said.

"No. Because it was his little girl's stuff and she likes her privacy. He said he knew I'd understand. And I do."

"Where is it now?"

144

"Tapley School."

"Tapley!"

Madeline burst into sobs. "I'm sorry. I didn't know. I still don't know why you're both so freaked. I'm sorry."

"Shush. Stop it," Ben said. "Where did you put it?"

Madeline sniffled. "Mr. Luther said she'd pick it up when she got back from the beach trip. Told me to put it at the round-about in front of the school."

"Where the buses go." Cannon looked at Ben. "When're they coming back from the beach?"

He rubbed his temples, trying to think. "Two o'clock. That's what all the flyers said. The buses would leave Nahant at one and be back here around two."

Ben flipped open his cell phone and dialed 911. Nothing. He grabbed the phone from the kitchen. No dial tone. He went out to the balcony and peered down the avenue to see if any cruisers or emergency vehicles were around. Nothing but people sitting in lawn chairs or on porches, as if they expected a parade. Where were the cops when you needed them?

"Cannon, we've got to get to the school and move that knapsack to where it can't do much harm if it blows."

"Blows? What do you mean, blows?" Madeline's eyes widened. "It's a bomb? I carried around a bomb?"

"Yeah, it was a bomb," Cannon snapped. "You moron."

Ben turned to Maddie. "How heavy was the knapsack?"

Madeline bit her lower lip. "Pretty heavy. I thought there must be books in it. I'm sorry, I'm sorry, I'm sorry—"

"Stop it. We'll take care of this. Just tell me where you put it. Exactly."

She drew a ragged breath. "At the flagpole, under the flowers. So no one would steal it."

Cannon swore.

"Shut up," Ben snapped. "Let her talk. OK, Mad Dog—I mean, Madeline—this is important. What does the knapsack look like?"

"Dark blue with a big pink flower on the flap. And pink straps."

"OK, that'll be easy to spot," Ben said. "Let's go, man."

"Do you want me to come, too?" Madeline asked. "I can show you exactly where."

Ben shook his head. "Your job is to pick up the phone every minute or so. When you finally get a dial tone, dial 911 and tell the cops to send the bomb people over to Tapley."

"No way," Cannon said. "She ain't takin' the hit on this. And no way is this bouncing back on me."

"OK, OK, let me think. Here's what you do. Tell the cops that you heard someone down in the stairway talking about it. You got scared, thought you'd better call someone. Make sure they believe you, OK? And you can tell them what Luther looks like, but say that you overheard that. This is important—Luther never came to this apartment."

"I don't know, man," Cannon said. "This is too close to snitchin' to sit well on me."

"Are you crazy? You'd rather keep to the code than turn in a terrorist?"

Cannon raised his hands. "Just sayin' we got to play this smart. You got that, Mad Dog? Luther never came here. I don't know him, you don't know him. You just heard this from some other kids. OK?"

She nodded, eyes wide.

"Stay inside, OK? Until Mama gets back."

"Or you guys. Right?" She looked to her brother, and then to Ben. "Tapley's not far. You'll be right back."

Ben smiled. "Yeah. We'll be back before you know it."

chapter twenty-eight

WHEN LOGAN AND PAPPAS WERE A COUPLE BLOCKS from the Tower, Hilary ran out of the crowd and into Logan's arms.

"Oh, Jae," Hilary said. "I'm so scared."

For a long moment, all he could do was hold her and surrender to the vibrant memories her scent aroused.

Their first date, hot dogs and beer in the bleachers at Fenway Park. At nineteen, Hilary Sousa was sick of college boys and eager to be with a real man. At twenty-two, Jason Logan had already served as a marine in Bosnia, aced the police academy, put a down payment on a two-family house, learned plumbing and carpentry, and taken night courses in criminal justice.

Excelling in all the things real men did.

From a hardworking Portuguese family, Hilary was sick of slackers, irked by posers, and bored with football players whose only brush with danger came on Saturday mornings in pads and helmets. She was no adrenaline junkie, but she said something about him in his patrolman uniform made her feel safe.

Hilary liked to feel safe.

Logan told himself to break out of her arms—there was work to be done, people to help, a bomber to track. But as long as her body fit his so perfectly, he held on.

On their wedding day, he breathed in the lilies of the valley in her hair as he spoke his vows. Her voice wavered as she promised to remain faithful forever.

147

The morning of her first day at a real job, she smelled of cinnamon mouthwash. He kissed the tremor in the soft spot below her lower lip, as if he could take away her fear while leaving her sweetness.

Studying for the sergeant's exam, it was months of coffee for him and Diet Coke for her. They celebrated when he passed, a night with too much champagne and no birth control because it was time for a baby anyway. Nothing happened, and then the world skidded to a stop. Two days after September 11, Logan was called back into the Marine reserves for four months of duty in New York City. Hard, brutal work, but he was a good fit for it because he was both soldier and cop. A couple quick trips back to Massachusetts meant a positive pregnancy test in his Christmas stocking.

Then two months of ginger ale and saltines and Hilary pushing him away because she didn't want him to smell the vomit on her breath. His only regret was having to hide his giddy joy while she was so miserably nauseated.

The sweet scent of lotion during her labor as he rubbed her belly and back. Kimmie born six weeks early but at a healthy seven pounds, three ounces.

Holding his breath and the sour taste in his mouth when Ma held her granddaughter for the first time. She didn't utter a word of doubt about how a Korean man could father such a fair-haired infant.

Mary Logan sang a Polish lullaby and clucked over Kimmie as if she had her father's eyes. And she did, Logan knew, though he never said a word because he adored his daughter and loved his wife.

And so he forgave Hilary the worst of betrayals.

They agreed she would quit the job as Carlton Reynolds's fund analyst to be a full-time mother. It meant giving up one of the cars and not moving out of the two-family as they had planned, but parents sacrificed for their children, didn't they?

For the first four years, they managed the ruse and squeezed out happiness. Each time he saw Kimmie's blue eyes and blonde hair, he only saw joy and only gave love.

In the past year Hilary had changed, finding fault with his work hours, his family, and finally his lovemaking. When Hilary asked for a separation, he wasn't surprised. Sandra Reynolds had died the month before.

It grieved him when Hilary filed for divorce.

But when she asked for a paternity test, he was shocked to his bones, and furious. To rock his and his daughter's world was so cruel and heartless. So wrong.

Just as she was so wrong now to cling to him as if he still mattered. He pushed her away. "Where's Kimmie? Why aren't you at the house with her?"

"I'm trying to get there, Jae. My car won't start."

"So walk up the hill. She shouldn't be alone right now."

"Can't you give me a ride?"

"We haven't found a car yet that's working."

"Even your cruiser?"

He shook his head.

"This is serious, isn't it?"

"It might be."

She clutched him, her tears dampening his shoulder. The bulletproof vest beneath his shirt was no protection against the memory of the last time she cried in his arms. She had stunk of Carlton Reynolds's cologne and cigar smoke. "Why can't you understand?" she had said. "It will better for Kimmie if her mommy is happy and fulfilled."

Pappas barked at him. "Logan, we can't wait any longer. Let's go."

"Hil, why don't you head over to Grace Church and wait for me there? As soon as I take care of business, I'll take you up to Walden."

She wrapped her arms around herself. "When would you expect that to be?"

"As soon as humanly possible, Hilary. As soon as help arrives."

chapter twenty-nine

"**W**HAT DO YOU MEAN, YOU CAN'T GET TO IT?" Kaya said. "Was there another bomb or something?"

She had sent Johnny Beck down to Rose of Sharon nursing home to ask if they could take some patients. He had come back a half-hour later, a stunned look on his face.

"I couldn't..." He dragged his hand over his face.

"Couldn't *what*?"

"I couldn't get past the... what's in the sky. Except it comes down to the ground over on Fourth and Lunenburg. I tried going down the block and taking Fifth over, but... it's too thick to see into. Like a solid wall, but not really because you can see stuff beyond, but it's stuff that's not supposed to be there."

"Johnny..."

"I know, it sounds nuts. It was like a million little strobe lights. But if you just focus, you see, like, trees and grass, but not *our* trees and grass. I decided just to suck it up and go into the stuff. I bent down, kept my hand on the curbing and tried to follow it in. But as soon as I got into that fog, the sidewalk just... seemed to disappear."

"I don't understand," Kaya said.

"I don't either. I saw some weird things back in 'Nam, but nothing like this. What if it's a chemical attack or something messing with our heads?"

Kaya couldn't think of that possibility, not now. Too much to do. "Thanks for trying, Johnny. We'll keep Grace our base of operations, do our best until help arrives."

151

"I'll get back to my shop and round up food to feed your volunteers," he said.

"Awesome. That would be a big help."

Kaya got back to work, praying for the moment she heard the sirens. She had sent volunteers out to canvass the streets, see if they could find a physician. For now, the responsibility for delivering high-level care rested squarely on her shoulders.

Word had gotten out that injured were being treated in the basement of Grace Community Church. People came from up and down University demanding to have their lacerations stitched, their bruises iced, and their fears soothed. Kaya refused to treat anything as inconsequential as a turned ankle or scraped knee and was already taking heat for it. Too many seriously injured to stop and put a Band-Aid on a cut.

Most of the serious injuries were from flying glass or the various car crashes. Kaya had splinted two broken wrists, hopeful that Tylenol with codeine and a quiet place to sit would tide these patients over until real help came. Some residents of Lindenwood Road had taken it upon themselves to haul their mattresses to Grace so the badly injured didn't have to lie on the floor.

She had two open fractures—one ankle and one tibia—that could rapidly devolve into trouble without the ministrations of an orthopedic surgeon. The best Kaya could do was wash the skin where the bone protruded, isolate the patients so they wouldn't move, and dope them up so they wouldn't care.

Though she had antibiotics, she hesitated to administer them. She was not equipped to deal with a severe allergic reaction. The elderly woman with the broken ankle was frightened and unable to assist in her care. The girl with the fractured leg was only fifteen and didn't know her own medical history. If help didn't arrive soon, Kaya would have to start both women on a broad-spectrum antibiotic and hope for the best.

Antibiotics wouldn't help the middle-aged plumber with internal injuries. His blood pressure inched steadily downward. A male college student had a pneumothorax in the left lung. If the other lung went, she'd have to try to insert a chest tube.

One man had a badly torn bicep. Kaya had had to pull the shard of glass from the man's arm and dress it with a pressure bandage. If he didn't start intravenous antibiotics in the next few hours, he'd also be in danger of sepsis.

Why was she thinking like that? These people would be at St. Vincent's or UMASS Medical by nightfall.

Chet Babin had come through big-time. His son guarded their pharmacy, shotgun across his lap, while Chet delivered medical supplies to Grace. In addition to betadine, sterile water, painkillers, and ice packs, he had also brought a full bottle of Valium. Kaya had administered the tranquilizers as appropriate.

People were starting to get scared. They turned to her for reassuring words, a gentle touch, and her clinical skills.

Where were all these people two months ago? During the whole debacle with the lawsuit, the city council, and the media, even clinic patients couldn't string her up fast enough. Very few came forward to speak on her behalf. Jason Logan was one, but he was just a cop—what did he know about civil liability and media relations, the council's attorney said.

All because of a lollipop.

The day it happened was well-baby clinic. Kaya checked ears, listened to hearts, and gave inoculations, too busy to notice when a mom gave a Tootsie Pop to her crying four-year-old.

The rush of sugar sent Matthew Lowe running around the waiting room. He tripped, driving the hard ball deep into his throat.

Kaya called 911 immediately, then dug for the candy. When Matthew fell, he had bitten the stick off. She could see the cherry-red ball, but it was slick and jammed in like a rock.

The seconds ticked by, the boy thrashing in panic while she tried to extract the candy. At one minute, he turned blue. At ninety seconds, he slipped into unconsciousness, his heart rate dangerously low.

At two minutes, her receptionist said dispatch had called back—the ambulance had been caught in a traffic jam, took to sidewalks until it got free, but was still at least a minute away. And then another four minutes to St. Vincent's. Matthew would be brain damaged in that minute, dead by the additional four.

Kaya performed an emergency tracheotomy—a procedure she wasn't licensed to do. The story made the local news, called in by a neighbor who saw the little boy carried on a stretcher. As paramedics bagged him, Michelle Lowe screamed at Kaya for cutting her son's throat. An unscrupulous lawyer persuaded the boy's mother that the city of Barcester owed her millions of dollars for what he called her son's *disfigurement*—the scar on the front of his throat where Kaya had trached him to save his life.

Spurred on by the insurance company, the Barcester city council settled the suit and closed the clinic. The bitterest pill had been the lack of support for Kaya from her patients. Some had called or sent cards, but most just faded away without giving her a second thought.

Too much loss in their lives, Jason Logan said last week in Bible study. Folks cope better if they just don't acknowledge it. He had shared almost nothing of his own loss. Did he know that it was clearly etched on his face?

She would get through this afternoon—protected by the state's Good Samaritan law—and then get out. A cushy corporate job in Framingham and a high-rise condo would be paradise after contending with the thugs on the streets and the slugs in City Hall.

The most important thing was that Ben would be safe. Enrolled at Brooks Academy, he would be with other bright kids. Kids with more on their minds than getting high or proving their machismo.

Kaya was checking the plumber's blood pressure when she heard Leah yell out, "I said *spread 'em!*"

Paul Wells had a big grin plastered on his face as Leah patted him down.

"Leah, he's a cop," Kaya called.

"I told you so," Wells said, laughing.

Leah stepped aside to let him in. "Sorry, man."

He made his way across the room. "I see Logan deputized Barbie. Sweet deal. Hope there's more where she came from."

"Is there something I can do for you, Officer?" Kaya asked.

Wells rocked on his heels. With more muscles than brains, he'd probably been playing hero up and down University Avenue. Hopefully he hadn't caused more trouble than he fixed.

"Yeah. Can you go over to South Spire?" he said. "Jamie Walsh and me don't have the number of casualties you got here. But we got a couple that have been pretty badly wounded."

"I've got my hands full. Jason—Sergeant Logan—said you'd bring them here."

"One looks like a broken neck. We're scared crazy about moving her. Poor kid's only about six—was on her bike with her mother when the bomb blew."

"What's the status of her mother?"

"There're a couple bodies up by the Circle. She's one of 'em. Pretty tough on a kid, being without her mother."

Kaya should be with Ben, if she knew where he was. Logan had headed off for the clinic with Pappas. Why hadn't she sent them to her house? That psycho Stone might been there now, lying in wait for her. Maybe Ben had finally remembered their disaster plan—*go home.*

Yet she was here, taking care of other people and their children when her own was missing. And she hadn't given Angelina another thought since leaving her with Alexis. At least the baby was safely locked behind Donnelly's grates.

Not like this place. Grace offered little as an infirmary but even less as a sanctuary. Leah McKellan might be twenty-six years old and a lieutenant in the army reserve, but she looked more like a veteran of information systems than the infantry.

Get a grip, Kaya told herself.

"Tell you what, Paul. I'll go over to South Spire if you'll run by my house."

"Why would I do that?"

Kaya gave a brief account of the shooting and Stone's threats.

Wells reacted with a long whistle. "I know that piece of trash. Tweaker—wouldn't put anything past him. OK, sure."

"Here's my address." Kaya scrawled it on a napkin. "If you see my son, bring him back here. Arrest him if you have to."

chapter thirty

"**T**HE TOWER'S ON THE NEXT BLOCK. When we get there, you need to give me a few minutes to go inside, chat up some folks." Logan slipped the M16 into his gym bag.

"I don't like this touchy-feely approach," Pappas said. "Not one bit."

"We go in with guns out, either someone will start shooting or most of the young male population will scatter like rats. A quiet approach works best. You should take your post out back, near the—"

"I know how to do a simple surveillance."

"Fine. Sorry. I'll call you if I catch up with Ben." Logan had dug out ancient walkie talkies from the basement, stuck batteries in them, and almost danced with joy when they actually worked. The range was limited, but they were better than nothing.

Pappas split off a half block away so he could approach the rear without being spotted.

The man moved like a cop, confident but watchful, taking in new surroundings with a practiced turn of the head without being obvious. Then again, Logan thought—wouldn't a terrorist have the same qualities?

A skinny boy on a skateboard whizzed by.

Within half a minute, three young men broke away from a small group on the corner. Too well trained to betray their urgency, they moved in different directions.

No way Logan would get in the front door without everyone in the complex being warned. And then he caught a break. He spotted a kid in a Celtics shirt walking away from the Tower with Elvin Sheffield—the kid they called Cannon. Neither one spotted him as they crossed University and went down Salton Street.

Logan hit the button on the walkie-talkie. "Pappas?"

No response.

After half a minute, Logan hailed him again. Nothing. They should have tested the range of the devices before relying on them. If he ran around back to get Pappas, he'd lose sight of the two kids.

Logan turned onto Prospect Street, a block over from Salton. Maybe he could get ahead of them. If they spotted him following, they'd break into a full run. With his bum back, Logan would never catch them. His sciatic nerve was a path of fire from his lower back into his foot. No time for babying it now.

Logan went a block, stopped, and peered down the cross street. There—a flash of that green shirt. He took off at a jog. The mist was lower here, brushing the tops of the triple-deckers. The sidewalks were deserted. People were either huddled inside their houses or had moved up closer to the Circle.

He went one more block and then cut down the cross street. Looked up and down Salton, found it deserted. He listened for a few moments but heard no footsteps. He scanned the houses on both sides of the street. No one moved in the windows, no indication that anyone was home.

A shadow flashed in the alley. Logan ducked around one of the triple-deckers, caught the runner coming out from between the houses. Clutching a ten-dollar bill in his hand, the kid couldn't be older than ten.

"Where'd they go?" Logan said.

He shrugged, face impassive. "Nobody here but me and the roaches."

Logan lifted the kid by his elbows. "Now!"

He swore, then said, "Down Cutter. But don't say I said."

Cutter was the cross street he had congratulated himself for sneaking across.

He went an extra block down Prospect, racing at the limit of his ability to endure pain. When he came onto Cutter, the boys were less than half a block away.

"Police! Stop right there."

The two of them froze momentarily, then raced away.

"I said stop!" Logan shot off a round into the pavement.

Ben grabbed Cannon's shirt, yanked him to a stop. They both raised their hands.

"Stay there. Keep those hands up," Logan said.

Cannon's head jerked to the side. With a startled look, he fell like a sack of grain. Ben let out a strangled yelp and began to run. Even from a hundred feet away, Logan saw the blood gush from Cannon's throat.

He ran to the kid, jamming the walkie-talkie as he went. "Pappas, come on, man. I need backup."

The walkie-talkie sparked. "Where the devil are you, Logan?"

The sight of a knife through Cannon's throat robbed Logan of a reply.

The kid was dead before he hit the pavement. Ben Murdoch raced away in mortal fear. Chase him? Or try to find the killer? Logan couldn't leave Cannon like this—young eyes empty, lifeblood pooling under his head.

He ran into the nearest house, startling an elderly woman who huddled in her living room. "Police business," he yelled and ripped a sheet off the first bed he saw.

Back out on the street, he covered the body. The sheet soaked up the blood, the angry crimson proclaiming another kid cut down too early.

Logan surveyed the area, going down one alley after another, checking yards and sheds for hiding places. The killer was gone, as was Ben Murdoch. He went back to the Sheffield boy's body. He shook his cell phone, willing it to work so he could call the medical examiner and start the wheels of justice turning.

Footsteps pounded behind him. Logan whirled around, ready to shoot. It was Pappas—running down Cutter Street, M16 pressed against his bad arm to keep his injured shoulder stable.

"Where have you been?" Logan said.

"Is this Murdoch? Or the other guy?"

"Elvin Sheffield. I asked you a question, Pappas."

"Piece of garbage walkie-talkies. I waited for your signal—finally went into the Tower on my own. The boys weren't there, but a little girl told me she'd been trying to call the cops. Obviously she'd been coached—said she overhead people talking, something about a knapsack that might have another bomb."

"Another bomb? Where is it?"

"Don't know. I pressed her—"

"You what!"

"We didn't have time for milk and cookies, Logan. I didn't beat her—just used my teacher voice. She got hysterical, told me her brother and his friend were going to get the knapsack. She was about to tell me the location when her brother's pals came in. Fools thought I was messing with her."

"And you escaped alive?"

"I flashed my credentials, which only made matters worse."

"Nice move, Pappas. Like dangling raw meat in front of tigers."

"Even the M16 didn't faze these boys, not with the firepower they packed. We reached a stalemate, guns trained on each other while they whisked her out of there."

"Where did they take her?"

"No clue. You'd have to go through every apartment in that place, and even then you likely wouldn't find her."

"We've got to track down Ben Murdoch, then."

Pappas rubbed his face. Dark circles ringed his eyes. Aging under the stress of the day? Or was this a different tension eating the man—the strain of maintaining a ruse? Was this whole account about the little girl even true, or just some fabrication to explain his absence at the same time Elvin Sheffield was murdered?

Logan had been an idiot to take the guy's credentials at face value. Then again, they were only planning to walk the bike path—not manage the aftermath of an attack.

"Where would he go?" Pappas said. "Some friend's?"

"You screwed this up royally, Pappas. You should've stayed put outside, waited for me to call for you. That was the plan. These kids would've trusted me." Logan slipped the safety off his gun and jammed it to Pappas's head. "Question is, can I trust you?"

Pappas didn't blink. "What exactly does that mean?"

"Let's just say I'm still tripping over too many coincidences."

"I pledge allegiance to the flag and to the country for which it stands. Is that what you need to hear, Logan?"

"The timing of your visit—an hour before the bomb blows—is a bit cute for my taste. Now you disappear, and a kid ends up dead. I had the plan, but where were you?"

"You listen to me, you pea-minded, muscle-bound sorry excuse for a cop. I've had all I can take of your accusations and your attitude—and your pulling rank—your scurrying left and right like some lame-brained chicken with its fool head chopped off—your running this show like it was your little toy circus and not a national security crisis. I'm telling you this, Logan: when this all shakes out, DC's gonna skin you inside out and hang you out to dry. And when they're done with you, I'll pick your bones clean and then grind 'em under my heel. You got that, boy? Because that's *my* plan, and *you'd* better remember it."

Logan burst out laughing.

"What the—"

He holstered his weapon. "Only a fed could spew such stinkin' garbage."

Pappas shook his head, then laughed with him. "Well, then. Glad that's settled."

"Yeah, man. Me, too." Logan clapped him on his good shoulder. "Let's go see a boy about a bomb."

chapter thirty-one

BEN WATCHED THE LIFE SPURT OUT OF CANNON.

Luther wouldn't need a knife for him—he'd self-destruct under his own thundering fear. A hero would yank the weapon out of the dead guy and chase down the assassin. But only in movies could a scrawny geek take a bomb builder who was good at tossing knives, too.

Ben took off at a dead run before his friend's blood soaked into his sneakers.

How had the day gotten so whacked? All he had wanted to do was walk with a pretty girl, hold her hand, and maybe—if Mom was right and there *was* a God in heaven—kiss her.

Now he expected God to jump from behind a building and yell, "Hey, dude. You've been punk'd."

Seeing a girl get blasted apart by a bomb was no joke. It was a nightmare. Seeing a buddy take a knife through the throat was beyond a nightmare.

Ben ran, his lungs screeching like someone had taken a blowtorch to them. No plan now, just get home. That was the family disaster plan. *Something happens, we both go home.*

Even though they were scheduled to move out tomorrow, the big old house on Townsend Street was the only home Ben had ever known. He and Mom had felt safe there, once the old man got sent to prison.

But no one was safe today, not with another knapsack still in play. Maybe the buses would just stay at the beach. Or go to Boston, or north to New Hampshire. Anywhere but Tapley

School. Yeah, that was it. Then second bomb would blow up a flagpole and nothing else.

But he really couldn't take that chance, could he? Mom would tell him what to do, whom they could trust.

Luther would come after him, just like he did Cannon. Ben's heart stuttered a beat—what about Madeline? She'd be OK. Luther could have gotten to all three of them in the Tower, but it was only when they headed for the school that Cannon got taken down.

A block away from home, Ben stopped to catch his breath. A mutt named Daisy was tied to a ratty doghouse. She lifted her head, sniffed once, then went back to her nap.

Even the dog couldn't care less about him.

He should just curl up in that broken-down doghouse and cry himself to sleep. The way Mom had done after the city council decided to shut down the clinic. For five nights running, she had closed the door to her bedroom and played the same song over and over. *Oh, come to me, Jesus. Oh, come and be my strength.*

Even over the music, Ben had heard her sobs. On the fifth day he couldn't take it anymore and went in to her. She was on her knees, her face to the floor.

"I hate to see you like this," he had said.

She looked up at him, her face swollen with tears. "Sometimes this is what it takes."

Was that true? Was this crazy thing happening to him what it would take—to do what? Not to save him. He was too far gone for that. If Luther didn't get him, the media, cops, court system would. What Mom had gone through with the lawsuit was nothing compared to what would come down on her because of him.

Ben crept through the backyards until he reached his own. This far from the explosion, the haze arched almost down to the ground, as if someone had inverted a giant crystalline bowl over this part of Barcester. Let someone else solve that, too. He was done being the brainy kid who thought he was hip and happening. The truth was, he was a minus factor.

He stopped, listened. Not even a breeze rustled the leaves, and the squirrels had disappeared. Dogs could be trained to sense a person's oncoming seizure. Some wildlife knew when an earthquake was imminent. Had the animals gone to ground, sensing another disaster to come?

Ben dashed for the back door of his house and slipped his key in. Time ticked like another bomb as he tried to unlock the door. If Luther wanted to take him down, this was the time. He might be a measly 140 pounds, but he felt like his back was as broad as Fenway Park's left field wall.

The key stuck.

Deep breath. Focus. *Come on!*

Waiting for that split-second crack before the bullet found its mark and the lights went out. Cannon was there one moment, but then a quick eruption of blood, and he wasn't.

Where did he go?

Mom said there was a God and a heaven and desperately wanted Ben to believe. But how could he decide? He wasn't even smart enough to know not to walk the bike path with Jasmine.

The lock clicked. Ben rushed through the door, then caught it before it slammed shut. His mother had pulled the shades so people wouldn't see that they were moving and be tempted to burglarize. The kitchen was crowded with boxes that cast long shadows in what little light there was. They had moved a lot of the furniture down to the first floor, providing plenty of hiding places if someone wanted to stalk and kill a stupid kid.

Light-headed, Ben sat on a box and tried to fold his hands to pray. His fingers couldn't seem to find each other. Fear had turned him into a slug, sitting in his own stupid slime because he couldn't get moving.

Our Father...

How was he supposed to know what else to say? He'd never had a real father. His old man was a slap across the face, a broken arm, and now a guest of the Massachusetts Corrections Department.

O God, please make sure Mom is OK. Help me not to die, and show me what to do about the blue knapsack with the big pink flower.

A peace like a warm blanket wrapped around Ben. It had no weight, but somehow it took the weight off his shoulders.

The way a real father would do, he realized.

chapter thirty-two

"**N**O WAY," LEAH SAID. "I'm coming with you."

"No way," Kaya countered. "I'm going alone."

Her bodyguard had already driven off a couple of young toughs looking to score painkillers at the makeshift clinic. They couldn't leave Grace unguarded.

Kaya tossed Percocet, ACE bandages, and other supplies into a knapsack, then shoved her hair up under a Red Sox cap and slipped out the back door. She cut through the parking lot and up one block before heading back to University Avenue and onto the bike path.

Paul Wells had warned her about the mist, but seeing it for herself made her queasy. She couldn't even bear to look at the fire. It flamed brightly, yet threw no heat, a phenomenon that ironically chilled her to the marrow.

Why should she have to do this? Jason Logan and Paul Wells had gone around the rotary, but they were cops. No one could expect such blind courage from a nurse.

Except for the little girl with the broken spine, still lying on the ground because Jamie had been afraid to move her. Her mommy dead, broken in half by a bomb.

One step, Kaya told herself. And then one more.

"Hey, you!" Stone rushed at her from the other side of the embankment. "What did you do with my baby?"

"She's in a safe place. So leave me alone."

"Where is she?"

Kaya shook her head. Stone raised the gun.

She dived into the mist, slamming against the pavement. She rolled and found herself on grass—*this was crazy, where was she*—of such a primeval green it was as if all the green in the world derived from it. The grass cushioned her fall and invited her to stop.

Keep moving, Kaya told herself, because someone—*why couldn't she remember who*—wanted to kill her. Suddenly four-year-old Matthew Lowe appeared in front of her, grasping at his throat. This place wasn't the clinic—Kaya didn't know what this was. But she comprehended Matthew's distress immediately.

His skin was a pearl gray and his lips were bluer than the sky. Perhaps he had swallowed the sky, because she couldn't see it, couldn't see anything except the mist overhead and a dying boy collapsing into her arms.

She tipped his head back and checked his airway. No lollipop this time—the red knot in his throat was the biggest blood clot she had ever seen. She wrapped her arms around him and performed the Heimlich maneuver. Over and over, her fist under his diaphragm, waiting for the clot to eject from his throat.

Nothing.

Matthew's lips, his fingers, the tips of his ears blued. Kaya laid him gently in the grass and then found a scalpel in her backpack. She couldn't remember packing one, wasn't sure even why she had a backpack full of supplies. There had been a bomb, she thought, but that was a lifetime ago. She sterilized the boy's throat, her own fingers, and the scalpel with an iodine wipe.

"Behold your second chance."

Kaya looked up. "What?"

Dressed in a designer suit, crisp shirt, and silk tie, this was the lawyer who had sued her and the clinic. Everything about him was gray—his sleek clothing, his bristled hair, his manicured nails.

His shrewd gaze.

The lawyer sniffed and wiped his nose with his forearm. Mucus streaked his sleeve but he didn't notice, didn't *need* to notice because it blended into the fabric.

"Behold Matthew Lowe. Your second chance," he said.

Under her hand, Matthew's heart stopped beating.

No time to lose. She raised the scalpel, found the space between his Adam's apple and the cricoid cartilage. Such a small boy, such a small space, but Kaya had steady hands and a steady head.

One slit would open the airway.

"Save him and lose the clinic," the lawyer said. "Lose him and save the clinic. You do the math."

"I'm a nurse, not a mathematician." Steady hands. Steady head.

"It's not a difficult equation. If you save the clinic, you can save many Matthews. If you save this Matthew, you lose all the other Matthews and Sarahs and Angelinas you otherwise could have saved."

"I can't make that decision."

The lawyer yanked his shirt cuffs, showing blazing gold cuff links, the same shape as the knot in Matthew's throat. "Ah, but that's the beauty of this situation. You don't have to decide. Simply let nature take its course, because this boy is going to perish anyway. You all do."

God sent His Son so we would never perish, Kaya tried to say. But the words stuck in her throat, a dry knot that tasted like blood.

"No one will know if you don't do it," the lawyer said. "If you do do it, everyone will know. And this time it won't be a civil lawsuit. It will be murder."

Kaya poised the scalpel over Matthew's throat.

"Murder, because once you cut him and spill his blood, you won't be able to stop spilling blood."

Spinning head, trembling hand, *but Lord, all I need is a steady heart.*

"Don't do it, Kaya."

"I have to." She sliced. Blood bubbled from Matthew's skin, a bubble so huge that it enclosed her and the child. She ignored the bubble, though it rocked her and the child like a ship in a raging sea. Kaya pried the wound open with her fingers, put her mouth to his throat, and breathed life into Matthew Lowe.

The mist flashed fire, and a bullet came her way, spinning so slowly she could see the striations in the steel and count the rotations.

"Behold your last chance," the lawyer said. "Let the boy take the bullet so you can live."

She sheltered Matthew with her body and continued to breathe life into him.

The bullet pierced the bubble of blood with a tiny pop. She still had almost forever before the bullet would slam into her. Long enough to fall aside and let the child take it for her.

"Remember, nurse. You all perish."

Her heart held steady, held *her* steady. The bullet slammed her, splintered her like clay, ripping her meager heart—

"Worm bait," he mocked. "No more than dirt."

—and spilling out secrets and sins, *but, dear Lord, not faith and never hope.* This she would hold to, even when her life spilled out because faith was being sure of what she hoped for and certain of what she did not see.

And so Kaya sang the words that would show her the way home.

Oh, come to me, Jesus.

HE HAD THEM ON THE RUN.

The cop, scurrying like a rat in a maze. No way out, buddy. Just keep knockin' your head against the wall.

The kids, a foolish attempt to undo his work. Bon voyage, Mr. Sheffield. Your friend has a ticket and will board soon.

Citizens, helping here and there, puffed with pride. You will all cower again soon.

The fog? Some things even *he* doesn't know. A nice touch on the part of those who engineered the event. The strange haze terrified these fools more than any bomb could. And it proved the cowardice of these people. With all the armed soldiers, puffed-up politicians, do gooder EMTs, doctors and cops and firefighters this society had to offer, not one had dared pass through the fog to help.

The mettle of this nation was plastic, as thin as the credit cards these people loved to wield—as if mortgaging your future were a sign of power. Sucking off the next generation like the cowards they were.

He waited at the prearranged meeting spot. In his own time, his superior stepped out of the shadows. In a hooded sweatshirt, tattooed throat, close-cropped hair, and piercings, he had his street persona goin' on, passing as a banger called DeLuxe.

DeLuxe was at the very top of the organization, one of the few who could enflame an entire nation with a whisper. So long in the war, so many battlefields—had DeLuxe also forgotten where he was really from and what he was really after? Perhaps not. Then again, perhaps—as for him—the journey had become sufficient to justify any means, no end required.

"Good work, Luther."

"Thank you." No need to crow. DeLuxe knew the brilliance of what had gone down in the last few hours.

"What about the next event?"

"I have the second device in place. But I wonder if the location has become irrelevant."

DeLuxe nods. "Perhaps. If I might make a suggestion?"

"Of course. I'm eager to hear anything you have to say." Nice words, but the truth was that he couldn't stop DeLuxe if he wanted to.

He wouldn't even dare try.

"**H**E'S GONE," LEAH SAID. "You're safe."

Kaya tried to stand, could only manage to stagger and hold on to Leah. "What happened?"

"Chet came by right after you left. Freaked when he heard you had gone off alone. He offered to guard the infirmary, so I came running after you. I saw Stone shooting and you jump into the mist. He shot at you, I shot at him—hope I took a piece out of that slime—and he took off. I came up onto the path and couldn't find you anywhere. Then I heard you singing."

"Singing? I don't remember singing," Kaya said.

"You're not ready for *American Idol*, I'll say that. You were in the mist and singing something kinda churchy. I groped around and found your hand and pulled. And here we are. Let's check you out."

"I'm OK." OK on the outside, even though it felt like an elephant had stepped on her. On the inside, Kaya wasn't so sure. What really happened in that mist?

Leah unstrapped the vest, lifted it off. "The vest is cracked. Look, here's the bullet."

Kaya ran her hands over her own ribs, sternum, and abdomen. She had no injury other than a whopping contusion on her side where the vest had stopped Stone's bullet. "I'm OK," she said.

"You've got blood in your mouth. It might be an internal injury. We've got to—"

Blood from breathing life into Matthew Lowe, but not a boy's blood or a hallucination's blood, and certainly not her own blood. This was the blood of the God who protected her in the mist from Stone's bullet and from something far more devious and predatory than a madman or even a terrorist's bomb.

Kaya would explain it to Leah when the time was right. For now, she said, "I bit my tongue, that's all."

Without a single backward glance, Kaya stepped between the mist and the fire and continued on to South Spire. Fifteen minutes later they headed back the way they had come, leading a strange procession of wounded and volunteers.

The worst injury was Natasha. A broken thoracic vertebra, Kaya guessed, praying it was only severe inflammation and not a severed spinal cord causing the child's loss of sensation and movement. With careful help she had slipped a neck collar on the child, then rolled her onto a backboard. Two men had carried it as though Natasha were made of glass.

Apart from the little girl who was paralyzed, Kaya was most concerned about a middle-aged executive type who had pulled a shard of glass out of his own eye. The glass would have driven dirt and debris deep into his eye socket. If he wasn't in a hospital setting in the next few hours, he'd be well on the way to a septic infection.

Though Damon Johnson's situation was dire—and his eye destroyed—he had insisted on walking on his own rather than being pushed along in one of the office chairs they had commandeered as makeshift wheelchairs.

Kaya brought two open fractures back with her. One was a slender woman with a broken leg, the other an extremely obese man with his ulna protruding from his forearm. She had acquired three more head injuries, including a comatose woman. So many hurting people, and so little she could do for them.

She almost wept with relief when they came out of the Circle and saw Grace Community Church a block away. So close to the explosion, but only the windows had been blown out.

Otherwise, the church stood as it had for over a hundred years, a classic New England church with white clapboard and black shutters. Set back from the street, its rolling lawn and stone wall gave it a real country feel. The bell clock in its steeple had rung the hours for as long as she could remember.

Kaya led her charges along the fieldstone path and to the back of the church. Leah took her post again at the door while Chet came inside. A foul odor wafted throughout the fellowship hall.

"The toilets?" she said.

"The water's out. I told people not to use them unless they absolutely had to but..." He shrugged. "What am I going to do? Shoot them?"

"Can we use bottled water to flush?"

"You could. But...people are using up water like it's...well, water. We already used up my stock. I sent a couple kids over to the convenience store. Pauline gave me half of what she's got. She's passing out the rest for people on the street."

"What about Donnelly's?"

"Negative on that. My runner came back, said Alexis will only release water to you. Not to me, because, as only she could put it, 'Tell that man he's the competition.' Oh, and she said the baby is fine. Sleeping nicely."

That was good news, though Kaya was ashamed that she hadn't thought about Angelina or Sarah for a good hour now. "What do we do, Chet?"

"Clean the johns out manually. Then we spray 'em down good, give 'em one flush. Tell people they're just for peeing. People will have to poop in bedpans. I've got plenty of those at the store. And I'll bring over the one bedside commode I keep in stock. We'll take the feces out, bury it."

"The Board of Health will love that."

Chet scratched his nose, looked anywhere but at her. The longer he kept silent, the more goose bumps broke out on her arms.

"You don't think anyone's coming," she said.

"I don't know what to think, honey. Best to just live in the moment and see what the next moment brings. I'll head back over to the store, bring over those bedpans and whatever else I have that will help."

He left Kaya standing in the middle of the room, trying to organize her thoughts.

The church's fellowship hall had seemed so big when she opened it an hour ago. With the influx of the South Spire wounded and their volunteers, she was running out of room. The walking injured would have to go up to the sanctuary. She'd have the nurse's aide—what was her name? Patricia, that was it.

Patricia could diagnose simple headaches, bumps, and sprains, and dispense Tylenol and ice as needed. She'd have to ask Chet to bring her notebook paper or something so they could chart what they had done for whom.

Bridge Liquors had sent over three bags of ice. How long would that last? They'd already run out of the dish towels they used as compresses. She'd have to send a volunteer to canvass the neighbors and ask for donations of towels and facecloths. They needed more mattresses, sheets, pillows.

First priorities—taking vitals on everyone. Patricia could do that, determine those patients well enough to go upstairs to the sanctuary. Kaya needed to check on Natasha, then wash out Damon Johnson's eye. Try to figure out what she could do for the open fractures beyond dose them with OxyContin. Both she and Chet had passed far over the line on dispensing hardcore drugs. They could only hope the state Samaritan laws would protect them against any lawsuits.

What choice did they have? They couldn't leave these people writhing in pain. She would just pray that no one was allergic to the medication she dispensed without benefit of medical records.

Pray someone would come soon and take this off her shoulders.

Pray that she wouldn't be the one to have to tell Natasha her mother was dead.

Best to live in the moment, Chet had said. How could Kaya do that when this moment was so dire? She swallowed, no longer tasting the blood.

A heavyset woman touched her elbow. Ruth—a waitress at the Starlight Diner. "I'm praying for you," she whispered.

"I need it."

"You do what you have to do. I'll cover you, hon. Scoot now."

Natasha had been put in a corner where they could pull a classroom divider for privacy. Her volunteers had laid the backboard on a table. Kaya was surprised to find a little girl in with Natasha, chatting away.

"Miz Kaya," Natasha said. "Look! My friend came to visit."

"Hi, honey," Kaya said. "Mind if I sneak in for a moment and check Natasha?"

The girl—not more than five or six—slid her chair away from the table.

"On the other side of the curtain, OK?"

She scurried out.

"No!" Natasha cried. "I need her to hold my hand."

"Can you feel her hold your hand?" Kaya kept her voice even.

"No. She...feels it for me."

"We'll get her back here as soon as I take a look." Kaya pressed the stethoscope to Natasha's chest. Elevated heartbeat but strong pulse. She slipped the head of the stethoscope as far under Natasha's back as she could without moving her.

Was that a whisper of fluid she heard? Not a good sign.

Her pupils were reactive. Her skin was very dry. She should get some fluids into her, but Murphy's Law decreed the minute she gave the child some juice, an ambulance would show up and rush her off to surgery.

"Why are you looking like that?" Natasha said.

"Just thinking, sweetheart."

Natasha frowned. "You're not going to give me a needle, are you?"

"Not unless you want one."

The child squeezed her eyes shut.

"It's a joke, sweetheart."

Natasha blinked back a tear, mustered another smile. "I knew that."

"I have to check out some other people, but I'll be back in a few minutes."

"I'll be here."

Kaya searched for a reply.

"It's a joke," Natasha said.

"Best one I've heard all day." She squeezed Natasha's hand, devastated to see no response.

"Miz Kaya, can my friend come back in now?"

"Let me go see."

Kaya found the child on the other side of the divider, in heated whispers with a dark-haired woman. The woman nodded at Kaya. "I'm sorry, doctor. I told her not to be a nuisance."

"I'm Kaya de los Santos. A nurse practitioner."

"Ah, you're the clinic lady. I'm this one's nanny. She wants to go see her friend, but I told her not to be in your way."

Recognizing a fellow Latina, Kaya switched into Spanish. "Her friend has a broken back. She's paralyzed."

The nanny stifled a gasp. "One so young. Shouldn't be."

"These two know each other?"

Still in Spanish: "From kindergarten."

"I don't mind if they stay together, but I don't want to burden such a little one with that kind of a task."

She laughed. "Don't worry—she's a tough little kid."

As if to illustrate, the little girl tugged at Kaya's shirt. "I know you're talking about me."

Kaya switched back to English. "Natasha would like you to keep her company."

The child looked up at her nanny. "I told you."

"Do you understand that she's been injured?"

"She can't move," the child whispered. "I know. That's why I want to stay with her. To help take care of her until her mommy comes for her."

Oh, God, Kaya thought. *How can I do this?*

"I'll let you stay for a few more minutes. OK?"

"OK."

Kaya extended her hand. "I'm Ms. Kaya. What's your name, honey?"

The child—an adorable blonde with big, blue eyes—shook her hand with solemnity. "I'm Kimmie. Kimmie Logan."

chapter thirty-five

CUPCAKES AND SOFT DRINKS HAD SEEMED LIKE A brilliant PR move.

Alexis's generous offer of food and drinks was based on the expectation that the authorities would be rolling in within an hour or so after the blast. People would be sent home warm and fuzzy because Donnelly's had made them welcome.

No one had come.

In the hours since the explosion, a couple hundred people had clustered in her parking lot.

Alexis was a pragmatist. She didn't worry about why aid hadn't yet arrived. Her concern was what to do next. If night came and help still hadn't, she would be stuck with all these people.

Turning on the lights in the parking lot would suck up a tremendous amount of diesel. The way things were going, it might be days before power was restored. She had fifty thousand dollars' worth of meat inventory to keep cool.

But if Alexis didn't light up the lot, all these people would expect to be let into the store. That would be a complete disaster. She didn't mind having the kids in here. Kate, Jenny, and Tripp had been very helpful. The baby had been no trouble.

But strangers? No way. At the very least they'd chew through inventory. At the worst, some thug with a gun would sneak in with them, hold someone hostage, and demand Alexis give them money and beer.

She had to make these people go away, but how? It wasn't like she could just tell them to leave. It would be disastrous PR if she did.

Sergeant Logan's informational meeting at two o'clock was the key. As was Alexis's computer and photocopier.

Alexis peered through the grates. Teens in gang gear hung out at the food table, chatting up Jenny and Kate. She needed to get those two inside before they fell for that bad-boy routine. She'd do that after she put her plan into place.

She sat at her desk, fired up her computer. The lights came on, but the blasted thing wouldn't boot. The photocopier powered up, but stared at her with a blank screen.

OK, so she'd do this the old-fashioned way. Alexis counted out the marquee letters and numbers, arranging them in order before going outside.

"Miz Latham?" Tripp called from the sales floor.

She slid open the window and looked down at him. "All done?"

He grinned. "Yep. People really like this. What we're doing."

"How about you?"

"Never did anything like this before. It's rad, man. Totally. So Miz L, whassup with the bomb? Out there they're saying it's the trains the terrorists were after. But the people that made the trains said nothing could touch 'em."

Sad that the kid hadn't comprehended what had been obvious from the first window-shattering boom. "Of course it was the trains. What else in Barcester is there that matters?"

Tripp's eyes held a startling sadness. "We count for something. Don't we, Miz L?"

She wanted to grab Tripp and hold on, promising to take care of him because he didn't have the sense to take care of himself.

"You count for a lot, Tripp."

"Anything else you want me to do?"

"Can you get me the big ladder from out back? It's inside the loading dock. Meet me in the front of the store."

Two minutes later, she and Tripp went out to the parking lot. Those tough boys were still hanging at the food table. Let them have their five minutes of fun—once Alexis got this job done, she'd bring the girls back into the store with her and lock down.

She was partway up the ladder when Tripp said, "Can I do that, Miz Latham?"

"Sure."

He climbed up, took down all the letters proclaiming this week's specials. That big discount Alexis had gotten on fresh halibut this week seemed rather ridiculous right about now. When he had cleared the marquee, she passed the letters up one at a time. One side done, they moved the ladder and loaded up the other side of the marquee. The sign read:

> INFORMATIONAL MEETING 2:00 P.M.
> GRACE COMMUNITY CHURCH
> REGISTRATION OPENS AT 1:45 P.M.

Sure enough, it took less than a minute for someone to ask her: "What does that mean—registration?"

"The authorities want to register people who are around so they can let family members know who is where. Try to figure out who was injured or..." Alexis shrugged, unable to continue. The registration might be a little white lie, but the pain she felt for those who had been injured or killed was genuine.

No time to cry though. Too much work to do. Life going on was the only rational response to irrational terror.

People read the sign, peered up the block. Some put their paper cups in the trash—thank you—and headed for Grace.

Alexis would leave the remainder of the cupcakes and drinks on the table. Time to button down and wait it out. She'd keep

Jenny, Kate, and Tripp under her watchful eye. And the baby, of course. Help would come this afternoon, she'd replace her windows tonight, and tomorrow morning she'd open the store for business.

"Kate, Jenny. Let's go."

A muscular kid with a parade of gold hoops along his left ear grabbed Kate's arm. "Hey, come on. Hang awhile."

Kate glanced at Alexis. "I haven't had my break yet."

"Inside, Katherine."

"Sorry," Kate said to Hoops, trying to pull away.

"No one's working today," he said. "Chill with us."

Another boy—wearing a red hoodie—took Kate's other arm. "We could have us some fun."

Alexis unlocked the grate, shoved Jenny inside. "You too, Tripp."

"Miz Latham, you might need me out here."

Two hundred fifty pounds of little boy—trying to be a man. Alexis couldn't take that away from him. What was left of the crowd was silent, watching the drama unfold.

She turned back to the toughs. "Off my property. Now!"

A third kid grabbed Kate from behind. "Fun's just startin'."

Kate shivered with what must be the dawning realization that she'd made a terrible mistake in flirting with these guys.

Alexis pushed open her coat and rested her hand on the handle of her gun. "Get your hands off her."

Hoops laughed. "Right. An old witch like you is gonna be strappin'."

"I'll count to three and then I'll shoot."

"Let me have it, mama. One. Two."

"I mean it."

"Three, witch. Flippin' three."

Alexis shot him in the foot.

Hoops screamed, fell onto his backside. His friends took off at a dead run. Tripp grabbed Kate, hustled her into the store.

"Get off my property," Alexis said. "Before I shoot you somewhere you'll regret for the rest of your life."

"I can't walk," he cried. "I need an ambulance. And the cops. I'm gonna sue you so hard, you won't know what hit you."

"Then I guess I'll make it worth your while." Alexis leveled the gun at his crotch, willing her hands to hold steady.

Hoops hopped away, cursing and moaning.

"Good for you!" someone called out.

She bowed her head. Not good, not good at all. Just something that had to be done. She composed herself, looked at the crowd.

"Sergeant Logan wants people to head up to Grace Community Church so he can get some notion as to who needs help. We'll send you along with a drink and a treat, compliments of Donnelly's. By tomorrow..."

Alexis scanned the faces, trying not to blush at all this attention. She raised her arm in the air, surprised herself by making a fist.

"By tomorrow, the United States of America will have wreaked havoc on whoever did this to us. And by tomorrow, Donnelly's Supermarket will be back open for business."

A huge cheer went up. Someone in the crowd started singing "God Bless America."

Alexis joined in, finally letting her tears flow.

chapter thirty-six

LOGAN CUT OVER A BLOCK SO HE COULD SNEAK UP TO the back of Kaya's house. Pappas would go in the front way, but only after he got the signal. They had tested the range on the walkie-talkies again to make sure communication was firm.

The backyard was overgrown with weeds and untrimmed bushes. Good cover for Logan and good cover for a killer. Poor kid was on the run from the bomber, but what about that scum Stone? Unstable meth head like him could create even more havoc.

Logan took his time working his way onto the porch. Standing to the side of the door, he jiggled the knob.

Locked.

He knocked forcefully. "Ben. It's Sergeant Logan. We need to talk."

Nothing. He pressed his ear to the door, hoping to hear footsteps, a voice, a door slamming.

"I need your help. Could you open the door, please?"

Nothing.

"We know about the other bomb. But we don't know where it is. Please."

The deadlock clicked.

Logan clicked on the walkie-talkie. "Pappas, he's letting me in. Stand down. I repeat, stand down."

A burst of static, then, "Copy that."

187

A boy with shaggy hair and anxious eyes peered through a crack in the door. "Is my mother all right?"

"She's awesome, Ben. Working for us down at Grace Church, caring for the injured." Logan pressed his palm against the door. The kid still had the chain on. "Can I come in? We need to talk."

"You sure she's all right?"

"She's fine. I have a guard for her to keep her safe." Stupid—why did he say that?

The boy drew back, a wounded animal crouching in shadow. "Why does she need a guard?"

A man could only be so many places at once, Logan thought, but guilt still ate at him. Despite his promise to Kaya, they hadn't been over to the clinic. Hopefully neighbors would do the decent thing and cover Sarah Nolan's body.

Too many kids dying today.

"Was it the bomber?" Ben said. "Did he go after her?"

"No, no. There was an incident at the clinic this morning. But your mom's safe. And she's helping all of us right now. Like I'm asking you to do."

"You're not here to bust me?"

"Just to talk, Ben."

"I didn't mean for this to happen. Any of it. The bomb. Cannon. Jasmine and me didn't know what was in the backpack until right before I called you. I tried to do the right thing, keep trying, but I keep messing it up."

"I believe you, son. Please, can I come in?"

Ben slipped the chain and opened the door. Logan stepped into the kitchen, glanced about to get his bearings. The shades were pulled, casting everything in gloom.

"Are you alone in here?"

"I don't know. I just came in and then kinda froze. Trying to figure out if I was safer inside the house or outside. I knew

I should look for Mom in here in case something happened, but...I'm sorry."

"No, it's OK, Ben. And your mother is OK."

Logan took in the scene. Too many places to hide in here. Boxes were piled everywhere. A mattress and box spring leaned against the stove. An oak armoire blocked the door to the dining room. The air was hot, stale. Logan smelled old coffee in the pot on the counter. Salty fear radiated off the kid, his breath raspy and shallow.

He'd get Ben calmed down and get him out of here.

There was a whisper of a footfall in the hall.

Logan knocked Ben to the floor. Bullets tore through the boxes, raining down scorched cardboard.

He rolled with the boy to take cover behind the armoire. More bullets, feeling the concussions before hearing them, ears already battered, making it hard to hear Pappas yelling from somewhere outside.

Logan whispered into the walkie-talkie. "Where are you? I don't want to fire if you're in line."

"Still on the front porch. Let me creep up on this skell. Wait, watch the—"

Bullets peppered the walls, shattering windows. Got to get out of here, but the back door was in a direct line with the hall. Too exposed.

The back stairs then. Sneak into the cellar, come out through the back. The rhododendrons were overgrown, might provide enough cover to sneak Ben away from the house.

Logan nudged Ben to his knees. "We're going down the stairs. Got to be perfectly quiet. Stay with me. You run, you'll catch a bullet. Understand?"

Ben nodded.

Logan tossed a chunk of cardboard at the door. Gunfire splintered the doorway.

They slid down the stairs, keeping low, Ben squirming to get free. The kid was a mere wisp, skin and bones and terror. When they got to the bottom, Logan pushed him under the stairs and pressed him flat against the wall.

Moving him toward the stone steps leading out of the cellar.

Gunfire thundered throughout the house. Pappas's return fire was sporadic. He yelled from outside raw obscenities mixed with an order for the shooter to surrender.

Logan could fire the M16 up through the floor, but he'd provoke a storm of return gunfire. Even without a direct hit, they'd be struck with frags ricocheting off the cement floor.

Ten feet to the door. Looked like sixty.

Someone in the kitchen. A box tumbled, more boxes. Searching.

Opening the door to the cellar.

On the concrete steps, Logan spat on the rusty hinges of the door. He pressed his shoulder against it. It jammed—thing probably hadn't been opened in twenty years.

He pulled Ben to him, whispered, "I'm gonna go back, try to take this guy out. When I shoot, you kick that door open and get out of here."

Ben nodded, pressing his hands over his own mouth as if he didn't trust himself not to cry out.

Logan crept back into the main cellar. Through the steps, he could see a man's shadow, blocking what little light came down from the kitchen. Logan raised his gun, counting off heartbeats until it was time to take his best shot.

Something bounced down the stairs. Cop becomes marine, training becomes instinct—*grenade, gotta move, move, move.*

He leapt back at Ben, bursting with him through the door—light exploding—cellar erupting—rocketing them upward—

—thundering—searing—blinding—

Fire.

chapter thirty-seven

FIRE RAINED DOWN ON BEN.

Someone picked him up, someone strong. *Please God, an angel lifting me out of this fire because I don't want to go to hell.*

He let himself be carried because he had no will to rebel. A hard smack against the dirt—*please, don't bury me*—and then the angel or devil or hand of God lifted him.

Rolling him, dull pain as his skin and muscles flattened into his bones. Up again, air to breathe but he still couldn't see because there was too much light. The angel or devil or savior whispered in his ear, *You're OK, but don't move,* and so Ben didn't.

He held still, someone's heart beating against his back, fevered breath in his ear, explosions overhead. Somewhere deep in his heart, his mother's voice—*be good and do what Sergeant Logan tells you.*

Fire crackling, wood popping, sparks spitting everywhere, but still Sergeant Logan would not let him up. Not in hell, then, close enough, a verdict handed down by Luther who blew up houses and bike paths and pretty girls.

Logan crouched over Ben, squinting against the smoke, shirt charred and hanging off his shoulders. Someone groaned on the far side of the porch roof. It was in the middle of the backyard because, as Ben dimly realized, the blast had blown it clear off the house.

"Pappas," Logan said.

"Here," the man named Pappas said, his voice lost in the snap of flames.

"You OK?"

"Caught a bullet."

"How bad?"

"Left forearm. In and out. Scored my ribs on its way, but I'll deal."

"OK. Good."

"You?"

"Burned. Hurts like blazes, which is a good sign. Can you see anything?"

"Negative. What was that?"

"Concussion grenade. You clear?"

"Of the fire. I've got cover behind what's left of the porch."

"I'm coming your way," Logan said. "Ben, be still and don't run. OK?"

Ben nodded. If he spoke, he'd cry. A baby blubbering while the men did the work.

Logan helped him up, pressing on the back of his neck to remind him to keep low. Ben stumbled over one of the metal doors that had landed nearby. It was a miracle it hadn't taken their heads off.

How could miracles happen while hell kept exploding around him?

The porch roof had blown off in a single piece and landed against the maple tree. Taking cover behind it was a narrow-faced man with cold eyes. The sling on his left arm was bloodied but he seemed not to notice, so intent he was on scanning the yard.

Somehow Ben knew that his mother had put that sling on this Pappas guy. That brought him comfort.

"Ben, this is Agent Pappas. Secret Service," Logan whispered. "Stay here with him while I check things out."

"I've got your back, man." Pappas raised his rifle. An Uzi or something like that. Ben couldn't remember, though he should be able to. Cannon would know in an instant—but where was Cannon now?

Logan crept away, burns on his shoulders, neck, and upper arms. Burn in the singular—all the skin above his bulletproof vest was one big red welt.

Pappas crouched next to him, eyes everywhere at once. Gun in his good hand, blood oozing down his side. "Did you see Luther—in the house or anywhere else?"

"No. I think he's seen me a couple times, but I've never seen him, at least that I know of. I only heard what he might look like."

"You carried a bomb for a guy you never saw?"

"We didn't know. My friend Cannon—Elvin Sheffield—hooked up this girl for a quick courier job. Jasmine Ramirez. She asked me to go along."

Pappas frowned. "I don't make you for the bodyguard type, Ben."

Eyes like a wolf, Ben thought. Good if he's on your side. "As insurance. She thought she was transporting pot or something. I've never been arrested, so if something came down, she thought I'd take the hit."

"Must be some chick to get you to roll for her."

Ben bit his lip. "She died in the explosion."

"Oh. Sorry, man. We didn't find..." Pappas's voice trailed off. He must know why they didn't find her body.

Ben tried to wipe his tears with his shirt, ended up with soot in his eyes.

Pappas cleared his throat. "You warned people away. She didn't listen?"

"She saw Luther and panicked. Ran toward the Circle instead of away."

"But you didn't see him?"

Annoyance now, quickly turning into suspicion. Pappas looked like a cop, and probably all these questions were normal. But the guy just rubbed him wrong. No way would Ben spill his gut to anyone but Logan.

Pappas probed him with an icy stare. "I'm talking to you, young man."

"No, sir, I don't have much to tell you. Sorry." Ben resisted the urge to look away. Instead, he pretended to be Cannon, the tough guy who could maneuver any circumstance. His neck twitched, wanting him to shrink away from the guy's knifelike gaze. He searched for a greater strength, found the image of his mother on her knees.

Pappas blinked, turned back to watching the house.

Flames poked out of the windows. The smoke barreled into the mist overhead, darkening the veil that hid the afternoon sky.

Afternoon. Time ticked on a desperate task that Ben had almost forgotten. He jumped up. "Sergeant Logan!"

"Get back here!" Pappas shouted, but didn't have a free hand to yank him back.

Logan met him partway, pushed him toward the neighbor's yard.

"The other bomb," Ben said.

"I know. We need to know where," Logan said.

But Pappas had followed them, and Ben wouldn't trust anyone he didn't know. The roof came down, a *whoosh* that dampened the fire. Ben flinched at the shower of sparks, but Logan didn't move. Just kept staring down on him.

"I'll take you there," he whispered into Logan's ear. "But only you."

"We're wasting time," Pappas said. "We've got to get that backpack."

One of the bike cops rode up and skidded to a stop. "Sarge! What the heck is going on?"

"Long story," Logan said. "What're you doing here, Wells? You're supposed to be helping Jamie."

"Long story short, Ms. de los Santos sent me. Is this him? Her kid?"

Why was his mother involved with the cops? "Is she OK?"

"Yeah, dude. She's rockin'." Wells took a long look at the fire. "That their house?"

"Was." Blisters bubbled on Logan's forearms.

He had taken the fire meant for Ben. And Agent Pappas had taken his bullet.

Why had anyone even bothered?

"Some serious stuff goin' down here, huh?" Wells said. "Hey, I made a deal with his mother. She said she'd go over to Spire and bring back the wounded, and I was supposed to come find him. She wants me to bring him back to her."

"You promised I could go with you." Ben grabbed for Logan's shoulder, made him cry out. The guy's shirt was burned off his back. "I'm sorry, sorry—"

Logan doubled over, took a few deep breaths, then said, "Ben will stay with me. Wells, you take Agent Pappas up to Grace so Kaya can sew up that arm."

"No way. I'm coming with you, Logan," Pappas said.

"Time out," Wells said. "Where are you all going? Maybe you need me. I'm the only guy not walking wounded. What do you need, Sarge?"

"What I need is for someone to do what I say!"

"I was just sayin', Sarge. You don't need to bite my head off."

Ben felt like some interloper listening to these guys work out how to clean up his mess. He thought he was going to help by getting information on Luther, but now he'd gotten Sergeant Logan burned and Agent Pappas shot.

No wonder Gus Murdoch thought he was a major-league loser.

195

"OK, let's work this through for a moment," Logan said. "Pappas, you're little use to me with those wounds."

"I got a good right hand. You'll need me, Logan."

"Not if you're passing out from blood loss."

"Grace Church is almost a mile away. Too far."

"The clinic," Ben said. "It's not even halfway there, and my mother has some supplies still out in case of emergencies. Like that baby that came in today."

"Baby?" Wells said. "Were you there when—"

Logan waved the guy quiet. "Wells, take Agent Pappas over to the clinic. Try to bind him up best you can. And while you're there, clean up what was left on the sidewalk."

What was left on the sidewalk? These guys were talking in some sort of code, but Ben was just not getting it. "Are you lying to me? Did something happen to my mother?"

Logan's smile didn't begin to mask his pain. "She is fine and at Grace. You have my word on that. She's doing heroic work, son." He turned back to Pappas. "Once you're fixed up, you can head back to help."

"Be glad to if I knew where I was supposed to go," Pappas said. "Young man, you have got to tell us where the second bomb is."

"There's a second bomb?" Wells said.

Ben inched backwards. Wells was known in the Flats as a braggart and a bully. "I only want to talk to you, Sergeant."

"Enough of this garbage!" Pappas pressed his rifle to Ben's head. "Talk."

Ben froze. "Tapley School."

"Put the gun away, Pappas," Logan said.

"We don't have time for this kid's games. We need everything he knows."

"Do it!"

Pappas glared but lowered the gun. "Did you see a detonator? A timer?"

Ben didn't answer. Couldn't answer with his heart in his throat, was barely able to shake his head.

"This is how we play it," Logan said. "Wells, you take Pappas over to the clinic. Pappas, if your bleeding can't be controlled, you have got to get up to Kaya so she can stitch you."

"It won't come to that."

"Hopefully not. If you're up to it, you can head back this way on University. Take the right on Connor Street, then a left on Townsend. That'll bring you to Tapley. If you're going up to Grace instead, then send Officer Wells back to me. Got it? One of you needs to be up at the church to help out there, and the other can come back to me."

"What about the meeting?" Wells said. "What should we tell people up at the church?"

Sergeant Logan rubbed his face. "We'll hope that help has arrived before that. The response team can't be much longer."

Ben was doomed if they did, doomed if they didn't. When the authorities finally showed up, he'd be carted off to some jail where that hungry wolf Pappas would interrogate him. And if they didn't come soon, eventually Luther would get him. Maybe he should run for it. Take a bullet in his back and be done with it.

Sergeant Logan put his hand on his shoulder. "We'll be OK, son. We do this together, and we'll all be OK."

"Let's go," Ben said. "I'll show you where it is."

the fourth hour

chapter thirty-eight

I T WASN'T MUCH OF A PLAN, BUT IT WAS THE BEST JON could come up with.

He volunteered to hike the three miles east to the next access stairway. Hansen had the bad ankle and, though Chloe wanted to, no way would he let her do it. They both swore they'd keep far away from the fire.

He had been trudging now for half an hour. Sweat poured down his back, as much a product of anxiety as exertion. How had all this happened?

It was supposed to be the best day of their lives—other than the day Chloe told him she loved him, of course. He had been too shy to say the words first, so she passed him a note in their advanced quantum mechanics course. He turned so red, Dr. Hagstrom thought he was having a stroke.

So many best days to choose from...

The day they eloped, Chloe looking amazing in a peach sundress, her cheeks ruddy with excitement. Though it was mid-July, Jon wore the only jacket he owned, a heavy tweed. He matched it with a turtleneck because it was the only shirt he had that wasn't a T-shirt. As they walked into the town hall, she carried the orange day lilies he had picked outside their dorm as if they were prizewinning roses.

The day the pregnancy test showed positive, Jon had already practiced the words *We'll do whatever you want.* Two grad students with a hundred thousand dollars in loans had no right to have a baby. Words he never had to utter, because Chloe wrapped her arms around his neck and called him *Papa*.

They had begun this day with every intention of having many more "best days." What had they brought down upon themselves with their stupid, idiotic little experiment? And if they had killed or even just injured someone in the train, how could they forgive themselves?

There would be an investigation, of course. If Hansen hadn't been with them, they could have torn up their pipe and wiring and thrown it into that fire. Even then, the hack job might be tracked back to them. At the very least, their careers were over. The worst-case scenario was that they'd be in jail for manslaughter.

Wrong. At the very worst, they'd die down here.

What was that up ahead? The mouth of the tunnel looked as though someone had hung a glittering curtain over it. He took off at a run, his diaphragm cramping mercilessly. Perhaps what he saw was light reflecting from another train moving towards him. A rescue, oh please. Or maybe the rescue had already begun, and this was some sort of barrier hung over the tunnel.

Jon stopped, bent at the waist, and gagged. Should have gone out for cross-country instead of the chess team in high school. He breathed deeply, allowed his gut to relax, and straightened up.

Oh no. This couldn't be.

The tunnel was blocked by a wall of rocks.

The rocks were sheared off so impossibly flat that they appeared, against all reason, to be machine-carved. Even the margins where the rock walls intersected with the walls were absolutely flush with the tunnel. There was no breakage or fissures in the concrete; it was as if the tunnel had simply ceased being where the rocks began. Even where stones and dirt filled in around the boulders, the surface was smooth.

How could anything spawned by a catastrophe be so perfect? And where in blazes did these rocks even come from?

Think. *Think!*

In areas closer to Boston and New York City, the tunnels were reinforced because of marshy areas, rivers, or the Atlantic Ocean. Barcester sat on a solid ledge of granite—another reason why Quanta had chosen this area for the crossing of the train lines.

No way these rocks were any form of granite. They were translucent, glittering with veins of crystal, like mica or muscovite. Meteoric rock, perhaps. A meteor strike would explain the blast—and get Jon and Chloe off the hook. But anything large enough to penetrate the earth's atmosphere and plunge a hundred feet underground would have been visible for weeks before its strike. Nothing had been reported...unless, by some vast government conspiracy, the existence of a massive meteor had been kept secret.

"Don't go there, idiot." Jon's voice echoed off the walls, a lonely sound. He shivered, suddenly feeling like someone—or something—was watching him.

He needed to stave off panic by exerting reason. Observe, measure, deduce, decide.

Mustering his courage, he walked up the wall of rocks. As he ran his hand over the surface he marveled at its flatness, as if it were the very definition of that concept. He rubbed, and tiny pebbles trickled out of the hard-packed mass. Turning them over with his finger, he imagined that even these grains were leveled on one side.

Yet as flat as it was to the touch, visually the surface seemed to shimmer. A trick of light, he had assumed, but something spoke from inside his head or maybe from the tunnel walls: *Can't make your own reality, lad.*

"Crazy," he whispered.

Jon poked his fingers into the dirt, touching the edge of the tunnel. So flawless that he imagined even under electron microscopy he'd see no bumps or cleavage. He dug deeper, hooking his fingers around the edge of the tunnel.

It ended right here.

He resolved not to even think the word *impossible*. He dug more dirt and rocks out at the margin, reached in to try to find where the tunnel had gone. But even six inches in, all he felt was more dirt and stone.

Pop!

Jon hit the walkway, instinct from living down in the Flats. You heard gunfire, you hit the floor. A stone had popped out where he had dug. Sand flowed now, destroying the perfection of the rockslide, and then—*bang*—a rock the size of a melon popped out.

Shot as if from a cannon, a second rock smacked the walkway, followed by a cloud of dirt.

Jon jumped back just in time to avoid getting hit by a spray of water. The pressure was incredible, the kind of flow that was used to etch glass or metal. Hard enough to have taken off his face had he not been looking the other way.

It was only a matter of time before the entire wall of rocks and sand let go.

Jon ran, trying not to think about burst dams or flash floods. How far would he have to go to be able to withstand a collapse?

Rocks popped out of the slide with regularity, clattering on the floor of the tunnel. Jon glanced back, saw one boulder smash the magnetic track, followed by a blast of water. It shot straight down the guideway like a high-pressure hose wielded by a giant.

Was there enough water behind that wall of rocks to fill this tunnel and drown them? Judging by the pressure—yes.

What hope was left?

Jon jogged on, the water roaring in his ears. Should he pray? He'd never even been to church. His parents had been adamant atheists, his father a graphic artist and his mother a chemist. Bill Percy's faith was in the metaphysics of color and form, and Nancy relied on equations balancing for her spiritual stability.

In chemistry they do balance, Jon thought. Even in elementary physics, they want to zero out. But not in quantum physics, where the uncertainty principle was a certainty. It was impossible to measure simultaneously and exactly two conjugate quantities, such as both the position and the momentum of an electron.

Did that hold true for science and religion, too? Was it impossible to measure one against the other because they were related? Or would never the twain meet between the unknowing and the all-knowing?

How could he ever know God when he hadn't even considered that God might exist? What was the last refuge of the hopeless but a shedding of all rationality and a begging of the unseen to reach down and rescue?

Oh, God, I don't even know how to doubt and how to believe.

Someone called his name.

"Chloe? Is that you?" Jon waited—it was difficult to hear with the water blasting and his heart thundering.

Jonathan. My son.

OK, the delirium was official now. Because the fact was this: his father had never called him *son*. His parents were on a first-name basis with him from the time Jon could say their names. Never Mum and Dad. Always Nancy and Bill.

Jonathan David Percy. A son who wasn't a son.

Jon. My child.

Delirium was bad enough, but it should never be so tender.

"Chloe!" Jon screamed. "Help me!"

He almost belly-flopped with joy off the walkway when he heard her call his name.

chapter thirty-nine

L OGAN JOGGED WITH BEN, EVERY STEP AGONY. The burns on his shoulders were blistered, and being blown out of the cellar hadn't done his ruptured disk any good either. It felt like a barracuda was chewing on his sciatic nerve.

Ben slapped at his wrist. "My watch isn't working. What time is it?"

"Why? Got a date?" He tried to get the kid to smile and maybe stop shaking.

"The buses that went to the beach were due back to Tapley at two. If there's another bomb in that backpack..."

"Yeah, man. I gotcha on that." Logan wore the Timex his father had given him when he went into the Marines. A good, old-fashioned, self-winding watch with real hands and no digital parts. "It's quarter after one. I don't think the buses will come back to the school."

"But we can't take that chance."

"No. We won't take that chance."

"People won't care that I didn't know. They'll blame it all on me."

"We won't let that happen, son. Let's just keep moving."

Left foot, right foot—*agony*—pretend the pain belongs to someone else. Carlton Reynolds would be a great candidate. His kind had plenty of money to wield the legal system to his own advantage. Plenty of charm to wield a beautiful woman like Hilary Logan to his own lust.

If God was the real deal, how could He let this go on? He had to understand Logan's desire to protect his own daughter from a man who only wanted her because his girlfriend—Hilary Sousa *Logan*—wouldn't come without her.

Surely mercy didn't exist in a vacuum—it had to include justice.

Logan couldn't think about this now. He had to put aside Walden Estates and pay attention to where he was at the moment.

Old maple trees lined Connor Street, cracking the sidewalks with their roots. Logan could see the trellis in the backyard of what used to be Frank's Market. Though it was now a computer repair shop, it cheered him to see the grapevine still thriving. Mr. Francolini had let him and his brother pluck those grapes when they were kids. They'd suck down the juices and then spit the seeds at each other.

His grandparents had grown up in a neighborhood like this in South Boston, then moved out to Barcester to work in the factories. His parents were the first in either family to go on to college, his mother getting her RN while his father got an associate degree in machine technology.

Ma and Pop would be safe now, he knew, because they lived four miles south of the Circle—beyond the mist. Pop would pace, worrying himself silly, but Ma would bring coffee and cinnamon rolls up to the fire station, then demand to know when someone was going to University Avenue to help her son.

As they turned onto Townsend Street, Tapley came into view. The bus roundabout circled a lush flower garden. The sight of the Stars and Stripes on the flagpole gave Logan goose bumps.

Ben raced ahead and ripped through the marigolds, zinnias, and geraniums. Logan bent down with him, pushing through petals and foliage, searching for a glimpse of a blue bag with pink straps.

Time ticked on. Eighteen minutes after one. They found nothing but a candy wrapper and a soda can. Twenty minutes after one. Rocks, dirt, and ruined flowers—but no backpack.

"Could Madeline Sheffield have made up the story?"

Ben shook his head. "She was straight up, Sergeant."

"Maybe she meant the bushes and not the garden."

"She was specific. At least... I thought she was."

"We need to make sure. Let's go." They moved to the school and searched the bushes that lined the front walk and around the entry. Time was passing, with no results.

A chill ran down Logan's spine. "Did you hear something?"

Eyes wide, Ben nodded.

A razor-edged voice called from the east side of the school. The mist reached all the way to the ground there, a perfect veil for anyone wanting to keep out of sight. "You want it, you're going to have to come get it, Sergeant Logan."

Logan shoved Ben to the ground, then raised the M16. It had to be Luther taunting them. He could spray the area with bullets, hope to hit the guy. But with the senior center on that side of the school plus a row of triple-deckers, he could take down innocent people.

He lowered the gun.

Luther laughed. "Yet again, you prove yourself to be a decent man. Tell you what—I'll give you an opportunity to prove your courage. Come chat with me. I give you my word that you'll not be harmed."

"And what is your word worth?"

"I'm many things, but I'm not a liar."

There it was—the oldest and grandest lie of all.

Logan nudged Ben. Eyes scrunched tight and skin clammy, the kid had gone beyond terror into hopelessness. "If Luther was going to kill us, we'd be dead by now. We're going to move behind the school. Keep behind me."

Ben nodded.

Logan shuffled sideways, glancing back to make sure the kid stayed with him. Sheltering him with his own body was an exercise in futility. Luther could take them both down in a barrage of bullets, cutting through them like tissue paper. Not that he would at this point. Terror was more about the survivors than the dead. Terrify the cop on the beat and everyone else would tremble with him.

Around the side of the school, Logan scanned the parking lot and playground. Trash, a deflated basketball, and a couple of water bottles littered the area. There was no sign of a blue backpack with pink straps.

As if reading his mind, Luther called out, "Don't you want to know where I moved the package to, Sergeant?"

"Sure. Why not."

"Speak to me face-to-face and I'll tell you."

"Don't," Ben said. "It's a trick."

"He had a clear shot and he didn't take it. He's after something else." Logan stepped into the open. "Go ahead. Tell me where you put this alleged bomb."

Luther laughed. "*Alleged*? Perhaps you're resorting to law-enforcement clichés because you're scared to have a tête-à-tête with me. Is that it?

It wasn't Luther whom Logan feared. It was the mist.

"I give you my word, Sergeant. I will not harm you. However, many people *will* be harmed if you let time keep ticking on like this."

"Don't do it," Ben said.

Logan stepped back behind the building. "I want you to go to the clinic. Find Agent Pappas or Officer Wells. Tell them what's going down here. I need you to do that, son. Get me backup."

Ben's eyes ached with a raw longing Logan had seen in too many kids without dads.

"OK." Ben gave him a little wave and took off across the parking lot.

Logan turned back to Luther—and the mist.

chapter forty

BEN HAD RUN OUT OF HIMSELF HOURS AGO.

Nothing left of the Benedict who had tossed on a Celtics shirt at eight this morning, grumbling because he had to hang at the clinic with Mom instead of with his friends.

Nothing left of the Benjie who had walked with a pretty girl to the Circle, thinking he'd steal a kiss, only to have his dumb hope and the pretty girl blow up in his face.

Nothing left of the *brotha* who had hung with his friend, tried to do what was right, only to see that friend's blood rush out onto the street and his life rush out of his eyes to who-really-knew-where?

Nothing left of the little boy who cowered in his house, only to have that house spit him out on a tongue of fire.

All that was left of Ben Murdoch was the blind instinct to run to Mom, who had never let him down, never stopped praying for him, never stopped believing he could be more than he dared to dream.

But because Mom had done all this—and in this moment, still must be doing it—he resisted running up to Grace Church. Instead, with what little strength he had in his wobbly legs, he ran to the free clinic.

Find Pappas, find Wells. Get someone to help Sergeant Logan.

The streets were deserted. Right after the explosion, people had congregated on sidewalks or in their yards. They probably

211

had given up, gone inside just to wait it out. He cut through the little parking lot in the back of the clinic. His mother's car was out front, doors open.

He went in through the back door, into the kitchen. "Mr. Pappas? Officer Wells?"

His voice echoed off the walls. They were bare now, stripped of the colorful pictures that the kids loved. Boxes were strewn everywhere, spooking Ben because it reminded him of what had happened at home. How could Mom ever forgive him for getting their house blown up?

"Anyone here?"

Nothing. No whispers, no footsteps, no breathing except his own. The place was deserted. He should just head up to Grace.

But Pappas had come here to get stuff to tend his bloody wounds. The least Ben could do was check all the rooms, make sure the guy wasn't passed out somewhere.

He found Pappas's bloodied splint in one of the exam rooms. A roll of gauze draped off the counter, and blood-soaked paper towels filled the trash. So much blood—it filled his vision, all red and rushing; Jasmine in a cloud; Cannon in a river.

His knees gave out and he toppled backwards, bumping his head against the examining table. Dumb, stupid, no good for anything. He had to man-up here, get back to Tapley. He pushed up from the floor, went into the bathroom to splash water on his face—but there wasn't any. He turned to leave when he saw something in the bathtub—

—oh God, not her, too—

That girl who had come to the clinic this morning, a girl he remembered from grade school, now a dropout with a baby—Sarah staring up at him, eyes open but no fire of life, not even a flicker, a hole in her throat, blood crusted on her neck and chest.

Her body was what Logan had told Wells to clean up in front of the clinic, veiling the language so as to not upset Ben.

But he was beyond upset, beyond hope, beyond believing in anything but blood and more blood.

Breathe, Ben told himself, but a part of him wanted *not* to breathe so he could just be done with it. Jasmine. Cannon. And now Sarah.

This had to be his fault, too, because death clung to Ben Murdoch like a disease. He was beyond a boy whose own father despised him. He had become a rampant cancer, spreading death like confetti in a parade, but his parade rolled with bombs instead of drums, bullets instead of balloons. He was a freak, a loser who tracked violence wherever he went.

This was sick, just staring down at the body. But his measly strength had again drained and he couldn't move, though he knew he had to.

Kaya de los Santos believed that life was eternal, that God loved Ben even when he screwed up, that Jesus could make good out of this unholy mess they called life.

Ben couldn't believe that, not with dead Sarah lying in the bathtub, blood crusted on her chest where her baby should be.

He sprinted from the bathroom, out the clinic, and down the street. Running as fast as he could to find his mother.

chapter forty-one

JASON LOGAN MIGHT NOT BE THE BRIGHTEST GUY AROUND, but he was no fool.

With the M16 in his right hand and a handgun in his left, he moved around the far side of the school. Luther would likely anticipate this, be watching for him to sneak through the playground. But unless he had scouted the school thoroughly, he wouldn't know about the culvert.

Built to carry spring runoff away from the soccer fields, it was a hundred feet long, dumping into a brook. This time of year, the culvert would be bone dry, though a likely refuge for snakes and rats. And wouldn't that be fitting for an encounter with that slimebag terrorist?

After pulling away the sticks, trash, bottles, and dried mud, Logan kicked out the screen that covered the mouth of the culvert. Beyond lay darkness. Logan patted his back pocket, not surprised that he no longer had his penlight. Being blown out of a cellar would do that. Amazing that the letter from the DNA lab was still there.

Why not just turn around? Jog down Townsend, meet Wells or Pappas coming to help him. Two sets of eyes, double the firepower, they could surround Luther and beat the truth out of him, if need be.

"Tick-tock, Logan." Luther's voice was closer than expected.

Logan crawled up the embankment, scanned the area. Was that a swirl in the mist? Why wasn't Luther disoriented from it? Maybe he had been immunized against its hallucinogenic properties.

No time to waste. Either run straight at Luther or go belly-up under him.

Logan rolled down the embankment, dived into the culvert. Pulling with his left arm, he aimed the M16 with his right. The light behind him faded too quickly. Something moving next to his ear—beetles maybe. There was a *click-click-click* of claws as rats scurried ahead of him. The opening should be visible by now, but it was probably blocked by muck and trash at that end, too.

More *click-click-click*. When he got to the opposite end, how many rats would he have to paw through to kick his way through the screen?

Something silky brushed Logan's face, made him jerk back. *Idiot—just a spider's web.* He'd endured worse in the service of his country and the service of this city, seen things no man wanted to see, borne things no decent human could bear. Yet many men and women did bear such things—not just cops and soldiers and EMTs, but good people who healed the sick and fed the hungry.

Logan loved justice and doing good, but there was too much wrong with the world and too little he could do to fix it. And that angered him.

He pressed his face to the musty culvert. If Kaya were here, she'd say to pray for wisdom. No time for that—deliver me *to* evil, Lord, so I can do my job.

Logan pushed forward again through more silk. Not spider webs—this was the mist, somehow penetrating the earth and steel to find him, even here.

Before he could back out of it, it spun him so he lost sense of time and space. Blood pounding in his ears, he grappled for his bearings. The culvert had become a dank room, smelling of mold and vomit and cheap antiseptic.

There were rows of beds, separated by dirty curtains. Behind one curtain, a Korean woman with skin like cream looked down at an infant. Her slow smile showed dimples that Jason—*Jae Sun*—Logan saw in his mirror every morning. A shadow fell over her, a hulking darkness of a man. She fumbled for the blanket, expending precious energy to cover her baby. The blanket smelled like milk, a sleepy smell that made Logan want to drowse.

A rough voice jolted him awake. *I can't take that thing*, the man said. *Why would I want to?*

The woman's head lolled to the side, her breath a hollow *whoosh*. Time ticked on, but she didn't take any breath back. The man snorted his disgust, then bent over the baby. Logan clenched his own fists now, but his muscles couldn't remember how to raise his hands, defend the baby, protect the meager hope the woman had let slip with her last gasp.

Logan could smell the man's breath, rank with booze and cigarettes, but shadows blurred his face. The man put a grimy pillow over the child and said *You're better off dead.*

The baby kicked and thrashed, trying to breathe. Logan wanted to free him, but his arms couldn't remember how to work. The best he could do was shrug his shoulder and watch the child do the same, the pillow tumbling off until his tiny chest rose and he could wail.

He's all alone, Logan said, and pushed himself through the mist.

His hands almost brushed the baby's when he popped out of the culvert. He suddenly rolled down a slope that was not—never had been—on this side of Tapley School. The hill was studded with massive rocks, clear and hard as diamonds, rocks that had never been worn down by wind or rain. At the bottom was a rolling river, so blue it looked bottomless. It terrified Logan, as if it could strip away all he was so as to reveal what he could never be.

He dug in his heels, skidding in the dirt to stop his plunge. He wrapped his arms around a small boulder and hung on, the burns on his arms pure agony.

Luther stepped out from behind another boulder, an ocean-green stone with sharp points, as if a rare gem had been split by a massive stone cutter and discarded on this hillside. "Surprised?"

"Yeah, you might say that."

That this was also a hallucination seemed likely, and yet he knew it was not, that the culvert—and not the mist—had somehow birthed him to this strange place. He glanced up and saw a blue sky but no sun, yet he felt a sun's rays on his shoulders. Since he was willing to believe the ground under his feet to be real, then he'd also accept a sun that gave light and warmth without commanding the sky.

Deliver me to evil, he had prayed, and so he trained the M16 on Luther's face, thought mean and hard about shooting until he remembered why he had agreed to meet with this slime.

The second backpack.

Luther's face was so deep in shadow of a hood that Logan couldn't even describe him, let alone recognize him. The sweat-shirt he wore was oversized, the pants baggy.

"What do you make of this place?" Luther said.

Now was not the time to debate what manner of experience this was. The only reality that mattered was time ticking on. Eighteen minutes before two o'clock, according to his watch. "Where's the backpack?"

"You're not much of a poet, Sergeant Logan. Nor are you a strategist."

"You said you'd tell me."

"And you believed me? How droll."

"Spare me the dialogue from *Masterpiece Theatre*. Yes, I believed you. Because you want me to know."

"True."

"So tell me."

"I moved the backpack. To where it will do the most—"

A roaring whirlwind came over them, flinging both men to the ground.

The jets have been scrambled, Logan thought, though this must be a new kind of jet because the dark form passing over their heads filled a quarter of the sky. He jumped to his feet and saluted, risking Luther's wrath—and firepower—to demonstrate a marine's burning pride and a cop's vast relief.

The fighter banked and came back their way, its shadow so oppressively black that it swallowed light as it approached.

A new kind of stealth, Logan thought. The old stealth bombers sucked up radar, this one drinks in light. Nothing to be afraid of, and so he stood tall and watched—

—as the thing flapped its wings.

chapter forty-two

J ON REACHED CHLOE AND HANSEN JUST AS A LOUD *BOOM* shook the tunnel.

"What the devil is that?" Hansen shouted.

"Run!" Jon grabbed Chloe's hand and rushed back toward the mudslide. The rocks had let go and now a flood roared down on them from the east.

Water flooded over the guideways and onto the walkway. With a flood coming from the east and mud to the west, there was no way out. They were going to drown.

The tsunami white-watered in the guideways, spilling up on the walkways so that they had to link arms or be swept away.

"It'll put out the fire," Chloe said.

"No. Look."

They looked back, saw that the glow from the fire was as bright as ever.

"Maybe we can climb on top of the train," Hansen shouted. "Hold out until help comes."

A last-ditch plan, but what choice did they have? Moving east—no choice with the water pushing them—they could see the car now. The roof was bowed, but it had stood against the avalanche of mud.

We were just pushing one particle, Jon thought. Did we really deserve this?

What happened to him was irrelevant, but Chloe shouldn't die, not with their son's life yet unseen. Would he be an artist like Jon's father or a physician like Chloe's mom? Would he tinker with his hands like Chloe or live in a theoretical cloud like Jon?

Maybe he'd inherit some throwback athleticism and play baseball. Or sing in a chorus or do stand-up comedy. Maybe he would discover the cure for cancer or live a quiet life, raising his own vegetables and homeschooling eight kids.

"Breathers," Jon yelled. "I forgot about the breathers—masks and oxygen bottles. Packed under the seats. In case there's a release of toxic gas or carbon monoxide."

"Yes!" Hansen pumped his fist. "They'll buy us time."

They *whooshed* on, half walking and half bodysurfing. The emergency lights still burned. If the lights went out, it would be horrific down here, Jon thought. Or would the fire provide enough light to—*do what*? To die by?

With the current pushing them, it was only a minute before they reached the Quanta car. When the magnets had powered down during the blast, the car had sunk between the guide-ways.

The door was underwater.

Not only would they have to dive for the breathers, they'd have to dive just to get in. Mud leeched into the flood, making the water a chocolate brown.

They grabbed on to the top of the door, holding on against the current.

"This could be tricky," Hansen said.

"There're probably air pockets near the ceiling," Jon said.

Chloe shook her head. "It's too bowed in the middle from the mud. I don't think there's space left in there for air."

"OK. Give me some idea how to open the seats," Hansen said. "I'll go in and get us masks. Then we can all go and collect all the oxygen bottles we can find."

"I'll do it, Tom. You've got the bad ankle," Jon said. "If I'm lucky, I'll find a breather on the first try."

Hansen narrowed his eyes. "You said they were in all the seats."

"Will be. For now, there's only about ten per car. I'll have to search."

Jon hugged Chloe, then kissed her. Did he imagine the flutter in her abdomen, or was his child kicking, telling Papa that there were not just three lives but four at stake? How could he ever let Chloe and their baby go?

"If you don't come back, I'm coming after you," she said.

"I'll come back. That is an absolute." Jon kissed her one more time, took a deep breath, and dived into the car.

The lights inside had shorted out, but it didn't matter. The water was so muddy, he'd have to feel his way along anyway.

Bang! He knocked his head against the lavatory door.

Calm down. Save the adrenaline for saving the world. Pretty ironic that a flabby, nearsighted geek was about to save the day.

Jon counted up ten rows, popped the seat, and came up empty. He did two more, his lungs about to burst, when he found a breather. He shoved it into his shirt and swam for the door.

There was a loud groan from above—more mud loosened by the flood. The roof held, though now it bent almost to the tops of the seats. It would be a bitter irony to be trapped in here, with all the oxygen bottles for himself.

Jon kicked harder, knocking again into the lavatory door.

Had to focus, but his mind was muddied. Ha-ha—fatal puns would be the death of him. And now life was turned upside down. He and Chloe had wanted to peek into the fabric of the universe, but instead of it bowing to their will, the world was having its own way with them.

Mythology held that the world was created from four elements: *earth, air, fire,* and *water.* Maybe their experiment had unloosed the power of creation—they had all of those elements right here.

Which one would win in the end? Because it sure as spit wasn't going to be the high-and-mighty physicists and the flash-and-dash Quanta guy, weak vessels of nitrogen and carbon and oxygen about to be reabsorbed into the very mud they had crawled out of eons ago.

"Jon. Jon! Breathe!"

God roaring at him to take a breath? No, that was the water bearing down on them. It was Chloe who pulled him out when he got confused and couldn't figure out which way was up.

And really—wasn't that what love was about?

chapter forty-three

WHEN ANGELINA WOKE UP HUNGRY, KATE, JENNY, and Tripp fought over who was going to feed her. The world was in chaos, but they wanted to play with the baby.

Innocence in the time of crisis.

Alexis strapped the baby—carefully, because of her arm—into a stroller from the lost and found. She gave Angelina another dose of children's Tylenol, as Kaya had directed. Then she gave the kids clear instructions on how to feed her.

She left them in her office and went downstairs to check her security measures. The grates on the front windows and door were all locked. Through the slats she could see that the parking lot was empty except for the stalled cars. Off the main floor, she checked the customer bathrooms, the deli, and the bake shop, smiling at Jenny and her silly notion of something in the drain.

At the back of the store, the cavernous storeroom was uncharacteristically still. No trucks making deliveries, no employees taking breaks, no produce staff opening crates. The customers only saw the sales floor, but this was the true heart of Donnelly's. A crew of five worked overnight to restock staples, and Clint, her meat manager, came in at four every morning to take inventory and plan for the day's needs.

She needed to make sure the doors were tight, the generators were locked down, and that no one was hiding out here. That had happened once before—some bully who beat one of her stock boys before the shift supervisor clobbered him with a canned ham.

Her last stop was the meat room. It was vital that the temperature hold steady to protect her inventory. When the kids were done feeding and playing with Angelina, she'd have them unload the meat and dairy cases and move everything in here. No reason to run the open refrigerated cases in the aisles when no one was shopping.

Good thing the bombing had taken place on a Monday. This was a meager day, almost a loss leader. Donnelly's had to stay open, but the store made very little profit, what with salaries and utilities. Not that she'd pay Kate and Jenny for any time past one-thirty. Once she brought them into the store and they clowned around with Tripp and the baby, they became guests and not staff.

The meat room had been left in a mess. Her butchers understandably wanted to get home, but that was no reason to leave ground beef in the grinder and knives crusting with chicken. Clint was her highest-paid employee—she expected better from him. It would take an hour to wash and sanitize the cutting boards, slicers, knives, drains. Longer if what Jenny said was true and water was out to the entire store. What good were the high-pressure washers and steam hoses if they didn't have water?

Alexis turned a faucet. Nothing. This was ridiculous. This part of town got water from the tower high on the Ledges. No need for a pumping station to keep it flowing downhill.

Something scraped under the cutting table.

She grabbed a cleaver from the rack. This wouldn't be the first time she'd clobbered a varmint. Donnelly's was a clean store, but pigeons, chipmunks, squirrels, and rats sneaked in occasionally.

She bent down, found a pile of rib and leg bones under the table. Some fool had tossed his waste under there instead of bagging it. She and Clint would have a long talk tomorrow.

Scrape. A high-pitched noise, like fingernails on metal, but she couldn't see anything. Perhaps the invader had crept into the drain. The pipe was a good eight inches wide, a washout for scrubbing down the tables, walls, and floors.

This was nuts—Alexis had better things to do than go on a mouse hunt. She should just clean up the best she could, then go play with the baby.

What would happen to Angelina now that she was orphaned? Couldn't worry about that now. Today was all about getting through the moment. Keeping safe. Which was why this scraping drove her crazy.

A shrink would say Alexis was displaying transference, shifting her anxiety from the terrorists to a rodent. But an invader was an invader, whether it had two feet and a bomb or four feet and sharp teeth. And a defender was a defender, whether she carried a Lady Smith & Wesson or wielded a cleaver.

Alexis shoved the table out of the way and looked down into the drain. Couldn't see anything through the grate, so she used a filet knife as a screwdriver to remove it.

"Miz Latham?" Tripp had come into the meat locker, with Kate and Jenny right behind him. Jenny held a teary-faced Angelina.

"I thought I told you not to lift her out of that stroller," Alexis said.

"She did a stinky," Kate said. "We were going to change her, but when Jenny picked her up, that ACE bandage on her arm shifted and she began to cry. We calmed her down, but we thought maybe you should change her diaper."

There you have it, Alexis thought. It always fell to her to change life's stinkies.

Alexis took her from Jenny, smelling the diaper but also her baby sweetness. And wouldn't it be heaven, Alexis thought, if there were more sweetness than stink in the world?

Kate screamed and pointed.

Something thick and sinuous glided out of the drain—*this can't be*—covered with what looked like shining hair, but the bristles sparkled—*we're seeing things*—with a fierce beauty in their razor-sharpness—*move, run, get out.*

But like the kids, Alexis froze in the horror of the moment, the disbelief that the drain had spawned something beastly, something that even when seen could not be believed.

The razor creature moved with such quickness that even Tripp, standing in the door, did not have time to escape before it had encircled all four of them. Not four—there were five of them because Angelina was also in the circle of this snaking beast that seemed to have no end.

It continued to push out of the drain, showing thicker bristles that tapered to a point like filet knives. That beast could squeeze and shred them, just as it must have done to that side of beef, leaving its bones under the table.

Alexis could shift the baby to her left arm and grab her gun, but would bullets even work against this thing?

It twined up her leg, not cutting her; it had a different intention she might comprehend if she didn't have to think through the ice block of horror numbing her mind. She managed to cover Angelina's eyes, because the poor baby had seen too much of the monstrous today.

The beast was eye to eye with her now, because surely that was an eye at its very tip, searching her out, examining what manner of beast she might be.

"Get out of my store," Alexis yelled.

The creature whipped her across the brow. Blood streaming over her eyes, she could only feel Angelina being torn from her grasp, only cry, "No! Take me instead!"

Only pray, *God, help me keep her safe!*

chapter forty-four

THE WOMAN IN THE COMA HAD JUST DIED.

If she had been taken to a hospital, she would have had neurosurgery. Bone fragments removed from her brain, massive IV steroids, other sophisticated measures to reduce swelling and give her time to heal.

There wasn't one thing Kaya could do for her other than to take her blood pressure, pray for help to come, and move on to the next patient.

She had so many, with more trickling in. People further away from the blast had been injured in vehicle accidents or endured other medical crises.

She slumped into a chair, sipped water, and tried not to smell the fear or listen to the agony. Ironically, Natasha was the most comfortable, because she couldn't feel the pain. And that blessed Kimmie Logan had helped take away the child's fear by showing none of her own.

Did Jason know his daughter was here? She hadn't seen him for almost two hours, hadn't seen Paul Wells for an hour. And where was Ben?

Hung on the wall near the kitchen was a child's drawing, a shaky brown cross on a dark-blue background. Yellow rays stretched across the paper in a crude representation of a rising sun.

This is the day the Lord has made, Kaya thought. And this is what He set before me.

First order of business—deal with one of the most funda-mental functions of living.

She stood up and yelled, "I need a volunteer to empty bedpans!"

Everyone got comically busy with their injured. Leah kicked the backside of a strong-looking young man who had helped transport patients from South Spire. "Hey, you. What's your name?"

"Nick. Nick Suarez."

"The lady's looking for volunteers."

Sheepish, he raised his hand. "I'll do it. But...how? There's no water."

"Get some big spoons from the kitchen for scooping. Then scrub 'em out with dirt."

"Oh, this is just too gross."

"Hey. It's your chance to be a hero," Leah said.

"Dig a hole way behind the shed," Kaya said. "We'll dump the feces in there. Maybe you can run over to the hardware store and get me some lime."

"Hold on. Time out here," Nick said. "Lime is a long-term solution."

"Just common sense."

"You know something the rest of us don't?"

"I'm just thinking ahead," Kaya said.

Leah shoved him. "Come on, let's not waste any more of this lady's time. Go scoop some poop."

Chet Babin came in. He was the real hero of this day, emptying the shelves of his pharmacy to treat the injured. "Hey, I thought you were sending over another list."

Kaya resisted the urge to sigh. "I haven't had time."

"Tell me what you need."

"Broad-spectrum antibiotics. An ocular antibiotic rinse. And whatever you would recommend as a prophylaxis for tetanus," Kaya said. "Oh, and adult diapers."

Chet raised his eyebrows. She nodded toward Natasha's corner.

"What else?"

"Baby wipes. Antiseptic hand wash. Be thinking of what we'll do if we have to set those fractures."

"I don't have anything in the store that'll provide that level of sedation. We'll have to go over to the liquor store. If it hasn't been trashed."

Could this day become any more of a nightmare? Kaya curled her fingers into her palms. If she couldn't squeeze out the fear, she'd trap it. There was work to be done.

"Do you have any casting materials?" she said.

"No. You'll have to send out to..." Chet stopped, rubbed his head, then wiped the perspiration on his pants. "I was going to say a medical supply store. The closest one is three miles down on South Spire. This thing is insane. Maybe I should try going through that—"

"No. Don't even think it. I got lost in it and..." Kaya caught his arm. "Chet, how long can we keep this up?"

"I'll let you know when inventory is running thin."

"I mean us. You, me, the injured, the cops, the people helping. All of us."

Chet wrapped his arms around her. A father figure to so many in this neighborhood, he had resolutely stood by her during the lawsuit. "I figured you needed a break, so I brought you something. Left it outside so no one else would grab it."

"There's too much work—"

"Young lady, I said *now*."

Chet steered her through the fellowship hall. Meant for potluck dinners and youth group meetings, it was now a makeshift hospital. Less than an hour ago, her patients had all listened intently for ambulances while they waited for their pain medication to bring them some relief. Back then, they had been running thin on patience. The blank looks and sallow eyes made it clear these people were now running thin on hope.

"Make sure she sits for ten minutes," Chet told Leah. "And makes sure she eats."

On the picnic table was a cooler filled with ice and cold drinks. Kaya popped open an iced tea and drank it down thirstily. Chet passed her an insulated carton from La Hacienda. They had a wood-fired grill—one place to get hot food with the power out. Manna couldn't have been more welcome than chicken and green-chili enchiladas.

She dug in, the spicy flavors giving her a rush. She'd skipped breakfast, tussling with Ben to get him out of bed and to the clinic with her. This morning seemed like a lifetime ago.

After she demolished the second enchilada, she wiped her fingers with the napkin and got ready to go back inside.

"Oh, no, you don't," Leah said. "Mr. Babin said you were to sit for a full ten. You wolfed that chow faster than a marine. You've got eight minutes left."

Kaya stretched out on the bench, eyes closed as she listened to the strange sounds of the afternoon. The shifting of Leah's feet as she kept watch. An occasional shout from the Avenue. Moans from inside.

Fear itched under Kaya's skin, but no—she would not scratch. She searched for Scripture, settled on her favorite.

Neither death, nor life, nor angels, nor principalities...nor terrorists, nor terror...nor bombs, nor fear...shall be able—

Screams coming from University Avenue jolted her to her feet.

"My son," she said. "My son is in trouble."

chapter forty-five

ALEXIS GRABBED THE CLEAVER AND WHACKED THE BEAST a foot below where it coiled around Angelina.

It was a perfect cleave because she knew how to cut through flesh and bone with a single strike. Tripp picked up Angelina and sheltered her as, in its death throes, the beast torpedoed its bristles outward.

"Get her out of here!" Alexis yelled. "Get up to my office and stay there!"

The kids didn't have to be told twice.

She flipped the table upside down onto the drain and weighted it with as much meat as she could lug out of the cooler. She locked up the meat room, jammed a chair against the door handle for good measure, then allowed herself one long, voiceless scream.

She went into the ladies room and dumped a bottle of water over the cuts on her brow. The water swirled red in the white sink.

Something deep in the drain clicked and scraped.

Alexis ran to the men's room, the bake kitchen, the deli, and the maintenance closet. The beast or beasts—*what insane thing could they be*—were in all the pipes, under the store—*get out, go now*—maybe even in the small pipes over her head. She could take the kids and run away—*anywhere but here*—go up to Grace maybe.

But Alexis hadn't gotten where she was by thinking irrationally.

If her store was on a well and septic system, she might conclude that the beasts were her problem and no one else's. But she was on town water and town sewage, so if these monstrosities were here they could be anywhere.

What horror had the bomb shaken loose from the bowels of Barcester?

•••

A secret weapon, a mutant bird, a monster—no time to decide or define, but just get out. Logan dived back into the mist, Luther somewhere beside him, terror now driving the terrorist.

Deliver me from evil, Logan prayed, and maybe he got it right this time because his head bumped the edge of the culvert. No reason to crawl through it now; he scrambled up the embankment. He ran past the school and through the parking lot. What had Luther said about the backpack? *I moved it to where it would do the most—*

One word unspoken but comprehended in an instant.

—damage.

Logan had unwittingly set up survivors as the perfect target by sending them to Grace Church for the bogus two o'clock meeting. He ran down University Avenue, plagued by pain and cursing himself because people had taken his word to heart and gone to the church.

Fourteen minutes before two, and Grace was still a quarter mile away. Passing by Donnelly's, he saw the sign proclaiming the meeting.

Should he look for a bike so he could get there faster? Searching backyards, sheds, and garages would take up a minute, maybe longer. He had to run on and pray that someone would be around, a kid or Wells or anyone who could move faster than he could and tell all those people at Grace *to get out; there's a bomb!*

Time ticking, bomb ticking, eleven minutes before two as he neared the church. A knot of men stood on the sidewalk.

"I need help! Help! Someone help!" Logan yelled.

But they didn't hear him because they were packed together like coyotes, shrieking at some poor soul.

•••

"Leave him alone!" Kaya cried, but one man wrapped Ben in a headlock so another could punch him.

She flung people out of the way with superhuman strength, screaming, "Stop it! Why are you doing this?"

"He's the kid who did the bombing," said the puncher.

Kaya ripped Ben away from the man who held him, resisting the urge to slam the brute's head into the pavement, though in this moment she had the strength to do it.

Ben collapsed against her. "I didn't mean it," he said. "I just went for a walk with Jasmine."

"Shush. Don't talk." She glared at the men. "What is wrong with you? He's only a kid."

Ben spit blood, both eyes already blacking. "Sergeant Logan needs help."

"He's lying," a kid yelled out. "We saw him go into the Circle, come back out, and tell people to get away. And then we heard he was the one who carried it."

Kaya had to get Ben away from here.

The puncher—a guy with a blond buzz cut and reddish goatee—blocked her way. "You're not going anywhere."

"Oh, yes, I am. Get out of my way."

"Sergeant Logan," Ben sputtered. "Someone has to go to Tapley and help him."

"Why, honey?" Kaya said.

"There's another bomb."

The crowd imploded on them, pulling at Ben so violently that she fell with him. She covered him with her body, took blows and kicks meant for him.

A shot rang out.

"Back off," Jason Logan yelled. "Now!"

The puncher waved his fist. "This kid's the bomber."

"He's working with me. Now back off or I'll shoot the whole lot of you."

The men stepped away, glaring poison at Ben.

Kaya helped him to his feet. "We've got to get inside so I can look at those injuries."

Logan yanked her around. "No time," he whispered. "We need to evacuate the church."

"The bomb," Ben sputtered. "It's in the church."

"Jason...it's too much...I can't." How could she when she couldn't even catch her breath back?

"Yes, you can. Get your volunteers moving; take the injured out. Move them at least half a block away. I'll go upstairs, clear out the sanctuary. We have eight minutes, Kaya. Move it—please go!"

Kaya helped Ben around to the back of the church. Leah stood in the sidewalk, made sure no one followed them.

"Mom, they're gonna kill me," he said. "As soon as Logan's not around, they'll get me."

She wanted to tell him that was ridiculous, but she knew he was right. "Can you walk?"

"Yeah."

"Remember that place on the Ledges we used to picnic? Can you get up there?"

"I think, yeah. I'm fine."

"Go there and wait for me. As soon as I help evacuate the injured, I'll come get you."

"Mom, come with me."

She hated the thought of sending him away, especially as battered as he was. But she couldn't leave all these injured people to the fury of a bomb. "Honey, I can't right now. Do you understand why?"

Ben met her gaze, something shifting in his so that she knew she was witnessing a miracle in this time of terror—her son had just gone from boy to man.

"I do understand," he said.

Kaya kissed him. "I love you. Now go."

Holding his side, he ran through the lilac bushes behind the church. Beyond the dirt lot and overgrown brush lay the path up to the Ledges.

Ben would be safe there.

chapter forty-six

THE SANCTUARY OF GRACE COMMUNITY CHURCH WAS standing room only. The pews were packed, the side and center aisles jammed.

As Logan ran up to the pulpit, applause broke out. He shook his head, waved them quiet. "We need to evacuate this building immediately."

"Why?" A weary-faced woman struggled to hold on to her twin toddlers.

A bald man with a beer gut yelled out, "Another bomb?"

"Just a precaution. Start with the back rows, one row at a time. We'll have enough time if we're orderly."

"Is it OK if we get the children out first, Sergeant?" This from Dorothy, the woman who volunteered to help get cars moved this morning.

"It's got to be a bomb," someone yelled, and the panic started. A tsunami of people, trying to push into the crowded aisles. Children were separated from their mothers or lost underfoot, the elderly crushed against walls or pews.

"We can go out through the basement," the bald man said.

Logan fired three shots into the ceiling. "No one goes through the basement. We're evacuating the injured that way. You will go out the front. Back rows first and orderly. And if you're able-bodied, I expect you to assist the elderly and children."

"Stupid pig, you got us into this in the first place," an over-the-hill hippie yelled. "Everyone just get out."

"Hey!" Logan trained his gun on the front entrance. "Back rows, move out, a steady pace. I will shoot the next person who pushes out of turn."

"You're not gonna shoot anyone." The bald guy pushed by an elderly couple and headed for the door that led downstairs.

Crack! Chunks of plaster rained down from the ceiling onto the bald man.

Pappas stood on top of the piano, glaring. His arm was bandaged and resplinted. "Maybe he won't, but I will. And the next shot isn't into the ceiling, trust me. Any takers?"

A stunned silence took hold of the crowd.

"Let's do this in an orderly way now. Pass the babies and kids over the tops of the pews. Let's go, folks." Logan moved into the center aisle and met Hal Monroe moving against the tide of people.

"What do you need, Sarge?"

"Stand at the door, make sure they don't stampede."

Hilary pushed by Pappas, coming up from the basement. "Jae. Jae!"

"Not now, Hil." Logan was the stopgap keeping people from pushing too hard. If one went down, more would and there'd be casualties.

Hilary climbed over pews to get to him. "I can't find Kimmie."

"She's up at Walden. That's what you said."

"I went up there, Jae. Marita left me a note, said she was scared because she was all alone. So she brought Kimmie here. She went to the bathroom downstairs and just disappeared."

Logan went cold into his bones.

"You have to find her!" Hilary shrieked. "Why aren't you looking for her?"

"We've got to get these people out or we won't be able to find her."

Hilary slapped him across the face. "This is why I couldn't stay married to you. I knew I always came last. But your little girl?"

"Go look for her," Pappas said. "I'll keep these people moving."

"Thanks, man. And keep your eye out. She's blonde, blue-eyed, only five."

"I will, I will." He lowered his voice. "How much time do we have?"

Logan flashed five fingers, and then followed Hilary down the back stairs. He was dismayed to see how slowly the evacuation of the injured was going. Only half had been moved out of the fellowship hall.

"Kaya, you can't move everyone. You've gotta triage," he shouted.

She looked up from an elderly patient. "Jason, your little girl is here. But I don't know where."

"I know. You've got to choose who to save and then get out."

"I can't."

"You have to, Kaya. You're too important to all of us."

"Jae!" Hilary screamed. "You're wasting time."

Logan broke off to search the utility room and storage closet. Hilary and Marita went through the classrooms.

Four minutes left. He crossed the fellowship hall and found Hilary in a classroom. "Time's short. You go out. I'll keep looking."

"She's my daughter, too."

"And what if she's outside trying to get in? Get out, search the crowd!"

Logan dashed upstairs, found Pappas sending people out the windows now—still too many to get out the door. The *tick-tock* pressed in on him and he looked around, wondering if everyone could hear it.

Time ticking, bomb ticking, and the church too big to search for a child who was not in plain sight. Pastor's study, main office, music room, maintenance closet, upstairs kitchen, balcony, and upper classrooms—where should he go next?

"Kimmie," he bellowed but *tick-tock* answered him, so insanely loud that it battered his eardrums. So ridiculously loud that suddenly Logan understood.

He ran up to the balcony, took a narrow stairway into the steeple to the sound-system room. Climbed the ladder into the clock tower, a bizarre place of giant gears for the bell and the guts of the clock.

In the corner—a pink strap.

Logan opened the backpack and saw a sophisticated plastique explosive device on a windup timer, one minute and twelve seconds away from detonation. What looked like trip wires meant if he yanked the timer or tried to reset the time, the bomb would blow immediately.

Even if he wrapped his body around the bomb, the steeple would bring the roof down—on Kimmie and Hilary and Kaya, Pappas and Hal, too many people and *God, I'm just one man.*

Time unbearably ticked on.

Logan took one second to kick out the front clock face. Counting as he worked—two more to climb out onto the steeple. People everywhere below. If he tossed the bomb, he'd kill twenty or thirty, maybe more.

It took five seconds to go back into the sound system room and grab the rope ladder that served as a fire escape. More time to sling the backpack over his shoulder and drop the rope.

Tell people to move and just drop it? No, they'd stampede, and there were too many toddlers and infants down there. And it still might take down the church, with Kimmie somewhere in it.

Twenty seconds coming down the rope to the ground. A half a minute now, counting off the ticks—twenty-eight, twenty-seven, as Logan ran west toward the Circle.

Fifteen seconds, fourteen, thirteen as he scrambled up the embankment and onto the bike path.

Sprinting straight for the fire. Ten, nine, eight, seven—

—three, two seconds left when Logan heaved the backpack.

Only then did he spot Kimmie, gazing into the fire.

One last second while he grabbed his baby and then dived with her into the mist because it was the only cover he could find.

chapter forty-seven

THE WORLD EXPLODED.

Kaya held Natasha, running from sanctuary to find sanctuary, but none could be found, not with the air hissing and the ground shaking and the sky ripping—

—the store buckled, throwing Alexis off her feet so she could only watch as the pipes over her head stretched thin, like a balloon before bursting, but she could only pray they wouldn't because they were all that stood between her kids and the beast—

—the street rippled and cracked, and Luther thought, *What a glorious, horrific thing have we wrought*—

—the mist shredded so that every depravity and hatred was unleashed and Logan couldn't stop the onslaught, ashamed that the best he could do was to cover Kimmie's eyes and press her to his chest so she would only hear his heart beating and not the shrieks of a world vomiting its darkness—

—the mud exploded, the water filled what little expanse Jon could claim, stripping away their breathers, pulling his arms out of their sockets, but he willed himself to stretch because he had a hold on Chloe and would not let her go—

—Ben huddled behind a boulder, all the boulders ever created coming down on him, driving him into the ground so that the world he had always known had gone dark—

—vanished from sight.

the fifth hour

chapter forty-eight

LOGAN HAD LOST HIS DAUGHTER IN THE MIST.

"Kimmie? Kimmie!"

"I'm here, Daddy."

He peered through the mist. Was that flash of color the fire in the Circle?

"Where, honey?"

"Over here. Can't you see me?"

If he told her the truth, she might panic. "Keep talking, baby. I'm coming your way."

"Not so fast, Jae Sun." The mist parted to reveal a man slouched on a bench, his head lolling drunkenly to the side.

"Where's my daughter?"

The man squinted up at Logan through greasy strands of hair. His skin was like jaundiced leather, forehead creases so deep they looked black. Cracked teeth, almost rotted to the gum so only sharp points were left. An end-stage drunk, Logan knew. He sucked on a hand-rolled cigarette, smoke so thick around his head that it was impossible to tell where the smoke ended and the mist began.

"Kimmie!"

"She'll be along in a while. After we have ourselves a chat."

"Who the blazes are you?" Logan swore under his breath, then yelled, "Kimmie! Where are you, baby?"

The bum stood, almost as tall as Logan. "It's my blood running through your veins."

"You're insane." He tried to push by, yelling, "Kimmie!"

The man grabbed him, his grip like iron. "What kind of father abandons his child?"

"I didn't abandon her—she's lost. Kimmie!"

"I'm not talking about you, fool. I'm talking about me."

"I don't give a flying flip about you." The guy was all scab and smoke—why couldn't Logan get free?

"That's because you think I'm a worm-infested drunk, rotting from the outside in and inside out. But the truth is this, Jae Sun. You—and that tramp of a mother—weren't worth the ground I spit on then. And you are worth less even now."

"You're insane. I'm a good man."

"And that's the problem, wormspit. You got rage in your heart. Plenty of guns, and a vomitload of self-righteousness. But when it comes to being a man and putting down that dog who stole your wife and now wants your girl... you don't have what it takes."

"Shut up! Just shut up!"

"And you wanna know why that is?" The guy laughed, rancid smoke belching from deep in his lungs. "Because, Sergeant Jae Sun Logan, you don't think that little trinket you pretend is your daughter is worth dirtying your soul for."

Logan clenched his fists, nails biting so deep into his palms he drew blood. What had he heard about wounds in another man's palms?

Fury taken, justice delayed, grace given.

"Oh, God," he cried out. "Oh, Jesus!"

Suddenly Kimmie was in his arms, her fingers digging into his back. "I knew you'd find me, Daddy."

The man in the mist laughed himself away, smoke and mist, but the accusations kept coming, darts from every side scraping Logan raw. He covered Kimmie's eyes and held her tight, shielding her while he had to look upon what was ugly and terrible and true.

He was stubborn—holding tight when he should let go. Let go and leave Hilary to her rich-and-famous lifestyle. Let go and leave the gangbangers to rule the very streets that would kill them. Let go of law and justice and peace because they all were stolen long ago, and only a fool like Jason Logan would believe otherwise.

More accusations—and temptations—sticking like barbs.

He was a fool—letting go when he should be taking. Take the revenge that even now smoldered in his gut. Take his wife back and make her submit to him. Take Kaya de los Santos because she was his for the asking.

He was stupid—risking his life for others when he should live only for himself. Live as a man does, and not as a weak-kneed fool in pursuit of a weak-willed dead man.

"Daddy," Kimmie whispered, "don't be scared."

Logan fell to his knees under the burden of rage and fear, trying to keep it from falling on Kimmie. He tightened his grip on her and begged for God to spare her, even though he understood that the almighty God had not spared *His* own child.

Oh, Father. Oh, Jesus, save me.

Kimmie wiggled, freeing one arm so she could point to something. He was afraid to look, but she wouldn't hold still. "Daddy! Daddy, let's go."

Logan couldn't see what she did, but he put her down and let her lead him, feeling the indictments fall away like dead leaves.

He opened his hand—opening his heart—and left law and justice to the One who held it anyway.

He closed his hand—sealing his heart—to take that which never could have been earned but was offered freely.

He promised to live this new life—the life of Christ—in this moment and every moment to come in his Father's sight.

chapter forty-nine

THE MUD HAD EXPLODED, SPITTING THEM OUT OF THE tunnel and into a rushing river so powerful that Jon was helpless to stand.

No time to wonder or fear why they were suddenly in a strange land and under a piercing sky, or why such mud-filled dreck had erupted into a crystalline river—there was only time to breathe and flail and try to survive.

Hansen wrapped one arm around a rock jutting out of the water and grabbed Chloe with the other. She held to Jon just as she had promised—for richer or poorer, in sickness and in health, in the mud and the fire, in relative reality and absolute impossibility.

But this water ripped at him—*wanted* him—so, at the risk of it claiming Chloe along with him, he let go.

"Jon!" she screamed, but the roar of the water swallowed her voice.

As he was carried away, he saw Hansen dragging her onto the riverbank. She tried to run after Jon, but the water was too fast for her to keep up with, so she could only yell words he didn't need to hear to believe.

Wasn't it better that he be separated from her? In his passion to rip apart the fabric of the universe, he had brought this terrible thing down on them.

What—or why—this thing was, he couldn't even begin to guess. Either their little experiment had somehow shifted them spatially into a different part of the world, or temporally into the past or the future, or horrifically into a different reality altogether.

One thing hadn't changed. Chloe loved him and he loved Chloe. As soon as he found another rock to grab on to or the current lessened enough so he could swim to shore, he'd get out of this river and find his way back to her.

Until then, he could only muse on this irony: rather than pushing one particle, wasn't it fitting that *he* was now the particle being pushed?

chapter fifty

OGAN CLIMBED UP THE FRONT STEPS OF GRACE Community Church. Pieces of the broken clock face were scattered at his feet. He glanced up, saw the rope ladder still hanging. Further up, a simple cross topped the steeple. He had seen that same cross every day of his life, but from this moment on he would never look at it the same way.

Even from here, he could see the fire in the Circle. The second bomb hadn't dampened it or fed the flames—it simply *was*. The mist blossomed around it and stretched over their heads, but it had changed. The sky was now visible through it.

Logan shrugged his shoulders, feeling the agony of his burns but also a shifting of the burden. The cross above his head and the grace in his heart pointed to the only way any of them would get through this.

Hal Monroe yanked on the pull rope to ring the church bell. Over and over, the solemn peal called people to attention. This same bell had rung for the Armistice after World War I, for Pearl Harbor and Kennedy's assassination, and on the night of September 11 to call people to prayer.

Snuggled in Logan's arms, Kimmie jolted with each toll of the bell. Hilary clung to her from the other side and, for this moment, they were the family they had vowed before God to be.

Pappas stood on the steps with them, blood from his wounds already seeping through his clean shirt and splint. Ever watchful, he scanned the crowd as they gathered on the lawn and spilled out onto the street.

255

The injured had been moved back into the fellowship hall. Kaya was assessing what further trauma they had suffered during the evacuation.

Logan signaled Hal to stop. The last peal hung in the air, people seeming to hold their breaths until the next one came.

What could he tell these people to bring them assurance that made even a smidgen of sense? He turned to Pappas and whispered, "You want to take this, Pappas?"

"They're scared, man. They don't know me. They're all looking to you."

"What's going on?" the hippie cried out. "We have a right to know."

"Is help coming?" someone else shouted. More voices, clamoring for answers.

Kimmie burrowed into his shoulder. "Why are those people mad at you?"

"They're not mad, sweetheart. They're just scared." So was he—what could he possibly offer them?

Pappas blew the air horn. "Quiet down! Let the man speak."

Deep breath and a simple prayer: *Lord, give me wisdom.* "Folks, I don't know what's going on. But I'm going to find out. Give me an hour to check things out, and then I'll come back and report. Can you do that?"

"Yes!" Dorothy called out.

"Thank you, Sergeant Logan," Johnny Beck added.

"This is Agent Pappas, with the United States Secret Service. He'll be coordinating..." Logan searched for the right word. *Rescue* wasn't appropriate, but *recovery* was way off. "...coordinating..."

Pappas touched his arm, spoke to the crowd. "Relief efforts. We're gonna work together, make sure everyone's OK."

People nodded, murmured among themselves. Volunteers moved into the crowd with clipboards borrowed from the church classrooms. Donnelly's had advertised registration, a fib that they had decided was a good idea. At least it would keep people busy for a while.

Logan turned aside to Pappas. "I'm going to survey the margins of the affected areas. Maybe create a quick map. Meanwhile, you still need to get stitched up."

"Are you going up to Walden?" Hilary said.

"I'm going wherever I can without getting into that mist."

"Then we're going with you."

"Absolutely not."

Her face flushed. "For goodness' sake, we almost got blown up. I want to take Kimmie home. To Walden. It's not safe down here in the Flats."

"Why do you alwa—"

Kimmie burrowed her face into his shoulder, stopping him cold.

Hilary softened her tone. "Up there we have armed security, guard dogs, an alarm system. We've even got a generator. No bombs, Jae."

"Let me check it out, make sure nothing's going on up there. When I get back we'll discuss it. Please, Hil."

She bit her upper lip, blessedly showing restraint. "OK. Fine."

Logan passed Kimmie to her. "Stay right here with Mommy, OK? And no wandering off."

Minutes later, the disaster team—Logan, Pappas, Wells, Hal Monroe, Chet Babin, and Kaya—gathered in one of the classrooms. As they discussed how to allocate the few resources they had, Kaya stitched up the wound in Pappas's forearm.

They put together a duty roster for the next three hours. Hal would give Leah a break guarding the back door, and Wells would go over to South Spire to spell Jamie. Pappas would do another sweep of the church, make sure there weren't any surprises, and then get out on the street.

"Not until I'm sure we've stopped that bleeding," Kaya said.

Pappas squinted at her. "Are you always this bossy?"

"Kaya, where's Ben?" Logan asked.

She bit her lower lip, trying to hold back tears. "He's somewhere safe. He can't be involved in this, Jason. Surely you believe that. I don't know why those people think he was...but he couldn't be."

Logan pulled her aside. "He thought he was going on a picnic with Jasmine Ramirez. She had a backpack, talked him into carrying it. She thought it was a drug drop, but when they opened it, they saw the bomb. Ben called me, Kaya, but it was too late. Kids just being dumb kids. Word got around that he was warning people out of the Circle."

"So...he tried to do the right thing."

"I'll make sure people know that, and then we can get him back here."

Kaya grabbed his arm. "You knew, didn't you? When I came to the substation and told you he was missing. You already knew."

"I didn't know it was Ben. Pappas and I put it together when you told us what he was wearing. I'm sorry, Kaya. We needed you desperately. And we weren't sure yet what Ben's involvement was." He met her gaze. "Can you forgive me?"

"It's a terrible day for all of us, Jason. We'll get through it."

Back at the table, the crisis team decided which volunteers could be trusted to go house to house. They needed to account for children separated from parents and bring them here to be taken care of, assist the elderly who depended on home health aides, or find people who may have been injured or suffered medical crises.

Paul Wells would take volunteers with him to do the same on South Spire. Logan said he'd worry about West University and North Spire as he did his survey.

"Those people out there have got to be getting hungry," Hal said. "I know I am."

"Johnny Beck took care of our volunteers," Kaya said. "Maybe he can get something going."

"Hey, Sarge. What're we going to do when the looting starts?" Wells asked.

"Maybe it won't," Logan said.

Pappas shook his head. "Come on, Logan—all these stores with their windows blown out? The owners are sitting in their shops even now, shotguns ready to blast the first thing that moves their way."

"Logan, you gotta get going," Hal said. "These people won't wait forever for the information you promised."

"Wait," Kaya said. "I want you on antibiotics for those burns. And you need a painkiller."

"I'm OK," Logan said.

She stripped off her gloves. "You are not OK. You will take your medicine and you will let me wash out those burns."

Pappas laughed. "Now we know who's really running this show."

Logan followed Kaya to the kitchen, where he pulled off what was left of his shirt. His bulletproof vest was crusted with ooze and, as she cut it away, it pulled at his blisters. He clenched his jaw, trying not to cry out.

"Hey, pal. That strong-silent thing gets old."

"What's it look like back there?"

"Ugly. Nasty first-degree, some second, but nothing we can't get started on."

As she poured bottled water down his back, he thought of the river he had seen on the far side of Tapley. If he were to dip into that water, would it wash away his pain—or would it strip off his skin and expose him to the marrow?

Kaya wrapped his burns, bringing the gauze up over his shoulder and around his upper arms. Each time she leaned over him, he smelled the salt of her exertion and the fragrance of her hair. Her skin was shiny with sweat, her eyes bright even though she had to be exhausted.

Logan cleared his throat. "Not too tight. Make sure I can use my arms."

"Shush. Relax." She kept working, her breath warm on his neck, her hands gentle.

Logan forced his focus back to the work at hand. He scanned the fellowship hall. There were twenty-nine people with significant injuries and nineteen volunteers to help care for them. The walking wounded were still out on the street—those who couldn't get home would have to be persuaded to go up to the sanctuary.

Kimmie sat in the corner with Natasha, helping her drink juice through a straw. Hilary—cheeks flushed with anger—huddled with Marita. Probably firing the poor woman even though Kimmie's disappearance wasn't her fault. She had told Marita she was going to the bathroom. Instead she had gone outside, looking for flowers to bring to Natasha. She spotted the fire in the Circle and was drawn to it.

His throat still clenched at the thought of her getting trapped in the mist. Logan had sheltered her with everything in him, but his strength and determination weren't nearly sufficient. All it had taken was a child's faith.

His faith was even less, and yet he had a man's job to do.

Kaya leaned over his shoulder, careful not to touch him. "You OK, big guy? You're a little green behind the ears."

Hilary looked over, caught his eye—caught Kaya pressing her cheek to his—and scowled.

Logan was too spent to do anything but whisper, "Pray for me. OK?"

"Yes, of course. By the way..." She came around so she could face him and took his hands in hers. Holding his gaze, she said, "I'm coming with you."

chapter fifty-one

BEGINNING AT GRACE, THEY HAD RIDDEN BIKES EAST, following the inside perimeter of the mist. Every couple of blocks they stopped and marked a map with the margins where the mist intersected the city.

By the time they had gone all the way down to Tapley School and then followed the mist back to the Circle, a pattern had formed.

"This is bizarre," Logan said.

"Like a wide flower petal," Kaya said, connecting the dots on the map. "The area bordered by the mist is narrowed at the Circle, gets widest about eight blocks down, and then narrows again."

"Egg-shaped might be a better description. An oval with the point at the Circle."

For a split second her gaze shifted north, and then back.

"You sent him to the Ledges, didn't you?" Logan said.

She brushed her hair out of her eyes and nodded.

"He'll be OK."

"As long as he..." She wrapped her arms around herself.

"What?"

"Nothing."

Logan put his arm around her. "Leah told me you were lost in the mist."

She nodded, her gaze again shifting to the Ledges. The mist arched down so that the top third of the rocky hills was obscured.

261

"Me, too. A couple of times. It was brutal. I can't explain it and I'm not sure how it happened, but I think this whole blast area is lost in the mist. And that scares me. Because things are in that mist. Terrifying, hellish things." A vicious chill seized him so that he pulled Kaya closer, not to comfort her this time but to be comforted.

"What else, Jason? I can see it in your eyes—there was something else."

"God was there, too. He found me. And somehow, I found Him."

"*Hmm*. Thought so."

"With all you had to deal with, you still prayed for me."

Kaya grinned. "Just doing my job."

"Speaking of which—we need to keep moving."

Unless they wanted to go through the mist, the only way to get to South Spire Boulevard was through the Circle. They made their rounds of that area and again marked the map, revealing a mirror image of the one they had drawn around East University Avenue.

As they headed back to the Circle, they spotted Paul Wells and some volunteers pushing elderly people in office chairs. "We're taking these people to Grace," he said. "But since you're here, Sarge—you gotta check something out."

Logan and Kaya followed Wells into the North Middlesex Bank building. Just a couple of hundred feet from the Circle, its top floors were obscured by the mist. The bank's bulletproof windows had withstood the blast, but the office windows had all blown out.

Wells led them up to the third floor. "We came up here to make sure that no one had been too injured to go looking for help. We didn't find anyone—this building is like a rock. I guess everyone's gone to Grace or tried to go home. But this is just so freaky, you gotta see it."

Wells opened a door marked Daniel Stevens, Attorney-at-Law. Pictures on the wall were askew and a vase knocked over, but otherwise nothing seemed amiss in the reception area. Then he opened the door marked Atty. Stevens.

The mist seemed to cut the office in half.

"I wondered, how the devil did this stuff come in here?" Wells said. "So I walked slow—really slow—toward it, keeping my hand to the wall. And that's when I felt it."

"Felt what?" Logan said.

"Nothing. That's the problem."

"I swear, Wells—"

"I can't explain it, Sarge. You just need to do it."

Logan glanced at Kaya. She offered no encouragement at first, just nibbled on her lip. Then she extended her hand.

He took her hand, inching along the wall with his other hand. When his fingertips touched the mist, Kaya squeezed his hand and he reached deeper in.

Suddenly the wall ended, a perfectly flat line going up into the ceiling at the same angle as the mist.

"It's gone," Logan said. "Just like that, it's gone."

Wells nodded. "Weird, huh? Like the mist was a giant sword that came down and—*whack*—cut us off."

Kaya squinted at him. "And this doesn't scare you, Paul?"

"What good is being scared gonna do me?" he said, but Logan saw the tightening of his jaw.

"OK, here's what we'll do," Logan said. "We'll get people settled and finish our map, and then we're going over to the Polytech. We're going to rouse a couple of those profs out of their labs or wherever they're hiding and make them figure this out."

"Wouldn't they have come to the meeting?" Kaya asked.

Wells snorted. "They live in their own little world. Even have their own so-called security force. Don't have the time of day for anyone without letters after their name."

"We'll worry about them later," Logan said. "For now, we've all got a job to do. So let's do it."

•••

Logan and Kaya took their bikes around the Circle to West University. A knot of people stood on the bike path, trying to get up their courage to go around the fire.

"We heard something about a meeting," a woman with frizzy gray hair said. "But we're afraid to go near that thing."

"The meeting has been postponed," Logan said. "And honestly—there's not much to report yet anyway. If you still want to go to Grace, you just stick to the bike path and you'll be OK. But it would be far better if you could help out here." He gave them a pep talk about organizing to go house to house and promised to send someone back in an hour or so to see if they had any injured.

"An hour? Why so long?" asked a square-jawed man in shorts and polo shirt.

"Because we're stretched a little thin right now."

"When are the ambulances coming?"

"We don't know."

"That's crazy. How can you not know? What're you covering up?"

"Listen, pal," Logan began.

Kaya touched his forearm and said, "With communications out, it's on all of us to be good neighbors."

The man nodded. "OK, then. We'll get to work."

"Was it so obvious that I was going to jump down his throat?" Logan whispered to Kaya as they pushed their bikes away from the knot of people.

"The guy was one comment away from you having to fight me for that pleasure."

They hopped on their bikes and rode through the neighborhoods, tracking the inside perimeter of the mist. When people waved them to a stop, Logan referred queries to the group by the Circle. There was far less traffic on this side of the Circle, which meant far less injuries.

They cycled through Hubbard Park. The playground was deserted. The sandy beach next to the pond was littered with toys and blankets. People must have grabbed their kids and ran when the bomb went off, Logan thought. He would have done the same.

"I haven't been on a bike in years," Kaya said. "In a strange way, I'm enjoying this."

Logan laughed. "You don't get out much, huh?"

"We used to come up to Hubbard all the time. Except back then, it was train whistles all the time. Remember when they ran aboveground?"

"Yeah, my brother Mike and I used to mess around, trying to jump onto the freight cars when they slowed down at the University-Spire intersection. One day my father caught us and... well, we didn't sit down for a week. And we weren't let out of our yard for a month."

"The good old days," Kaya said with a smile. "Back then, the tracks were natural boundaries. This neighborhood—single-family houses and the park, the Flats, the business district, the Tech. Even the Ledges and Walden Hills, high above all of it. We were all within an easy bike ride or walk, but we just stayed where we were. And now, the old tracks are torn up, a nice bike path in their place, but we seem more divided than ever."

"Bombs and philosophy," Logan said. "Way to rock it, Kaya."

They followed the mist boundary all the way back to the Circle. They stopped their bikes and marked up the map, not surprised to find that their survey of West University produced a mirror image of what they had seen on East University and South Spire.

"It's starting to look like a flower," Logan said.

"More like a clover. And I'm betting once we've been up North Spire, we'll have our fourth leaf. It's weird how it's so precise."

"Pappas thinks it's about the trains."

Kaya laughed. "Duh. Of course it's about the trains."

"No, not the bomb. The way the mist groups around the Circle. The midline of each of these petals, or eggs—however you want to describe them—is the bike path. And the paths are directly over the train line."

"Something to do with the magnets?" Kaya asked.

"Exactly." Logan explained Pappas's theory about electro-magnetic-pulse devices being planted in the Circle and detonated by the backpack bomb.

"That explains the shape, but it doesn't explain what's in the mist."

"I keep telling myself they're hallucinations."

"No," she whispered. "They're coming *because* of us, but not *from* us."

"We're supposed to...um...tell God whatever, right?" Logan asked. "Tell Him that He can do whatever He wants, even wrap us in a mist and drop-kick us, because He's still God and He'll catch us on the other side of the goalpost. Right?"

She laughed. "You give a good sermon, Sergeant Logan."

"Kaya—I went through the mist. To beyond."

Her smile died. "If you went through and couldn't get us any help..."

"I have to sit for a minute." Logan dropped the bike. His back and leg throbbed, and his shoulders seared with pain. He lowered himself carefully to the ground.

Kaya sat next to him and gave him a bottle of water. "Drink this."

He slugged down a couple mouthfuls.

"All of it." She waited while he emptied the bottle. "Good. Now talk to me."

"The thing is, Kaya...I don't think we're in Kansas anymore."

"What do you mean?"

"I went through the mist after Luther, the guy we think is behind this. We found ourselves on a rock-studded hillside. But not like any rocks we have around here. More like...this is insane."

"It's OK. Go on."

"They were like what I imagine uncut diamonds look like. And Luther—who I couldn't get a good look at—saw the same thing. Even so, he was in full mocking mode, told me he had moved the bomb to where it would do the most damage. And then this thing flew overhead. I thought it was a jet, a bomber even. It filled the sky, and then—"

Kaya rested her hand on his forearm. He took a deep breath and continued.

"—and then it flapped its wings. Whatever it was, it was real and alive and like nothing I'd ever imagined."

She dug her fingers in, her gesture of support now a cry for help. "It's like we're in some science-fiction novel," she whispered.

Logan nodded slowly. "The worst I had imagined about why no one came to help was that a big part of the Northeast had been destroyed. But now I'm thinking it's because there's no one out there *to* help. I don't know how or why this happened, but I think we're...all we've got."

Kaya linked her arm through his. "We're not alone, Jason. You know that."

"I know that. Now I have to practice believing it."

chapter fifty-two

NOTHING BROKEN—EXCEPT MAYBE THE WORLD.

Ben pushed up from among the boulders, shocked that none had actually fallen on him. There'd been a flash of light at the Circle, followed by a small *boom* and then a terrible ripping, as if Barcester was a scrap of paper and some giant force was tearing it to bits. For a moment he had felt every bit of his being—mind and body—being squeezed and stretched while someone pressed down on him.

What about Mom—was she all right?

Ben shook out his muscles the best he could and climbed up to the next ledge. From there he could see the steeple at Grace, and that meant his mother had to be OK. She'd be here as soon as she could.

He leaned back against a boulder, thinking maybe he could sleep. Sleep, and then wake to find out it had all been a horrible dream. Too many videogames and R-rated movies, too much talk about guns and knives, too much thinking he could be hip and cool. A drowsiness came on him, stones biting into his shoulder blades but not hurting nearly as much as the confusion and shame biting into his heart.

What a flippin' loser he was.

Footsteps pounded the path.

"Mom! I'm here," he called, then immediately regretted it. Just when he thought he couldn't get any stupider, he proved that he could.

No answer meant his worst fear—this was not his mother, but someone coming after him. He had nothing but rocks to defend himself with, so he picked up the biggest one he could throw. Hoisting it over his head, he crept around the side of the boulder.

There was a shuffling in the dirt on the other side, then a strangled cry. Had Luther brought his mother up here, choking her until Ben came out of hiding?

He howled like a warrior and rushed around the boulder with the rock held high, ready to crush the skull of whoever was on the other side.

"Don't!"

Ben dropped the rock, his heart pounding so hard that it took almost half a minute before he could even speak.

"Mad Dog. What are you doing here?"

"Elvin's dead. Elvin's dead, and I'm all alone." Madeline wrapped her skinny arms around him and sobbed. It took a good minute before Ben could calm her enough to continue. "His friends were trying to save me, but we saw this bloody sheet on the street. They all thought it must be you—"

"I wish it were," he whispered.

"They spooked and wanted to take me over to the warehouse on Factory Street. But we got lost in the mist and I heard them yelling. They were so scared, and I tried to tell them how to get out but they got deeper in. Then they started shooting—so I started running."

Ben instinctively looked north. The ledges continued for two hundred feet before a wall of mist cut them off. "Then what?" he asked as gently as he could manage. Madeline shook so hard, he had begun to tremble with her.

"Tripp didn't come home, and I didn't know where Mama was. There was this big blast, and I just started running and somehow ended up here. I don't know how; it's all kind of fuzzy. Maybe an angel was taking care of me. Right?"

Not by sending her to the biggest loser in the known universe, Ben thought.

He guided her to a small ledge of rock and sat with her. "Madeline, my mother's supposed to meet me up here. She'll take care of you."

"When?"

"I don't know. She's at Grace Church, taking care of the injured. As soon as she can, she's coming to get me."

"Why aren't you with her?"

"I...just needed to give her space, that's all."

Her gaze—too clear for a little kid—cut right into him. "You're in trouble. Right?"

"Yeah. I am."

"Because of the backpack?"

He nodded.

"Then I am, too. You had a backpack, and I had a backpack. And they both blew up, so people are..." She scrunched her face but didn't cry, only let out a ragged sigh.

"Sergeant Logan knows we didn't mean it," Ben said. "He'll stick up for us. But he's busy now. So we'll just wait here until my mother comes, and then we'll see what to do."

Madeline snuggled into him. "I'm scared."

If Cannon were here, he would flex his muscles and tell her that nothing bad could happen as long as he was *the man*.

But Cannon was dead, and Ben had run out of himself. So the best he could say was, "I'm scared, too. But we'll sit here and be scared together."

"OK," she said. "Hey, Ben."

"Yeah?"

"The angel wouldn't have brought me here unless God wanted it to. Right?"

"I guess," Ben said, wishing with his whole heart that he could do a whole lot better for her—and for all the mess he'd made—than *guess*.

271

chapter fifty-three

L OGAN AND KAYA WERE ALMOST DONE WITH THEIR survey of North Spire, including Walden Estates, when they ran into the woman with the broken wrist. When Logan had splinted her a few hours back, she had seemed fine. Now she was pasty-faced and sweating.

"It's hurt worse than I thought," she said. "I tried calling 911, but the phones are out."

Kaya unrolled the makeshift splint and examined the woman's wrist. "The phones'll be out for a while longer. I can stabilize this, give you a couple of painkillers. That way you can just stay home. Unless you want to come down to Grace?"

The woman stared down the hill. The mist was like a gray lump congealing around the Circle. The steepness of the hill made it impossible to see the fire. "I think I'd prefer to stay home. Could we do this up at my house? I think I need to lie down."

Kaya glanced at Logan.

"Sure," he said, a plan already forming.

The security guard had to open the gate to Walden Estates manually. He made pleasant chitchat with the woman but let Logan pass without comment.

He walked both his and Kaya's bikes while she laced her arm around the injured woman's waist. They passed by two splendid houses before turning up a winding driveway. The woman's house was a sprawling brick colonial with tennis courts, pool, and a gazebo. They entered a foyer with granite floors and a double stairway.

"Where would you be most comfortable?" Kaya said.

The woman scrunched her eyes closed. "My bedroom, if you wouldn't mind."

"Do you have children or any household help?" Logan asked.

"Grown kids. Clean the house myself." She forced a smile. "I take pride in that. My husband's in Europe, but I'll be OK if I can just get this bone to stop bouncing around in my arm."

He helped the woman upstairs, then followed Kaya into a huge master bath. While she rooted through the vanity for an ACE bandage, he said, "I'm going for a little walk."

"Why?"

Logan remained silent.

"Oh no. I can see it in your face—you want to go next door to the Reynolds house. Not a good idea."

"I don't even know if he's there. Marita thought he was in the office, but he didn't answer her knock. That's why she brought Kimmie to Grace."

"If he's not there, why go?"

"My job. Hilary wants to come back here. I need to make sure it's safe."

She turned to face him. "I have no use for that creep, but now is not the time."

"I need to," Logan said. "I don't know why, but I need to go over there."

"Fine. We'll go together."

"People are waiting for us back at Grace. You finish up here. I'll just run up, and then I'll come back in a few minutes."

"Don't get into anything with him." Kaya clutched his shoulders. "Remember who you are, Jason. And remember who you belong to now."

•••

The woman with the broken wrist lived in a house three times the size of Logan's old Victorian. Carlton Reynolds's house was twice the size of hers, designed to look like a thirties-era mansion with white cedar siding, floor-to-ceiling windows, French doors, a marble foyer, and Cinderella stairs. Going room by room, Logan half expected Katherine Hepburn or Cary Grant to pop out and start with the sophisticated chatter.

As Marita had said, no one was there. The housekeeper and gardener had hoofed it down to Grace with her and Kimmie.

Logan lingered in Kimmie's room, smelling her pillow. Wondering how long it would take her to prefer being in this room—decorated like a princess's castle—to her tiny room at his house. Eventually, she'd want all Carlton Reynolds could offer: a horse, piano lessons, her own cell phone, a fancy car, a super sixteenth birthday party.

He fingered the letter in his pocket. Until he opened it, she was still Kim Li Logan—his little girl.

But what if they were really cut off from the world they had known? If Reynolds hadn't been here to receive his letter, would it have gone back to the post office? No, the housekeeper would have signed for it, then taken it out back to his office.

Logan went out through the kitchen, surprised to hear the whir of the refrigerator. Had power come back? He picked up the phone. Dead. Marita must have started the generator before heading down to Grace.

Behind the swimming pool and patio was a high row of privet hedges. Logan's heart ached at the sight of beach toys he had bought Kimmie, now scattered on the patio and in the pool. He went through the gate to the back acreage, most of which was shrouded in the mist.

Carlton Reynolds's office was a one-story building with arched windows. The custody papers listed his occupation as *financier* and his annual income in the seven digits.

There was a mail slot in the door.

Logan walked onto the deck. The room beyond was dark. He knocked, waited. Getting no response, he knocked harder, then unholstered his weapon and used it to break a pane of glass in the front door.

With his heart thudding, he reached his hand in and unlocked and opened the door.

Carlton Reynolds lay crumpled on the floor.

Logan lifted the man's hand, searching for a pulse. Thready, if at all. Kaya would know what to do, but he only could guess.

Logan ripped open Reynolds's shirt, trying not to think about his wife pressed against this man's skin. A medical alert necklace—the guy was a type 1 diabetic, meaning insulin dependent.

Reynolds's blood sugar must be nonexistent to put him into a coma, Logan thought. He pulled open the desk drawers but found nothing. He went to the kitchenette and found the syringes, insulin, and testing device. He turned the device on but got only a glowing screen—fried by the bomb and whatever magnetic storm had followed.

Logan went back out on the deck, trying to figure out what to do. To the north, the mist swirled. Cold air blew over him.

He could just walk away and leave Reynolds to his fate. If he died, it wouldn't be at Logan's hands but because of his own illness. The custody issue would be moot.

What was it the bum in the mist—his father—had said? *You don't think that little trinket you pretend is your daughter is worth dirtyin' your soul for.*

How easy it would be to put this all behind him. Rather than risking the process to chance, Logan could go back in and cover Reynolds's mouth and nose with his hand. Within two minutes he'd be dead. Chances were, even an autopsy wouldn't show any cause of death other than diabetic shock.

Logan slipped his hand into his pocket again, fingering the letter from the testing lab. No matter what the test results read, he was Kimmie's father. He had the right to do this, didn't he?

No, son.

A father's voice, but not the bum in the mist or even Joe Logan's. Fatherhood was not a matter of DNA but of the heart—which was why he had to trust his heavenly Father's heart.

Logan went back into the office and dug through the cupboards until he found a pack of sugar wafers. He opened Reynolds's mouth and shoved a wafer into his cheek.

Then he sat back and waited for Carlton Reynolds to come back to life.

chapter fifty-four

KILL A MONSTER, CHANGE A POOPY DIAPER—ALL IN A day's work, Alexis thought as she swabbed the baby's bottom.

Cleaver in hand, Tripp leaned his bulk against the door.

"It's locked. And fortified," Alexis said. "Theft-proof."

"It ain't thieves I'm worried about," he said.

Kate pulled Jenny to the door to stand with him. "What're we going to do, Miz Latham?"

Angelina caught Alexis's finger and squeezed, her cocoa eyes seeming to ask the same question.

Leaving the store would be like cutting out Alexis's heart.

No—this was no time to indulge in melodramatic whimsy. Going up to the church made the most sense. She'd hand the baby to the nurse, settle Kate, Jenny, and Tripp with some responsible adult, and then come right back.

This was her fight—not the kids'.

"We're going to Grace with everyone else," Alexis said.

Kate grabbed Jenny, who in turn clutched Tripp's free hand. They didn't trust her anymore, Alexis realized. They had endured windows exploding, Ralph dying, thugs closing in, and being circled by a monster. Oh, and by the way, had lived through the stretching and shaking of yet another bomb. Were those cockroach terrorists done blowing up the neighborhood, or was there more coming?

She laughed. "All in a day's work."

"What?" Jenny said.

"Nothing." Alexis carefully picked up the baby and breathed in the smell of formula and baby wipes. The baby snuggled into her, ready for another nap. At least Angelina still trusted her.

"Get your stuff together," she said. "We're going up to Grace. Jenny, take the stroller down, please. Tripp—you take the baby, and I'll take the knife, lead us down and out."

Tripped straightened, and his chubbiness took on heft, as if he was transforming before their eyes from a fat kid everyone dumped on to a protector of women and children. The hand holding the cleaver trembled, but his gaze was steady. "I'll lead the way."

"Good enough. Kate, do you have the diaper bag I packed?"

"Yes, ma'am."

"You take the baby."

"I made her cry before. Because I held her the wrong way."

"And now you know better." Alexis smiled as she passed Angelina to the girl. "Go ahead, Tripp. Open it up."

He unlocked the door and stepped out onto the platform. He had to start down the stairs before there was room for the girls to get out.

Alexis slipped her gun out of her pocket and clicked off the safety. Just let some stupid sewer snake try to hurt these kids.

Slowly, slowly they crept down the stairs. At the bottom, Tripp turned and looked to Alexis. "Which way?"

"Go down two rows. There's no drains in the cereal aisle."

Tripp shuffled forward, Jenny and Kate practically climbing up his heels. Alexis scanned the shelves, watching for the Cocoa Krispies to topple and the sewer snake to lasso them again.

Focus.

They moved past the registers and toward the front door. Alexis unlocked the padlock and handed her gun to Jenny so she could raise the grate.

"What am I supposed to do with this?" the girl moaned.

"Point and shoot at anything that moves."

"Anything that ain't us," Tripp added.

Alexis lifted the grate, took the gun back, and stepped outside. For a moment, the sight of shopping carts in the corral disoriented her, as if she had made this whole nightmare up and life outside went on as normal.

Then she spotted Harry Stevens sitting in front of his store with what looked like a .45 in his hand. He shook his head at her, then nodded to his right.

The kids crowded out behind her.

"Want me to pull the grate?" Tripp said.

"Please," Kate said. "Before it follows us out."

"Wait," Alexis said, finally spotting what Harry clued her in to.

Hoops, Hoodie, and four other gangbangers stood at the corner of the store, fully armed.

"Get inside," Alexis whispered.

"Maybe if we're nice…give them money or something…they'll let us go," Kate said.

"It's not money they want," Alexis said. "You, of all people, should know that. Now, get inside."

"No," Tripp said. "They won't shoot. Not with all these witnesses and stuff. In daylight. They just won't. Right, Shawn? You ain't here to shoot anyone."

Somehow Alexis knew they *would* shoot because a few hours ago the bomb had blown apart more than the Circle, and it would take an act of God to put it all right again.

Tripp was still trying to play peacemaker. "We can talk this out. No shooting."

"Shut it, Sheffield," Hoops said. "That witch shot me and I'm here to return the favor." He limped toward them, blood seeping through the gauze wrapped around his foot.

He held the gun all wrong, like too many others who had never been trained and depended on spraying bullets instead of hitting their mark. Alexis could raise her gun and likely kill him before he could figure out how to sight down the barrel. But then his friends would unleash their firepower, and that would mean all of them dying.

"Tripp, take the girls inside," she said.

"Oh, no," Hoodie snarled, raising his gun. "No one moves."

Hoops stopped and leaned against a pole, his face distorted with pain. The bandage on his foot was soaked with blood. Unable to walk another step, he'd end it now.

Alexis would die, but she would not bow to fear. Never had, never would. Tightening her grip on the gun, she glanced sideways and locked eyes with Tripp.

You know what to do, she willed him to understand. *Just go inside, leave me alone.*

She looked Hoops in the eye, thinking somewhere deep inside that this was insane, hoping her fifty-three-year-old reflexes would somehow be faster than his.

Something flashed at his feet. He yelped and, instead of aiming for Alexis, shot at his own feet. The kid bellowed with pain, screeching to a fearful wail. His crew joined the shooting, blasting away so that Hoops nearly broke in two at the knees from the bullets.

Tripp grabbed Kate and Jenny and pulled them into the store—*bless him*—but Alexis couldn't move other than to shelter behind the concrete column and watch in horror as the monster wrapped around what was left of Hoops and pulled him into the sewer drain.

What felt like a lifetime couldn't have taken more than two or three seconds, long enough for Hoops's blood to run into the pothole that Alexis kept meaning to have filled. The shooting stopped, and the thugs—no more than frightened children now—stared at her in horror.

"I don't know," Alexis said, because, truly, she knew nothing except this one thing: it was safer inside the store than out.

She owned this place and knew it and would find a way to defend it and the kids.

Alexis backed into the store, pulled down the grate and locked it.

Let someone else worry about the rest.

chapter fifty-five

ARLTON REYNOLDS SAT IN HIS OFFICE CHAIR, SIPPING orange juice. His spite returned with his consciousness. "Get off my property."

"What, no *thank-you*?" Logan asked.

"My thank-you is not having you arrested for trespassing. Where's Kim?"

"My daughter is with her mother. Safe at Grace Church."

"Is Hilary there of her own volition?"

Logan bristled. "You accusing me of kidnapping?"

"I hate to think ill of anyone," Reynolds said with a smirk. "But I can't imagine why she'd go running to you when it's safer here with me."

"Your money isn't going to buy anyone's safety today."

"Is that a threat, Mr. Logan?"

"It's a fact. And that's Sergeant Logan to you."

Reynolds threw his head back and laughed. "We'll see about that, now that you've violated the restraining order."

Logan stepped toward him, hands clenched. "I saved your life."

"So what now? You going to shoot me?" Reynolds stood with the calm smile of the supremely arrogant. "This is what you've been waiting for, isn't it? The opportunity to prove your machismo. No restraining order or woman or little girl between us. Just you and me, Logan."

Give him what he deserves, every nerve in Logan's body howled.

You got what you didn't deserve, grace whispered.

Logan slammed his fist against the wall, then walked out the door.

"She'll come back to me," Reynolds called after him. "But you show up here again and I'll have you arrested."

Logan laughed. "Go ahead and try. Just go ahead and try."

chapter fifty-six

E HAD BEEN BEATEN AND STARVED, PURSUED AND abandoned, and endured all manner of training and torture.

But nothing had prepared Luther for what he had seen beyond the mist. The memory still riled his mind.

When that thing had flown over him and Logan, they had both frozen. A dim corner of his soul had almost rejoiced in understanding—finally—that this was what utter terror felt like. He had scrambled back through the mist. Logan was only ten feet from him, but it might as well have been hundreds.

Had the crying been the cop's or his own?

Since that episode a couple hours ago, Luther had banished fear from his mind, just as he had been trained to do, and got about his business. The bomb at the church had failed, but it had almost been worth it to watch that stupid cop scampering down the steeple like a spider with half its legs torn off.

Now that he'd had time to rest and reflect, he realized something was very wrong. Where were FEMA and the Feeble Bureau of Investigation and those blessed satellite trucks and news copters? Where were the finger-pointing politicians and the stern-warning generals? Where were the wailing citizens and their candlelight vigils?

Where was Barcester, Massachusetts?

Did DeLuxe know this would happen? Or had it all spiraled out of his control, too?

Too many questions.

Luther had sworn allegiance to this cause, promised to kill when called upon and die with glory when it became necessary.

Which was why he loaded up his weapons, sheathed his knives, and got ready to go back and do battle.

Whether they had landed in heaven, hell, or somewhere in between, he still had a mission and the will to see it through.

chapter fifty-seven

KAYA MET LOGAN COMING DOWN CARLTON REYNOLDS'S driveway. "You didn't do anything rash, did you?"

He laughed. "Trust me. I left that slimeball alive and kicking."

He filled her in on the man's diabetic coma. Kaya wanted to go back and examine Reynolds.

"He's fine," Logan said. "He doesn't want anything to do with us. Thinks he's safe in his fortress."

"Fool." Kaya looked up at the Ledges. "Jason, I can't leave Ben up there much longer. I have to get to him."

"Could I send Paul Wells up to bring him back?"

"No, not this time. He's my son, and he needs me."

As they had three times before, they followed the mist back to the Circle, then got off their bikes and walked them around the rotary. Kaya took his hand and held tight until they saw the opening for East University.

As soon as the crowd spotted Logan, they rushed around him. So many people, so many questions.

Pappas stepped in. "Back off, people. Give the man space."

Logan climbed the stairs to Grace, then turned and faced the crowd. He scanned the crowd until Hilary waved at him. Kimmie was asleep in her arms. He risked a smile, but Hilary just turned away.

"Did you find anyone to help?" someone yelled out.

Dear God, I can't do this without You.

"For some reason, the mist has cut us off from the rest of Barcester," Logan began. "We have to assume we're on our own for a while."

Logan expected shouting or cries, but the only response was a numb silence.

They're giving up, he thought. They can't—not yet.

Kaya stepped to his side and took his hand. Pappas—face tight and eyes hard—nevertheless managed a nod of encouragement.

Logan straightened, ignoring the agony in his shoulders and lower back. "We need to pray for strength and show mercy to each other," he said. "And act like Americans."

Dorothy Britain began to sing "America the Beautiful." The silence broke, voices joining in, Kaya with her lovely voice, tears in her eyes.

Logan saluted, and Pappas pressed his hand to his heart.

The anthem ended, but the people kept singing. "Amazing Grace" filled the air now. Logan wanted to linger, but he had a job to do.

He went inside the church, fell to his knees before the cross, and prayed for the strength to do it.

Oh, Come to Me, Jesus

by Victoria James

Here between the present and the not-yet-seen,
Future shores are just outside my grasp.
Longing for the land my feet have aimed to reach,
I'm tossing in the murk shadows cast.
>Though hope may be abandoned,
>You're the one that knows the way.
>You're the rescue, my belief among these
>waves.

Chorus:
Oh, come to me, Jesus.
Oh, come and be my strength.
Oh, come to me, Jesus.
Oh, come. Be near me.

The wind across the water has borne Your name
Through tempests rough and powerful to see.
Moving at Your calling, hearing of Your fame
As witnessed on the waves of Galilee.
>Like those You've called before me,
>You've the offer of the same.
>You're the hand that holds my own among
>these waves.

Bridge:
To think You'd leave the firmness of the land
To search a raging sea as if You were just a man
But the power of the waves bend at Your command.
You're so amazing. So amazing!

Chorus:
Oh, come to me, Jesus. Oh, come to me.
Oh, come and be my strength. You are the
    Rock of Ages.
Oh, come to me, Jesus. You are the Comforter.
Oh, come. I'm weary. Your hand holds my own.

Oh, come to me, Jesus. The heavens are Your throne.
Oh, come and be my strength. You are Lord alone.
Oh, come to me, Jesus. I will seek You only.
Oh, come. Be near me. Be near me.
Oh, come.

© 2007 vjames
www.victoriajamesmusic.com

12/10
↓